D0394811

SCHOOL FOR S.P.I.E.S.

PLAYING WITH FIRE

SCHOOL FOR S.P.I.E.S.

PLAYING WITH FIRE

BRUCE HALE

WITH ILLUSTRATIONS BY

BRANDON DORMAN

Disney • Hyperion Books

New York

Text copyright © 2013 by Bruce Hale
Illustrations copyright © 2013 by Brandon Dorman

All rights reserved. Published by Disney·Hyperion Books,
an imprint of Disney Book Group. No part of this book may be
reproduced or transmitted in any form or by any means, electronic
or mechanical, including photocopying, recording, or by any information
storage and retrieval system, without written permission from the
publisher. For information address Disney·Hyperion Books,
114 Fifth Avenue, New York, New York 10011-5690.

First Edition
1 3 5 7 9 10 8 6 4 2
G475-5664-5-13105

Printed in the United States of America

Library of Congress Cataloging-in-Publication Data
Hale, Bruce.
Playing with fire/by Bruce Hale; with illustrations
by Brandon Dorman.—First edition.
pages cm—(School for S.P.I.E.S.)
Summary: Reluctant orphan-turned-spy Max Segredo
discovers intrigue at the Merry Sunshine Orphanage
and must confront an international group bent on world
domination, while uncovering mysteries from his past.
ISBN 978-1-4231-6850-8
[1. Spies—Fiction. 2. Orphans—Fiction. 3. Identity—Fiction.
4. Racially mixed people—Fiction.] I. Dorman, Brandon, ill. II. Title.
PZ7.H1295Pl 2013
[Fic]—dc23   2012022296

Reinforced binding

Visit www.disneyhyperionbooks.com

SUSTAINABLE FORESTRY INITIATIVE
Certified Sourcing
www.sfiprogram.org
SFI-00993

THIS LABEL APPLIES TO TEXT STOCK

To Glynnis, a nice niece and a champion reader

FOSTERS AND FIRE DON'T MIX

CHAPTER 1

MAX SEGREDO stood by the curb and watched his house burn.

It gave off a cheery light, the crackling flames casting sunset yellows and cherry reds onto the manicured trees and tidy homes nearby. Sparks sizzled and popped like New Year's Eve fireworks. Clouds of gray billowed gracefully up into the night sky, and the homey smell of wood smoke filled the air.

But Max suspected that the house's owners didn't fully appreciate the beauty of it all.

Fifteen feet away on the lawn, Mr. Bumburger bellowed into his cell phone, his neck wattle jiggling. "I don't care how late it is. You get your bum over here right now and take this boy away!" As another crew of firemen rushed up to the house, dragging thick hoses, Mr. and Mrs. Bumburger

3

turned in unison to glare at Max. Bottom-heavy and block-headed, they resembled a pair of angry Russian nesting dolls.

Max decided this probably wasn't the best time to share that observation with them.

"No excuses!" Mr. Bumburger snarled into the phone. "I refuse to let this . . . this . . . *pyromaniac* spend another night with my family."

Rubbish, thought Max, fingers seeking the smooth weight of the gold-plated lighter in his pocket. They always invent some bogus reason. But his resentment felt dull-edged. He'd been through this sort of scene too many times.

Mr. Bumburger listened for a moment, and in the changing light, his pouchy face looked like that of deeply peeved cane toad. "No, that's *your* problem!" Ending the call, he jabbed the button with enough force to crush a flimsier phone.

Max hugged his arms and hunched his shoulders against the chill. Rain soon, he could smell it. True, he could dig his jacket out of the duffel bag at his feet, but really, what would be the point? He decided to make a game of seeing how long he could last before having to don his coat.

It wasn't much of a game, but it helped pass the time.

The red-faced Mr. Bumburger stuffed the cell phone into his pocket and strode across the lawn to where Max stood, well apart from the couple and their twin daughters.

"You'll pay for this, boy," he growled.

"Pay for what?"

Mr. Bumburger waved a hand at the merrily burning house. "All of this. You'll pay, by thunder."

Max frowned. "Leaving aside *why*, what would I pay *with*?" he asked. "My many stock market investments? In case you haven't noticed, I'm a kid."

"That's enough of your smart mouth." The toad-faced man planted his fists on his hips and glared down at Max, round belly thrusting forward like an angry beach ball. "I'll make certain Mr. Darny sends you straight to juvenile hall!"

"Juvie?" Max shivered, but he tilted his chin up defiantly. "For what?"

"Burning my house down, you little freak."

Max gaped. "But I didn't do it."

"Oh, really? Then pray tell, who did?"

"Do I look like Sherlock Holmes? I don't know!" Max said hotly. "But it's not my fault."

"Lies, lies, lies—that's all I've heard since you moved in." Mr. Bumburger gestured to where his wife stood with her hands on their daughters' shoulders. "And to think I let a creepy child like you endanger my little angels."

The angels, a pair of blond, perfect, eight-year-old brats, stuck out their tongues at Max.

"Look . . . *Dad*," said Max, trying to keep the sarcasm out of his voice, "I didn't set the fire. You've got to believe me."

The man's face slammed shut like a prison gate. "That's

Mr. Bumburger to you. You're not my foster child anymore. Not my problem."

"But, Mr. Bumburger—"

"It's pronounced *Bum-ber-zhay*! How often must I tell you?"

As often as it still gets a rise out of you, thought Max. But his heart wasn't in it.

"Stand right there while you wait for Mr. Darny. Don't move. Don't speak. Don't burn anything else down. And don't approach my family again, or I shall call the police." He stomped across the lawn, stumbling over fire hoses.

Max gritted his teeth and turned his back on the fire. Even after living in seven different homes, rejection still stung. But he shouldn't have been surprised. After all, Blame the Foster Kid was a game he'd seen played many times, and foster parents like the Bumburgers were masters at it.

He wouldn't miss them, with their fussy rules and their obnoxious daughters, their way of stashing him with a crusty old babysitter while the family went on expensive vacations. Max squeezed his eyes tight. The smoke was making them water.

What had really started the fire? The brats? One of his foster father's cigars? Their sinister cat, Mr. Waddles? He'd probably never know.

When he opened his eyes, the glint of light on glass captured his attention. A long black car was parked half a block away, just beyond the streetlights' glow. Two dark shapes sat in the front seat, and one of them was holding something reflective up to his eyes. Binoculars, maybe? A video camera?

Max squinted, trying to make it out.

From the other direction, a siren wailed its *wee-ooh-wee-ooh*, and a white police car drove into view, coming to a stop behind a fire truck.

The long black car pulled away from the curb. Light flashed again on whatever its passenger held as the vehicle U-turned down the wide street, drifting into the night. Max watched it go. Probably just some freaks who like to watch fires, he thought.

The chilly breeze knifed through his thin cotton T-shirt, and Max shivered again. Now his game changed to: *Can I wait until Mr. Darny arrives before I put on my jacket?* But it still wasn't much of a game.

Bundled in thick housecoats and robes, the neighbors stood on their lawns, watching the blaze with so-glad-it's-not-my-house fascination. Max hadn't even had time to learn their names. But they looked like nice enough folks, for a bunch of normals. A pity he'd never fit into their world.

Hoses blasted the fire from several angles. It seemed to Max that the firefighters had gained the upper hand. Sure, the second story would have to be rebuilt, but at least the blaze wouldn't spread. Damage would be limited to one house and one boy's life.

Max glanced at the Bumburgers and grimaced. It wasn't that he'd thought they were Foster Parents of the Year—not by a long shot. It wasn't that he'd hoped to be adopted— honestly, who would *volunteer* to change their last name to Bumburger?

It was just that they blamed him for a fire he didn't set. And *that* was deeply unfair.

Mr. and Mrs. Bumburger glowered back at him. An almost palpable wave of anger and loathing rolled across the lawn from his soon-to-be ex–foster parents. Great. Max could picture the glowing recommendation letter they'd write: *It was so hard for us to say good-bye to Max. We'll miss his friendly sarcasm and superior fire-starting skills.*

Then a sobering thought struck him. What if Mr. Darny actually listened to the beach-ball-bellied Bumburgers? What if, instead of another foster placement, Max drew a stretch in juvie? Juvenile hall made the worst foster home look like a lark in the park with unicorns and ice cream.

Max had seen the boys who came out of juvie. Hard boys; mean-eyed boys. Gang material.

That wasn't the future Max pictured for himself. He bit his lip and scrutinized the street, watching for Mr. Darny's car.

Could this night possibly get any worse?

Spit, spat, spatter. Cold droplets landed on his face and bare arms. Max raised his face to the sky. Thunder rumbled, and suddenly it was as if someone had turned on the sprinklers up above.

Rain. Just bloody perfect.

Max sighed. He squatted and dug through his duffel bag for his jacket.

All things considered, this wouldn't have been his first pick for the best way to spend his thirteenth birthday.

CHAPTER 2

NO SMOKING, NO GUNPLAY

THE CAB RIDE with Mr. Eugene V. Darny was every bit as delightful as Max had expected it would be.

"How *could* you?" the toast-brown, pear-shaped caseworker said for the fifth time. "After we talked and talked about your, er, pyromaniac tendencies and sent you to that expensive counselor?"

Max rolled his eyes. "Am I speaking Norwegian or something? I. Didn't. Do it. Understand?"

Darny huffed and tut-tutted and wobbled his head. As the cab forged onward through the rain, he yammered and jabbered, his pencil-thin mustache looking for all the world like a caterpillar doing calisthenics. But Max was far more interested in their destination than in rehashing an argument he couldn't win.

"Where are we going?" he broke in at last.

"Eh?" The caseworker stopped in mid-gripe. "Oh. I, er, found a sort of group home for you. More than you deserve? I'll say. And you'd better not mess this one up, boy, or it's juvenile hall for certain." He waggled a finger.

Max bit back a reply. He crossed his arms and settled deeper into the seat. At least he wasn't bound for juvie. That was something.

The rain had forced all but the hardiest of drivers from the roads. A few stranded pedestrians huddled under the awnings of all-night curry shops, and the tube stations stood deserted. Before long, the cab turned into a neighborhood of shabby redbrick homes and down-at-the-heels businesses, like Bangers & Sprods and Guido's House of Olives. Max had a hard time imagining their customers.

Halfway down one anonymous block, they pulled to the curb. Max leaned forward to inspect the nearest house.

"Out, out," said Mr. Darny, elbowing him. "I haven't got all night."

Max stepped onto the sidewalk, lugging his duffel bag. Torrents of rainwater sluiced off of his straight black hair, flowed down his jacket, and soaked his black high-tops. He couldn't have gotten much wetter by standing directly under a shower nozzle.

Darny reached a soft, pudgy hand over the seat back. "That's half," he told the driver. "You'll get the rest if you're still here when I finish my business."

Unfurling a purple penguin-themed umbrella, the case-worker stepped onto the sidewalk and closed the door on the driver's outraged squawk.

"Come, boy. Let's get you situated."

Max thought Mr. Darny sounded like a penguin with a head cold. But it didn't pay to tell your caseworker that. "Can't wait," he muttered.

Across the street, a long black car drifted past. Max wouldn't have sworn it was the same vehicle he'd seen at the fire, but he wouldn't have sworn it *wasn't*, either. The vehicle glided down the road, engine purring. Max slung his duffel bag over his shoulder.

Passing through a wrought-iron gate, Mr. Darny splashed into a puddle with a muffled curse and waddled up the short walkway. He even walks like a penguin, Max thought, trailing after. The grimy brick building was nearly identical to the other grimy brick buildings on the street—identical but for a few small details.

Max's sharp eyes took in the massive satellite dish squatting on the roof, the wicked-looking spikes and barbed wire decorating the rooftop edges, the barred windows, and the discreet cameras watching the street and walkway.

"Cheerful place," he said. "Who's their decorator, Martha Paranoid?"

"Hush." The caseworker climbed three short steps and rapped a claw knocker against a tarnished brass plate. *Bam, bam, bam!*

A faded, weather-beaten sign hung above the door. Max frowned at it. "'Merry Sunshine Orphanage'? I thought orphanages were extinct."

"Yes, well, apparently, you don't know everything. What a surprise." Mr. Darny straightened his tie and fussed with his overcoat.

Max surveyed the soot-stained windowsills, the bricks in need of a serious scrubbing, and the suspicious face peering through an upstairs window. On the whole, he found the entire place very *un*-merry sunshiny.

"Mr. Darny . . ." he began.

"Not now." The caseworker pounded the knocker more forcefully. At last, a tiny barred porthole opened, and a gray eye peered through bulletproof glass.

"Shove off," a man's voice growled. "We're closed."

"Oh, uh"—Darny bobbed his head nervously—"special delivery for the director. I called ahead."

"Well, nobody told me," said the owner of the gray eye. The porthole closed with a thunk.

"Bother," the caseworker muttered. He hesitantly raised his hand to the knocker again.

A woman's voice rang from behind the door. Max couldn't make out the words, but the tone was unmistakable—that of a battlefield general issuing orders. By her tone, an invasion of Poland was just around the corner.

With a buzz and a click, the door swung open.

Buttery golden light spilled into the night, making the

raindrops sparkle like Christmas tinsel. Framed by the doorway, a lean woman in black stood ruler-straight, one fist planted on her hip. Her face was ageless and Asian. She could've been anywhere from thirty-five to sixty-five, but her scowl warned foolish visitors against asking.

"Well?" she demanded of Darny.

The caseworker looked like he'd swallowed a spiny frog. "Miz Director, er, Annie . . . I, er, the boy . . ." He gestured limply behind him.

Max climbed the steps and extended his hand. He'd learned that it paid to be polite with authority figures—at least at the start.

"I'm Max Segredo."

"Segredo?" The woman's eyes widened briefly. She didn't shake, and Max noticed that her right hand held a sleek gray pistol.

"Nice arsenal," he said nervously.

The woman in black scanned the sidewalk. "Salesmen very pesky." Her accent was heavy and foreign, but nothing Max recognized.

Mr. Darny cleared his throat and got a grip on himself. "Max, this is er, Hantai Annie Wong. The orphanage director."

Max stuffed his hand into his pocket. "Charmed."

The woman grunted. "Get inside. It's wet." Her bright, birdlike eyes surveyed the street as she ushered the pair

over the threshold. They stepped into a ten-foot-long space watched over by two cameras above a second door. That door's narrow observation window was reinforced with wire.

"Expecting an invasion?" said Max, before he could help himself. Mr. Darny elbowed him.

"You never know," the director said darkly. She snapped her fingers and pointed at the coatrack. "Jackets."

Max and Darny hung up their coats. The inner door opened with another buzz and a click, and there stood the fellow who, presumably, had told them to shove off—a bear-shaped white man with a bristly crew cut and a face as round and crusty-looking as a steak-and-kidney pie. He held the door and stepped aside without a word.

Max edged past him into the entryway. The contrast with the house's facade couldn't have been more dramatic.

He found himself in a cozy, softly lit, semicircular space, with several doorways branching off to the left and right. The dark wood floor gleamed like a con man's smile; the antique rugs were spotless. Dead ahead, a flight of mauve-carpeted stairs curled up and out of view. The wallpaper sported a fleur-de-lis pattern in pale violet that must've been all the rage back when everyone wore powdered wigs.

Above a door to the left, another surveillance camera watched it all.

"*Oi, koi,*" said Hantai Annie. "Come."

She marched toward the nearest right-hand door, which

bore the word OFFICE on a brass nameplate. On the wall beside it, a framed needlepoint sampler displayed the motto: FAMILY IS WHERE YOU FIND IT.

Yeah, right, thought Max. Family is what you're assigned to. He hoped this wasn't one of those *Today is the first day of the rest of your ruddy life* type of homes.

Bear Man lumbered past and opened the door for them. The office looked homey and neat, boasting the usual assortment of desk, chairs, bookshelves, filing cabinet, and couch. Two samurai warrior masks hung on the wall, like the comedy-and-tragedy masks displayed at theaters. But both faces were scowling. Not a paper was out of place, and a mug of tea on a coaster sent wisps of steam curling toward the ceiling.

"Sit!" The director indicated the overstuffed sofa.

Mr. Darny perched on the edge of a cushion, briefcase atop his knees. Max sank into the couch with a faint soggy squish.

"So." Hantai Annie laid her pistol on the desk. Her ebony eyes bored into Max's hazel ones.

"So," said Max, tapping a sneakered foot.

He knew the drill. Whether they came on sweet as cinnamon or tough as buffalo jerky, they all wanted to know two things: Who is this kid, and will he fit in?

Unconsciously, Max slipped a hand into his pocket for his lucky stone, the chunk of obsidian he'd found at the beach that last sunny day with his mother, so many years before.

He rubbed its smooth sides, fingered the sharp edge. Then he leaned back against the velvety cushions and tried to act as if he popped into orphanages during thunderstorms every night of the week.

All that betrayed him were his shallow breathing and a certain tightness around the mouth. He was glad no one could see the sick feeling in the pit of his stomach.

Darny coughed nervously. "It's, er, all here, Director." He fiddled with his briefcase, withdrew a folder, and handed Hantai Annie a sheaf of papers.

She scanned the top sheet and studied Max's face. "Mixed race? What mix? You not Japanese, not Chinese."

This, too, was part of the drill. They took in his almond-shaped eyes, golden-brown skin, and features that blended East and West, and asked, *What are you?* Like he was some kind of strange new bug.

Max ran his thumb over the stone. "My mum was Thai. My dad . . ." He shrugged. "Some white guy. He ran off and died when I was little."

Hantai Annie read farther down the sheet. *"Simon Segredo?"* She exchanged a glance with Bear Man, who stood near the door. Something passed between them, something secret.

"What?" said Max.

"Nothing," said the director. "Now, why has one boy lived in seven different foster homes?

"Variety is the spice of life," Max heard himself saying. Darny winced.

"You think I stupid?" the director snapped.

"Of course not," said Mr. Darny.

"You think, this lady no talk proper English, so she *baka*?" Hantai Annie thumped her chest. *"Hontou wa*, I speak seven languages, I have master's degree."

"I believe it," said Max, thinking, I'll have to watch my step with this one.

"I learn English last," she grumbled. "Crazy language." Her gaze bore into Max. "So tell me truth. Why so many fosters?"

Max sat up straighter. "It's not my fault."

Mr. Darny blanched and tried on a halfhearted smile. It fit him about as well as bunny slippers on a bullfrog.

"Oshiero," said Hantai Annie. "Tell me."

The caseworker dropped his gaze to the file. "Well, his, er, first three fosters died."

"How?" asked the director, eyes on Max. He gulped.

"Let's see . . ." said Darny. "Devoured by crocodiles . . . executed by Gurlukh warlords, and . . . popped off in an accident involving a bathtub, a radio, and a yo-yo."

"Again, not my fault," said Max.

Hantai Annie pursed her lips. "And the rest?"

Mr. Darny grimaced. "They, um, released the lad for . . . er, starting fires or stealing. But he's learned his lesson, mum.

No trouble here." He shot Max a warning look.

"Fires? Stealing?" the director mused, her face cold. "You know what I say?"

Darny gripped his briefcase protectively.

Here it comes, thought Max. He wondered dully whether he could get into one of the better juvie gangs, and what their initiation would be like.

Hantai Annie held his gaze. "Learn to control fire," she said at last. "And if you stealing, don't get caught."

Max couldn't help gaping.

"Okay," she told the caseworker. "We take him on trial basis." Hantai Annie signed a form and thrust it at Mr. Darny. "Styx," she told Bear Man, "pay Darny. Bag goes in Room Five."

"Yes, Director."

Max did his best to hide his enormous relief. Could this Merry Sunshine Orphanage truly be a different sort of group home from the ones he'd known?

Styx lifted Max's duffel like a sack full of feathers, then shambled to the door. Mr. Darny's face split into a smile so oily you could've fried chips on it. He hopped to his feet and followed Styx, saying, "Thanks, mum. Knew you'd like him, I did. You're a first-rate judge of, er, character. Tip-top!"

The door clicked shut behind them. Hantai Annie studied Max carefully, as if memorizing him for a test on thirteen-year-old boys who appeared out of the night.

"Three rules at Merry Sunshine," she said. "No smoking. No unsupervised gunplay—"

"Gunplay?"

"And loyalty above all. You promise to obey?"

Max shrugged. "Sure."

"For now, this your family. Act like it."

Max nodded, but he honestly had no idea what she meant.

Up in his new room, gentle snores issued from two of the beds. Roommates. A thatch of blond hair stuck up from one lump of bedclothes, and a bare foot dangled from the other. Max yawned. He'd sort things out with them tomorrow. His duffel bag leaned against the third bed. In the dim blue glow of a night-light he undid the clasps and rummaged inside, pulling out a rolled-up T-shirt. He gently laid it down and unfurled it.

Nestled in its folds was a framed 3 x 5 photo of a smiling Asian woman. Max transferred his lucky stone from his pocket to the nightstand and stood the photo beside it. Flicking his lighter on with a practiced thumb, he held it to illuminate the image. Tenderly, he traced the woman's cheek with a finger.

Good night, Mum.

Then he reached into the bag for some dry socks and frowned. Out came a stiff square of card paper. Odd.

Max eyed his roommates, but both seemed truly asleep.

He angled the note and held it closer to the night light. The scrawled message read:

UKQN BWPDAN EO WHERA

It wasn't English. It didn't look like any language spoken by actual human beings. But an odd awareness tickled his brain. A familiar pattern lurked beneath the letters, waiting to burst to the surface like a shark from the depths.

A coded message, then. And something told him it wasn't just *Welcome to Merry Sunshine, old bean*.

Max shivered as a chill fluttered up his spine. What have I landed in this time? he wondered.

CAESAR'S CODE REVEALS ALL

MAX COULDN'T BREATHE. It was back—his old nightmare of suffocating in a tight space. Panic gripped him. Struggling up from the dark well of dreams, he felt like a great weight was crushing all the air from his lungs.

As things turned out, it was.

A beefy-looking girl with wild red hair sat astride his chest, trapping him under the covers.

"Who sent you?" she demanded. This redheaded troll leaned down into his face, treating Max to a close-up of beady blue eyes and a truly impressive demonstration of morning breath.

"Get . . . off, you . . . daft cow," Max wheezed in a pitiful whisper.

"Who sent you here to spy on us?" Beefy Red thwacked his nose with a finger. It stung. "Answer, you dimwat!"

Max's arms were tightly pinioned. In desperation, he tried thrashing his body to buck the deranged girl off. No luck. Someone else held his legs.

Max went wild. But no matter how he twisted, Beefy Red and her unseen partner kept him pinned. He began to feel light-headed. His lungs screamed for air.

"I said, talk, you little beggar," the girl sneered.

Max's unprintable reply came out in a faint hiss. He could make no sound.

A snide voice drawled, "Uh, Nikki, he can't answer you."

"'Course he can." She glared down at Max.

"Not if he can't breathe," said the voice.

"Oh," said Nikki. She shifted her weight just enough for Max to draw a gasping breath. He coughed.

"Now," the girl said, "who sent you, slant-eyed spy? China? North Korea?"

"Wee Willie Winkie and his dancing aardvark," said Max.

Her flushed face went slack in confusion. "Huh?"

"My caseworker, you moron. How else does a kid land in an orphanage?"

The girl's eyes narrowed, and she drew back a fist. "You little . . ."

"Nikki," the other voice said, in warning.

She glanced over her shoulder and vaulted off the bed in a flash.

"What's all this, then?" a new voice rumbled.

As Max rolled onto his side, sucking in a lungful of sweet air, he noticed Bear Man from last night—Styx, was it?—filling the doorway.

"We were just welcoming the new kid," drawled Nikki's companion, a scrawny, pale boy with silky brown hair and a face like a weasel. "Right, um . . . ?" He looked over at Max.

"Max," said Max, coolly.

"Is that so?" asked Styx. "They welcoming you?"

Max sat up. At a glance, he read the situation: Weasel Boy looking worried; Nikki beside him, glaring the message, *Tell and you die.* Max had passed through enough group homes to know the score—nothing was lower than a squealer, and half the time the staff didn't believe you anyway.

"Yeah," said Max. "Welcomed with open arms." *And closed fists,* he added silently.

The burly man sized up the scene with shrewd eyes. "Bloody heartwarming. Class starts in four minutes. Bugger off."

With a last warning glance at Max, Weasel Boy and Nikki edged past Styx and out the door.

"Class?" said Max.

"Morning Warm-ups. Room Three." When Max didn't move, Styx flung a towel at him. "Chop-chop. The director hates tardiness."

Max located a bathroom across the hall and splashed water on his face, considering his options. He only had to survive this loony bin long enough to avoid juvie and be placed with another family—hopefully one better than the Bumburgers. Then, in two or three years he could go to court, get emancipated, and live on his own at last.

He met his eyes in the mirror. Just stay cool, he told his reflection.

While slipping into jeans and a fresh T-shirt, he took stock of his new room. Three beds occupied the chamber, each with its own nightstand and cobalt-blue footlocker. The other two beds were immaculately made up. No sports banners or rappers' photos decorated the tan walls; no boy-type messes cluttered the floor.

Beside the door, a seriously old-timey poster showed a burning boat sinking into a blue sea. LOOSE LIPS SINK SHIPS, it read.

Charming, thought Max. Just the thing to make an orphan feel at home.

He could already tell this wasn't an ordinary orphanage; he just didn't know what flavor of weird it was. On impulse, he grabbed the coded message from the nightstand and stuffed it into his pocket. He hurried down the stairs and into the entryway.

Six numberless doors faced him. Which was Room Three?

Hearing a noise behind one of them, he turned the knob and stepped into the room.

Dead ahead, a lithe young woman with loads of glossy

blue-black hair was whipping her arms down in front of her. *Fwip-fwip*. Her huge brown eyes widened. Two objects left her hands—glittering knives headed straight for him!

No time to think.

Max ducked.

Thunk! One blade stuck in the door frame, a hairsbreadth away. The other sailed past, embedding itself in the baseboard of the opposite wall.

"Witless, brainless boy!" cried the woman.

"Me? You're the one throwing knives at doors."

She glared. "Never *ever* enter without knocking," she trilled in a musical, Indian accent. "Not in this school. And certainly not these days."

"Sorry," Max said, only a touch sarcastically. He noticed that the room had a conspicuous lack of other students. "Uh, Morning Warm-ups?"

The Indian woman pointed left with another wicked-looking knife. "Next door." As Max turned to go, she added, "You know, having a famous father doesn't make you special. You'll have to work even harder than the rest."

Max spun around. "You knew my father?" Hope quickened his heart. Simon Segredo had left when Max was so young, he couldn't even recall the man's face. If this woman could tell him . . . "What was he—"

The knife thrower jerked her chin. "Go!"

"But I—"

"It's not my place to say more. Now, hurry! Your class is beginning." When Max stepped out into the entry hall still dazed, the woman added, "And close the bloody door!"

Max did so, and immediately another knife thunked against it. He stepped over to the next door, rapped twice, and swung it open.

A lean body sheathed in charcoal spandex paced before a group of about fifteen kids who stood at attention on thin rubber mats. "You late!" Hantai Annie Wong snapped at Max.

"Yeah, well, nobody mentioned a class last night. Sorry."

"Don't be sorry." She reached down beside a rack of sports balls, produced a rolled-up mat, and tossed it to him. "Be on time."

Max found an open stretch of floor and unfurled his mat. He stood on it, copying the other orphans.

"Class, this is Max Segredo," said the director. "Introductions later. Now, forward bend!"

The students raised their arms high and bowed forward, folding at the waist. On his way down, Max noticed a deeply tanned older boy in a red tracksuit standing behind Annie, balancing a spinning basketball on his finger.

"Plant hands; jump your feet back!" barked the director.

Max imitated the student next to him, a wiry-haired girl with skin like pale chocolate milk. When she noticed him watching, she hissed, "Eyes front!"

"Oh, come on," he whispered. "How else am I—"

Bam! Something hard smacked Max right between the shoulder blades and bounced away.

He jumped to his feet, fists ready. "Hey! Who did that?"

Red Tracksuit Guy lifted a soccer ball off the rack, an exaggerated expression of innocence on his features.

"You dead, Max Segredo," said Hantai Annie.

"What? You're loony. Just tell me who hit me."

Someone gasped. The director picked up a volleyball, her face impassive. "Object of game is, don't get hit. When do you let your guard down?" she asked the class.

"Never!" came the answer.

"Take your position," she told Max.

"You—" A smart remark trembled on Max's lips, waiting to be said. He bit it back and remembered the threat of juvie. Just stay cool, he reminded himself. His fists unclenched. "Okay. I'll play your little game."

In triangle pose, a soccer ball smacked him in the belly. "Dead!" called Hantai Annie.

In crane pose, a volleyball bopped him in the bum. "Dead again!"

In seated twist, he got hit not once, but twice. "Dead, dead, you *so* dead," sang the director. She seemed to take an unhealthy delight in killing people.

Max clenched his jaw and put up with it. If the rest of the orphans could bear this stoically, he could too. Looking around, he noticed he wasn't the only one on the casualty list; nearly everyone had been hit at least once.

Class continued for what felt like hours, with stretches and thumps and a few muttered curses. By the end of it, Max's T-shirt was soaked through with sweat.

Hantai Annie clapped her hands. "Breakfast now. *Isoge!*"

The students rolled up their mats and stored them on a shelf. The wiry-haired girl reached past Max to add hers to the stack.

"Weirdest P.E. class ever," Max muttered to her.

"Really?" She cocked her head and surveyed him with an amused smirk. "You need to get out more often."

Wrecking yards and parrot sanctuaries were peaceful, quiet places compared to the orphanage dining room. All the kids from class, plus a few older ones, shouted, chattered, joked, and clattered plates. Rich smells of cooked meat filled the air, and Styx hustled back and forth from kitchen to table, bearing platters of eggs, bangers, and bacon, as well as baskets of muffins and tureens of porridge.

Max's belly grumbled. This orphanage beat Oliver Twist's all hollow.

A shaggy black-and-brown dog the size of a Shetland pony sat by the long table, watching every bite, ropes of drool dangling from its mouth. When Max passed by, it growled, rumbling like a distant avalanche.

"Nice puppy," Max muttered.

He loaded his plate with food and found an empty seat a little apart from the rest. Curious glances came his way, but Max needed space to think.

Why had that redheaded psycho, Nikki, attacked him? And what about his father? Why had the knife thrower called him famous?

Max barely recalled his dad, except for the faintest memory of ticklish kisses from a mustachioed mouth and the citrusy scent of aftershave. Details on the man were scarcer than snowflakes in July. *He left when you were young, he died soon after* was all Max had been able to glean.

He shifted in his seat and heard the crinkle of the coded message in his pocket. Had one of these kids slipped it to him? The orphans ranged from eight to eighteen and spanned a spectrum of skin tones from mahogany to ivory. Why would one of these strangers write him a note?

"Ease up, mon!" The voice in his ear startled Max. An athletic, teak-skinned boy with a downy mustache and a wraparound smile had claimed the seat beside him.

"Sorry?" said Max.

"You look like your life is full of botheration," said the teen, in a lilting Caribbean accent. He seemed a few years older than Max. "I'm Tremaine," he said, holding out his hand.

"Max," said Max, shaking it. "I'm fine. New place, that's all."

"Oi, Rashid!" Tremaine called to Red Tracksuit Guy.

"Muffin me!" At the table's other end, the solemn-faced boy reared back and hurled the baked treat, and Tremaine snatched it from the air with a spectacular grab. "So, did Nikki Knucks give you her bug-in-a-rug greeting?"

"How did you know?"

"Cho!" Tremaine chuckled as he broke the muffin in half. "Don't let it vex you, Maxwell. She does it to everyone—everyone she thinks she can push around."

"And here I thought I was special."

A heavy hand clapped his shoulder. "Right then, new kid," rumbled a deep voice.

"Ah, Mr. Styx," said Max, turning.

"No mister, just Styx," said the bearlike man. He jerked a thumb at the wiry-haired girl, who stood next to him, watching the room. "Director says stick close to this one. She'll show you the ropes."

The girl nodded at Max. "Cinnabar Jones."

"Max Segredo."

Cinnabar smirked. "So I gathered."

Styx thumped Max's shoulder with a hand like an anvil. "Right, then. I'm off to the salt mines." He lumbered away.

"You won't get assigned any chores until tomorrow," said Cinnabar, in a bored tone. "Drop your plate on the dirty stack and follow me."

"What's the rush?" said Max, eyeing his half-eaten sausage. But then he noticed most of the other orphans were finishing their meals and heading out the door. "Where are we going?"

"Maths and Puzzles. We can't be late."

He caught her arm. "Uh, think maybe you guys need to lighten up a bit? Classwork isn't a matter of life and death."

She stared at his hand until he released her. Then, for the first time, she looked straight at him. Up close, her eyes were luminous and golden.

"How do you know it isn't?" said Cinnabar.

A hodgepodge of mismatched chairs jammed the stuffy third-floor room. Built-in bookcases stretched from floor to ceiling, packed with enough musty old volumes to start a dust lovers' lending library. A pair of barred windows strained some weak daylight into the place, and the heat was cranked up so high it felt like noon in Cameroon.

Max claimed a hard wooden chair beside Cinnabar and eyed the stiff-backed older woman scribbling on a chalkboard.

"That's Madame Chiffre," said Cinnabar.

The woman turned, her bladelike nose parting the air like the prow of a great ship. Her clothes were simple and elegant: cream-colored slacks, dove-gray sweater, and a crimson scarf. Thick glasses magnified her watery green eyes. Her face was as pale as a blank page.

Madame Chiffre clapped her hands twice, and the orphans' chatter subsided.

"Eh, *bon*. Today, let us review ze Caesar cipher."

"Awww." The disappointed groan came from Nikki Knucks, who slouched on a love seat across the room with her weasel-faced friend. "Again?"

"A problem, *mademoiselle*?"

Nikki crossed her arms. "We already covered this. It's a substitution cipher where one letter takes the place of another, and blah, blah, blah."

"Then let us make things interesting," said the teacher. "First person to decode a message wins . . . one day free of chores." The students clapped enthusiastically, but Max's mind was elsewhere.

A *substitution code*? The mental tickle he'd felt at seeing last night's note grew stronger. Foster Parents #2, the Quinns, had been crazy about word games and puzzles, forcing Max to play along with them. Something about this reminded him of those days . . . but what?

Madame Chiffre called on Cinnabar to encode a message in the Caesar cipher. While the girl wrote on the chalkboard, the teacher explained the system. "Each letter in ze plaintext eez replaced by a letter some certain number of positions down ze alphabet. *Par exemple*, in a one-letter shift, ze *A* becomes what?"

"A *B*," said Nikki in a bored singsong.

"Correct, *mademoiselle*. It eez a *B* in ze coded text."

Max frowned. He pulled the note from his pocket and

doodled on it with a pencil stub. The teacher's description had shaken something loose in his mind.

UKQN BWPDAN EO WHERA . . . It wasn't a simple two-letter shift, where the *A*s became *C*s. Nor a three . . . What if it was a four-letter shift? The *U* became *Y*, the *K* became *O*. . . .

The sounds of the room faded into white noise as he scribbled away. Letters seemed to swirl before his eyes like a flock of starlings, and then all at once they formed a pattern.

Max blinked. He glanced up to clear his vision and saw Cinnabar's message shining through her code, clear as a copper penny in a reflecting pool.

"It says, *Where did my sister go?*" he blurted.

Cinnabar's mouth fell open in a perfect O. The other kids, halfway through their own decoding, turned to gawk.

"He cheated!" snapped Nikki. "She told him."

"I did not," said Cinnabar.

But Max didn't notice. He gazed down at his message and slumped in his seat, utterly and completely gobsmacked.

"What is it?" asked a stocky blond boy in the next row.

Max just stared. His message contained only four little words. But those four words were enough to rattle his world. The note read:

YOUR FATHER IS ALIVE.

CHAPTER 4

NEVER SASS THE LOCK MASTER

MUMBLING AN EXCUSE, Max staggered from the room. His heart thudded like wild hoofbeats; his thoughts swirled madly. Like any foster kid, he'd often played "if only." *If only my mum and dad were alive*, the game went, *my life would be normal. I'd have a real family.*

But it was one thing to play the game in bed on lonely nights, and another thing altogether to know that "if only" could actually come true.

Max trotted down the flights of stairs and knocked at the office door. Inside, Hantai Annie was scowling at the computer screen, red-framed reading glasses perched on her nose. A faint whiff of jasmine hung in the air.

"What you want?" she barked without looking up. "I'm busy."

Max strutted over to her desk and planted the decoded

message in front of her with a flourish. "Just this," he said, grinning. "My dad is alive, and I want to be with him."

"Eh? *Nanda?*" Hantai Annie scanned the note. "So?"

"So, I've got a real home now," said Max. "With a real family. You can ring Mr. Darny and have him take me out of here."

Hantai Annie snorted and gave the message a dismissive tap. "For this? Every orphan's daydream? *Baka yarou!* This fantasy, not proof. How do I know, maybe *you* wrote it."

Max flushed. "Compare my handwriting with the coded part. You can see they're different!"

Hantai Annie set the note aside. She paused and proceeded more gently. "Max. You don't even know who sent this. Do you?"

Max's eyes slid away. "Well, no, but—"

"So how you know it's real deal, eh? *Hontou ka?*"

Max shoved his hands into his pockets. "It's real, all right." It *had* to be.

The director said nothing, just raised her eyebrows and swiveled back to her computer.

"You don't care!" The words tumbled out of Max. "You only want me here so the government will keep sending you checks."

Hantai Annie turned and gave him the full effect of her glittering gaze. "So tell me," she said, her voice as flat as stale ginger ale, "if you father is alive, where is he?"

Max squirmed. "I don't know! But Mr. Darny can find him. And if he can't, I will! Just let me ring him."

The director flapped a hand at the phone on the desk. "Call. Who stopping you?"

Max lifted the receiver and punched in the only phone number he knew by heart. Darny picked up on the third ring.

"Mr. Darny, it's Max Segredo."

"Already?" said the caseworker. "What did you do?"

Max gripped the hard plastic receiver. "My dad is still alive."

"He, er, *what*?" Darny's nasal penguin voice jumped up an octave.

"You've got to find him and get me out of here," said Max, glancing at Hantai Annie. She'd gone back to glowering at her computer.

"*Out* of . . . ?" The caseworker choked and sputtered like he'd been gargling hot coffee. "Impossible. Preposterous. Who, er, told you this?"

"Someone slipped me a coded note," said Max.

"A coded . . ." Mr. Darny chuckled, sounding much more relaxed. "My dear boy, someone is having you on."

"What?"

"They're pulling your leg. Stop mucking about with this nonsense."

Max's fingers twisted the phone cord. "You don't understand. You've *got* to find him—*now*!"

The caseworker's voice grew as frosty as a November midnight. "No, *you* don't understand. This orphanage is *it*—the end of the line. You stay there and make it work, or you go directly to juvenile hall."

"But I—"

Darny's voice rose in crescendo. "Settle down, stop causing trouble, and make the best of your ruddy, miserable, wretched lot!"

Click.

Max listened to the dial tone for a long moment, watching Hantai Annie tap away at the keyboard.

At last she looked up. "Anything else? No? Next class starts in five minutes. *Hayaku!*"

Max hung up the phone, face burning. "This isn't over." He stalked toward the entryway. They wanted to treat him like a know-nothing, snot-nosed kid? Fine. He'd show them.

Closing the office door behind him, Max crossed to the front entrance and twisted the knob. Locked. He looked for dead bolts to turn, latches to undo. Just above the knob, a tall silver box sported six buttons, a slot for swiping a card key, and a matchbox-sized touch screen.

He pressed the buttons. Nothing. He poked the touch screen. More nothing. Its display read: INVALID ENTRY.

Max rattled the knob and growled. Then he hauled off and kicked the door. *Bam!* It didn't budge. Solid as a bank vault.

This wasn't an orphanage; it was a prison.

He paced the entryway, taking deep breaths. Get a grip, Max, he told himself. No matter how formidable its security, every prison had a weak spot. There *must* be a way out of Merry Sunshine, and whatever the cost, Max intended to find it.

Ignoring Hantai Annie's orders, he prowled the first floor, hunting for a chink in the building's armor. The house had more nooks and crannies than a king-size English muffin. His investigation revealed that every window was barred, and that the back door boasted the same complicated electronic lock as the front entrance.

Ten minutes into this search, Styx appeared, like a grouchy crew-cut genie. "Oi!" he grunted. "Don't be a git." He gripped Max by the arm and hustled him upstairs.

Max didn't struggle. This was merely a detour.

The bearlike man brought him to a cramped third-floor room that smelled of old sweat socks and machine oil. Cardboard boxes brimmed with doorknobs, lock mechanisms, and other metal paraphernalia. For seating, the room offered only four beat-up desk-and-chair sets scavenged from an ancient classroom back when Einstein was in knee pants.

By the time they arrived, the other students had already formed small groups clustered around the desks or sitting on the floor. A short, bullet-headed black man was pacing like a bored tiger in a cage, saying something about pins. The gleam of his single earring was outdone only by the shine from his bald dome.

The man's lecture broke off as Max entered. "Ah, the new lad. So nice of you to grace us with your presence."

"Nonsense," said Max, deadpan. "The pleasure is all mine."

"Ooh," said the man. "A cheeky monkey. Ta, Styxie."

Styx sighed and left without a word, shutting the door behind him.

"Right, boyo, I'm Roger Stones," said the bullet-headed man. He took a slurp from his coffee mug. "You can call me Mr. Stones or Boss Man."

A couple of students chuckled. Brownnosers, Max guessed.

"Welcome to lock—uh, Manual Dexterity class," Stones continued. "Join a group and jump in."

Max wandered over to a desk where Cinnabar and the heavyset blond boy from Maths and Puzzles were eyeing a doorknob. Cinnabar looked up, frowning. "Where did you run off to?"

"Had to see a man about a hippo," said Max.

Mr. Stones scowled at him. "Put a sock in it, sunshine. Unless I ask you a direct question, *I* do the talking in here. Now, you gormless bunch, where were we?"

The blond boy raised his hand. "Pins and tumblers, sir."

"Right, then. Open your kits and take out a medium pick and a tension wrench—that'd be the one with the ninety-degree bend in it."

Cinnabar unfolded a palm-sized black leather kit and selected the recommended tools from a gleaming array of metal picks.

"Wait," Max blurted. "We're learning *lock picking*?"

Cinnabar gave him a look that said "duh" in five different languages.

"Got a problem with that, sweetness?" growled the bullet-headed man.

"No." Max grinned broadly. "None at all. Tell me, does this kit work on doors with card-key locks?"

At that, the whole class guffawed. All except for Nikki and her weasel-faced friend, who stared at Max with incredulous contempt.

"You're a riot," said Mr. Stones.

"Well, does it?" Max said.

"Shockingly, you're not the first to ask that, peaches. And the answer is no. Now, everyone stop jabbering and start picking."

Max avoided the teacher's scowl, his eye happening to land on a bookshelf, where the title *Advanced Lock-Picking Techniques* caught his eye. *Hmm . . .*

The blond boy leaned closer and whispered in a nasal twang, "Cheer up, mate. First time with Mr. Stones, everyone wipes out. I'm Wyatt."

"Max."

"Mind if I have first go at it?" asked Wyatt.

Cinnabar and Max shook their heads. As Stones talked the class through the procedure, Wyatt inserted the wrench, applied tension, and fiddled with the pick. After an eternity of fumbling, the lock surrendered. He beamed. "Ripper!"

Max took his turn, then Cinnabar. After everyone had tried their hand at it a few times, Mr. Stones passed out wafer locks, and the orphans practiced picking those. By the end of the session, Max knew as much about lock picking as your average juvenile delinquent, maybe more.

He smiled. "This should come in handy."

"Like a chunk of Mr. Zog's on a surfari," said Wyatt.

Cinnabar raised an elegant eyebrow. "Let me guess: English isn't your first language."

Wyatt looked puzzled. "It's my *only* language."

As the students returned their locks to the cardboard boxes, Mr. Stones barked, "Listen up! Since you plonkers aren't completely useless at manual dexterity, Director Wong has authorized me to give you a treat."

Wyatt grinned. "It's not crumb cake, is it? I love crumb cake."

"Ooh, I couldn't tell, greedy guts," sneered Nikki, poking his soft belly. Wyatt blushed and twisted away from her.

"Neither cake nor pudding," said Stones. "But it's a right treat. You poppets have earned the privilege of practicing your skills off campus. Field trip after lunch."

Max's eyes lit up. The group erupted into excited chatter, and students began heading off to the dining room. Cinnabar shot Max a glance, but he lingered by the bookshelf, pretending to study the spines until she'd gone and the room was nearly empty. Then he leaned close, slipping the lock-picking book off the shelf and under his T-shirt.

When he stepped into the hallway, Mr. Stones was waiting. "Putting on some pounds there, boyo?" He rapped Max's stomach with a knuckle, thumping against the concealed book.

"Must be all that yummy orphanage food," said Max.

"This isn't a library, sunshine," said Stones, holding out his hand until Max reluctantly surrendered the volume. "And your nicking technique needs work. Perhaps I'll have a word with the director."

"Brilliant," said Max. "Can't wait."

"Cheers, then." The bullet-headed man nodded and then swaggered back into the room to reshelve the book. Max studied the doorknob.

"And don't bother casing the lock," came Mr. Stones's voice from inside. "I've got me own special rig. You couldn't crack it in a million years."

Max sighed and moved on. At the top of the staircase, Cinnabar was waiting. She fell in beside him as they descended the stairs. "What was that all about?"

"Oh, some extra-credit work," said Max.

"Right," she said. "Because you're such an ace student."

Max shrugged.

"Listen, Segredo," she said, tugging him to a stop at the second-floor landing.

"What?" The sweet fragrance of orange blossoms enveloped him. Her shampoo? Her perfume? He was acutely aware of her hand on his arm.

"The director ordered me to show you around," said Cinnabar. She released her grip. "It's not like I volunteered, okay? So next time you decide to disappear, tell me first."

Max put a mocking hand to his chest. "Ah, fair maid. I didn't know you cared."

"Don't flatter yourself," said Cinnabar. A dark thought flitted across her face, and she glanced away. Half to herself, she said, "I've got enough to worry about without adding you."

There was nothing to say to that, so Max said nothing. Foster kids have worries like dingoes have fleas; talking doesn't help. The two of them walked down to the ground floor in silence, side-by-side. As they entered the dining room, Max thought again about the after-lunch excursion.

Cinnabar's eyes narrowed. "What are you grinning about?" she asked.

"Field trip."

"But you don't even know where we're going."

Max shook his head, still smiling. "Doesn't matter. I love field trips."

What he really loved was this: field trips, by their nature, take place off premises. And someone who finds himself off premises might conceivably wander away from the group to pursue his own agenda. Like, for example, locating his missing, formerly-thought-to-be-dead father.

"Field trips," said Max, "can be *so* educational."

FUN AND GAMES WITH LASER BEAMS

BECAUSE THIS WAS no ordinary orphanage, Max suspected it would be no ordinary field trip. Exactly *how* un-ordinary became apparent right after lunch, when he spotted their chaperones standing in the driveway beside two silver Range Rovers. Styx hid his round face behind a false mustache and horn-rimmed glasses. Mr. Stones wore a dreadlocked wig with a green-and-red cap, looking for all the world like a Rasta gnome.

"Sporty," muttered Max. But it didn't faze him. He had already formed an idea about the kind of operation Hantai Annie was running—an idea that made sense of Merry Sunshine's many peculiarities.

"Get a wiggle on, you dawdlers!" Stones barked at the students leaving the house. "Let's go!"

The skies were as gloomy as a schoolboy at the end of

summer, but last night's rain had slowed to a halfhearted drizzle. The Puzzles teacher, Madame Chiffre, stood by the front door watching the street, one hand in her bulky purse. The Indian woman, whose name Max still didn't know, hurried them along to the waiting cars. As the ten orphans piled in, Max asked Wyatt, "Does the staff always wear disguises for field trips?"

"Depends on the trip," said the blond boy, munching on a Cadbury bar.

Max found himself wedged between Wyatt and Rashid, who was still wearing his red tracksuit. Cinnabar sat in the front seat, between Styx and a Chinese-looking girl with a spiky haircut. Nikki and Weasel Boy, thankfully, rode in the other car.

The Range Rovers swung out onto the road, taking a circuitous route that wound back on itself repeatedly and wove through several neighborhoods. Styx and Stones made sudden unexpected turns, almost as if they were trying to throw someone off their track. Looking back, Max couldn't tell if they were being followed. Come to that, he couldn't even tell where they were headed.

"So," said Wyatt, after the fourth or fifth turn, "what's your story, mate?"

"My story?" said Max.

Wyatt held up a finger to signal *Just a second*. He popped the last chunk of chocolate into his mouth and chomped away.

"My gran always said to chew everything thoroughly," he said around his mouthful. "It's healthier."

"Uh-huh," said Max.

Wyatt swallowed. "So, how'd you land at Merry Sunshine?"

"The usual way." Max looked out the window. "The stork brought me."

"My folks got sent to jail," said Wyatt, "so I went to live with my gran. Then *she* died, poor old thing, so I bounced through three different foster homes—each worse than the next. Totally shambolic. One of 'em used to lock me in my room, and only let me out for school and to use the loo." Wyatt paused for breath. "What's the worst foster you ever had?"

"Look, I don't really want to talk about it," said Max.

"Why not? Hantai Annie says we're like family. And family's got no secrets, right?"

In Max's experience, families had nothing *but* secrets. He lifted a shoulder. "No offense, but I don't plan on being part of this 'family' very long."

"Oh." Wyatt blinked rapidly. He looked like a surprised baby—all round cheeks, rosebud mouth, and big blue eyes. "Suit yourself," he murmured, turning to the window.

The drizzle finally drizzed its last drops, but flat gray clouds pressed down on the city like a massive iron, and puddles had collected at every dip in the road. After leaving the residential area for an industrial zone, the Range Rovers emerged in the port district. They turned onto a two-lane road, which snaked around the harbor and dipped down a hill.

Rashid leaned over and muttered, "Your name's Segredo, right?"

"Yeah," said Max.

The hawk-nosed boy regarded Max with a grave stare. "I hear your father was one of the greats."

"Great *whats*?" said Max, half turning toward him.

The older boy lifted a shoulder. "You know. He was in the biz, like us."

Before Max could confirm his suspicion of exactly which biz they were in, the cars stopped in a small parking lot and Styx grunted, "Out you go."

Rashid slid out the door, and the moment was gone.

On one side of the parking lot, behind a cyclone fence topped with barbed wire, squatted a long, low building. Its sides were gunmetal gray, completely anonymous. No graffiti marred its walls—unlike the grubby warehouse on the other side of the lot, which boasted some particularly creative (and rude) decorations. Drifts of trash lay here and there, and a rotten-fish smell overpowered the salty tang in the air, wrestling it to the ground.

"I can see why we'd want to come here," said Max. "It's lovely."

"The perfect vacation spot," Cinnabar agreed, deadpan. They exchanged a quick glance.

"Gather 'round, you plonkers," said Mr. Stones, straightening his Rasta wig and cap. "Look lively!"

When the students from both cars had formed a rough semicircle, he announced, "Theory is one thing—any git can learn a little theory—but practice is another can of worms, my lovelies. Practice makes . . . what, now?"

"Perfect," a few students muttered.

"Sheer genius. Today, your practice exercise is to break into that warehouse"—he pointed to the building behind the fence—"and out again, without leaving a trace. Clear?"

"What are we stealing?" asked Max.

Mr. Stones scowled. "Who said anything about stealing?"

Max raised an eyebrow. "Why else would you break into a warehouse?"

"You'll find out once we're inside, peaches," said Stones.

Max jammed his hands into his pockets. He was nearly certain now about the orphanage's real purpose.

"What if we wipe out?" Wyatt asked, round-eyed.

"Wipe out?" said Stones.

"You know, get caught?"

"Don't," said the teacher. "Other questions?" When nobody spoke, he continued. "Right, then. First off, how do you get past the fence?"

"Easy," sneered Nikki. "Just cut a hole in it." She bumped

fists with the weasel-faced boy, whom Max had discovered was called Dermot.

Stones folded his thick arms. "And exactly which part of 'don't leave a bleedin' trace' didn't you understand, sweetness?"

The orphans laughed. Nikki flushed redder than her hair.

"Anyone else?" said Stones.

Wyatt raised his hand. "Use a ladder?"

"And if you haven't got one?" asked the bullet-headed man. "Max?"

"Huh?" Max had been surveying the road and surrounding area, calculating his best escape route. "Oh, I'd uh, lay the car's floor mats across the barbed wire and just climb right over."

"Not bad," said Mr. Stones. "But how do you know the fence isn't electrified?"

"I'd let Nikki go first," said Max. The group laughed again, a bit nervously this time. Nikki and Dermot glared, but Max refused to feel bad. He considered it small payback for her nearly suffocating him that morning. "Or I'd test it with a metal screwdriver that had a rubber handle."

"One point for Young Einstein," said Mr. Stones. "Now, get cracking, you cack-handed mouth breathers! I can see five ways into that building from here; I expect you to find at least one."

While two students removed an extension ladder from one of the roof racks, Rashid tested the fence for live current and pronounced it safe. Up went the ladder, over went the floor mats. A grinning Tremaine led the way across, and the orphans followed one by one.

"Styx, watch the cars?" asked Mr. Stones.

The bearlike man made a sour face. "That's me. Always the glamor jobs." He leaned against one of the Range Rovers, ran a hand over his crew cut, and stared off into space.

"Coming?" Stones asked Max.

Max feigned indifference. "Thought I'd help Styx keep a lookout."

"Too late for cold feet," growled the Rasta gnome. "You're in it now, me lad." He none-too-gently hauled Max over to the ladder and nudged him onto the first rungs.

Max sighed. He'd have to find another way to wander off. Scaling the ladder, he squinted at the low gray warehouse. "The owners are okay with this, right?"

Mr. Stones snorted. "And what fun would that be?"

When Max and Mr. Stones had safely dropped to the ground, Styx handed the ladder over. Stones dug two pairs of binoculars from his bag and passed them around so everyone could survey the warehouse. "Someone tell me, what's the security setup?" he asked.

"Two cameras we can see," said Nikki.

"Three, including the one on the flagpole," said Max. Nikki glowered at him.

"Alarms on both doors," reported Cinnabar. "Maybe the

windows too." She gave them both a superior look.

Mr. Stones unzipped his day pack and laid it open on the ground. "So how do we slip in under the radar using just what's in the bag?"

The orphans rummaged through the jumble of tools, boxes, and equipment.

Nikki fished out a grayish chunk of some claylike material. "Ace! Plastic explosives." Her grin was wicked. Dermot made a sound like a bomb going off.

"No trace," said Stones, taking it back. "Remember?"

Wyatt poked through the bag's contents, looking glum. "You didn't bring a laptop? So much for hacking the system and redirecting the cameras."

As the group continued to argue over options, Max felt drawn into the caper despite himself. He scanned the road and the parking lot. Still deserted.

"We look like a bunch of kids breaking into a warehouse," he said. "How long before someone comes by?"

"The owners will be . . . distracted," said Mr. Stones, brushing back his dreadlocks. "But we don't have all day. So, class, what's our solution?"

Cinnabar held up a sleek black gizmo the size of a small pocketbook. "What's this do?"

"Beauty!" Wyatt cackled. "This bad boy causes a righteous controlled power outage." He took it from her, along with two leads. "Can I, Mr. Stones? Please?"

"Go," he said. "And take sunshine here." Stones indicated Max. "The rest of you lot, sort out the best entry point and get ready to rock and roll."

Avoiding the security cameras, Wyatt and Max circled the warehouse to the far side, where power lines drooped down to connect with the building. Wyatt donned green rubber gloves. He inclined his head at a thick cable entering a fuse box.

"Gotta go easy with this 'un," he said. "Make a blue and you'll get axed."

Max cocked his head. "They speak English where you come from?"

"Australia?" Wyatt looked puzzled. "All the time, mate."

Max boosted him up, and the blond boy gingerly connected two long wires to the line. Back on the ground, Wyatt plugged them into the device. "And to think, all I have to do is push this little button. . . ."

Foomf! Sparks showered from the fuse box above. They jumped back.

"Cool!" Max said, despite himself.

Wyatt hooted. "Epic!" He jerked the leads free, tucked the device under his arm, and took off running at an awkward gait.

"Wait," called Max. "What's the hurry?"

Wyatt called back over his shoulder. "The generator switches on in ninety seconds. We've got to be inside by then."

"*Now* you tell me," Max said, dashing after him.

By the time they rounded the corner, the rest of the group was clumped around the door. Cinnabar's picks were already worrying at the knob, while Rashid leaned over her, tackling the dead bolt.

Max and Wyatt panted up to them.

"Hurry!" gasped Wyatt.

Mr. Stones eyed his watch with a smile. "Plenty of time, cupcake. Right, girl?"

Cinnabar ignored him and kept fiddling with her picks. Her tongue peeked out of the corner of her mouth and a bead of sweat rolled down her cheek, despite the cool weather.

Click. Rashid's lock surrendered. He stepped back.

"Any time now," said Nikki.

"Get knotted," snapped Cinnabar.

"Fifteen seconds," said Stones. His smile looked a little glassy around the edges.

Cinnabar closed her eyes, made one final tweak, and . . .

Click.

The teacher turned the knob with a rubber-gloved hand and yanked open the door. "Everyone in!"

The orphans surged past him. "Freeze!" cried Stones. They stopped in a tight knot just inside the door. Mr. Stones slammed it shut behind them.

"What's wrong?" asked Max, who'd been jammed into the front of the group. He lifted his foot to move farther into the building.

The teacher snagged his coat collar. "Wait."

A *ka-chunk* reverberated deeper in the warehouse. An engine hummed, and four horizontal beams of red light winked into existence, mere inches in front of Max's nose.

"Cor!" breathed Wyatt.

"Laser detection," said Stones. "Very posh indeed."

Without moving, Max scanned the dimly lit space, which smelled of mothballs, scorched earth, and takeout curry. He noted the racks of steel shelves stacked with mysterious bundles and barrels, and some odd-looking contraptions hanging from the ceiling at various points.

"What are those?" he asked.

"Mantraps," said Stones.

Nikki grinned. "Brilliant. How do they work?"

"Hit the trigger and it snatches you right up in a steel claw." Stones shook his head admiringly, and his dreadlocks swayed like dancing snakes. "These blokes are thorough. They've got everything but lava and a shark pool."

After tucking his wig into the day pack, Mr. Stones showed the students how to slip between the lasers without breaking the light beams and triggering the alarm. When everyone had passed inside, he gave his last instructions.

"Here's what we're after, poppets: information. Any intel you can find on shipments from Argentina, or any mention of Nullthium-Ninety."

"Information?" Max blurted. "I thought you were training us to be criminals."

Mr. Stones chuckled. "Don't be daft. Merry Sunshine is

a school for *spies*, not crooks. There's a difference."

Max flushed. Nikki favored him with a mocking pout. "Aw, Young Einstein's a bit slow on the uptake."

Dermot sniggered.

The teacher passed out ten blue ballpoint pens to the group.

"We're taking *notes*?" Wyatt complained. "How old-school is that?"

"They're cameras," said Stones. "Click the button twice to take a picture. Now, spread out. Five of you cover the warehouse with me; five of you go toss the office. We've got fifteen to twenty minutes, tops."

The orphans jumped to their search. Max trailed behind Cinnabar and Wyatt in the group headed for the office, his mind whirring away like the paparazzi's cameras. If Merry Sunshine was a school for spies, and Rashid had said his father was in the same business *they* were, then . . .

My dad's a spy?

He wasn't sure how he felt about that. Yes, a spy was better than an out-and-out criminal, but what kind of agent was his dad, and whom did he work for? More to the point, where had he been all these years—on a mission? Imprisoned? At some kind of secret agent Club Med?

Max resolved to learn some answers soon. But first things first. Time to try out his new skills.

He shoved his way to the front of the group just as

Cinnabar was removing her lock picks. "I'll take the knob, you get the dead bolt," he said. Wyatt handed him a kit. In a few minutes, the office door creaked open.

A guy could come to like this spy stuff, Max thought.

Once inside, Tremaine and the spiky-haired girl tackled the filing cabinet. Max sat in the chair and rifled through the desk, while beside him, Cinnabar and Wyatt converged on the first of two computers.

Cinnabar switched the machine on. "It's asking for a password," she said.

"No worries." Wyatt smirked. "Reboot and toggle F8, then boot up in safe mode as the administrator. Works every time."

To Max, who'd rarely been allowed to use computers at his foster homes, the blond boy's instructions sounded as clear as a bus schedule in ancient Greek. But they seemed to do the trick, so he focused on searching the desk. Nothing but the usual office-supply junk cluttered the main drawer. The middle side drawer held more promise—it contained several notebooks.

"Here, let me," said Wyatt, trying to elbow his way onto the computer.

"No, I've got it," Cinnabar replied. She swatted his hand away.

Wyatt sulked. Max glanced at Cinnabar's determined profile, then turned his attention back to his work.

Picking up a red notebook, he leafed through it, snapping away with his camera pen. Most of the entries seemed to be written in some kind of alphanumeric cipher, but near the back he found a list of uncoded names. One jumped out at him: *Simon Segredo.*

A wave of prickly heat swept his body. He sat up straighter, galvanized.

Max scanned the list for a heading, some kind of clue about its significance. Nothing. He flipped more pages until a sharp word from Cinnabar caught his attention.

"Leave it alone!" she snapped.

Glancing over, he found that Wyatt was hovering by the second machine, eyes wide and mouth set in a half smile.

"Wyatt, you don't know what that does," said Cinnabar.

The other computer looked nothing like the desktop model; it crouched on the credenza, wide and solid, like an oversized mechanical toad. Insulated electrical cords linked it to a tall, gleaming device covered in knobs and LED displays. A bank of keys covered the lower third of its face.

Wyatt's hand wandered toward a yellow key. "I bet I could work this thingo and hack the—" He pushed the button, and all at once, two things happened.

First, an ear-piercing alarm began to *woop-woop-woop* at a volume loud enough to make rock-concert roadies cringe.

And second, a pair of enormous metal jaws sprang from the ceiling, plunging directly down on Wyatt.

CHAPTER 6

EVERYTHING GOES PEAR-SHAPED

WYATT STOOD frozen in shock. He gaped at the steel teeth about to chomp him like a fresh tortilla chip.

Without thinking, Max dove at the blond boy. He seized Wyatt around the waist, and both of them tumbled to the carpet. The jaws crunched down. They bit through the back of the office chair and hauled it up to the ceiling, casters spinning.

For a moment, nobody moved. The alarm kept up its *woop-woop*.

Wyatt croaked, "But it's supposed to *trap* you, not *kill* you."

"I'll mention that to the designer," said Max, rolling off of him.

"Everybody out!" cried Cinnabar. "Move it!"

The other two orphans slammed the filing cabinet drawers and shot through the office door. Max helped Wyatt to stand. The boy's legs were as wobbly as a first-time stilt walker, and his face hung slack. "Wha?" he mumbled.

"Hurry up, you berks!" yelled Cinnabar. "Look!"

A metal plate was descending from the top of the door frame like a slow-motion guillotine. In a handful of seconds it would seal them in the room, nice and tight, until the warehouse security team showed up to claim them.

Max shoved Wyatt at the door. The blond boy stumbled into Cinnabar, who slung him through the opening and darted after him.

Glancing back, Max saw the red book lying open on the desk. This was his first lead, his first chance for finding his father. How could he leave it behind?

"Max!" cried Cinnabar.

He lunged to the desk, snatched up the book, and spun.

The metal panel had reached waist height. It was accelerating.

Max dove for the gap and barely squeaked under the barrier. *Clang*—it met the floor, sealing the office. He tried to stand, but something held him. His shoelace was pinned under the plate. He tugged and tugged, but the blasted thing wouldn't pull free, nor would it break.

"I'm caught!"

Max cursed the Bumburgers, who'd bought him the tough hemp shoelaces in the first place. *They're ecofriendly and they'll last you forever,* Mrs. Bumburger had said.

Bollocks.

"Come on!" cried Cinnabar, propping up Wyatt, who looked a little green.

The sirens maintained their ear-splitting shriek. "I'll catch up!" shouted Max. He started unlacing his tennis shoe.

Cinnabar stared. "Of all the . . . *Cut it*, you bimble-brain!"

Max shrugged. "No knife."

Cinnabar growled in frustration, leaned Wyatt against the wall, and knelt by Max's leg. "Here." Her penknife parted the shoelace, and Max pulled free.

"Thanks."

Cinnabar and Max each gripped one of Wyatt's arms and hustled him toward the exit. In the main part of the warehouse the other students had covered their ears and were milling about uncertainly near the laser sensors, as Mr. Stones shouted unheard instructions. Thick yellowish smoke began pouring from ceiling vents.

"Don't breathe it!" shouted Max. "Anything that nasty-looking can't be good for you."

"Genius advice," Cinnabar yelled. "How can I *not* breathe?"

Mr. Stones bellowed something at the group, motioned for them to stand back, then hurled a chair into the laser beams. Another mantrap plunged from the ceiling and snatched up the chair in a heartbeat. The way was clear. He began shoving kids toward the exit, where, Max saw, a second steel plate was descending.

"Gee, you think they have enough security here?" he shouted to Cinnabar.

"What?"

Together, they bustled Wyatt through the door, ignoring his protestations of, "I'm fine. Fair dinkum, mates." They escaped just in time, Stones rolling under the plummeting barrier last of all.

Once outside, the students ignored the security cameras and ran flat out, making for the ladder. The cool air seemed to revive Wyatt, who shook free of Max and Cinnabar and moved under his own power. Max swiveled his head, expecting armed agents with savage dogs to pounce on them from every direction. But the parking lot remained empty, aside from Styx and the cars.

One by one, the orphans scaled the fence and dropped over. Max hung back, sensing an opportunity. He was the last to climb, and by the time he reached the other side, his fellow students were piling into the cars with Styx and Stones.

No one was watching Max.

He tucked the red notebook under his arm and sprinted for the road like a jackrabbit with a guilty conscience. The shoe with the broken lace flapped awkwardly, threatening to come off. But Max didn't stop. If he could only reach the roadside bushes before he was missed, maybe he could hide until everyone had gone.

Tires squealed behind him. Max ran harder—only ten more yards to go.

Styx's Range Rover pulled up on his left. A window buzzed down. "Get in!" yelled the bearish man as the car screeched to a halt and the door swung open.

Max veered away to his right. But the move made his shoe pop off, and as he stumbled, the other Range Rover swung in front, cutting him off. Tremaine leapt out and grabbed Max.

A wide smile split the older boy's face. "It's faster if you drive, mon!"

Trapped, Max had no choice. He retrieved his lost shoe, squeezed into the backseat with Tremaine, and the cars roared off, bumping along the access road.

"Did you get confused?" asked the girl with the spiky hair, leaning past Tremaine to see Max.

"Yeah." Max clasped the notebook to his chest. "Too much going on."

Mr. Stones's wise eyes found Max's in the rearview mirror. He knew Max hadn't gotten confused, but all he said was, "Well, sunshine, how'd you like your first field trip?"

Back at the orphanage, the two chaperones and ten students jammed into Hantai Annie's office, all talking over each other and trying to be heard. At last the director thwacked a ruler on her desktop with a loud crack and cried, "*Damare!* Shut up you mouth!"

The room fell quiet.

"Now," she said, "one at a time. Stones-*san*?"

The bullet-headed man winced. "The mission went pear-shaped, Director."

"Because of Max!" cried Nikki Knucks, elbowing her way to the front. "He sabotaged it!"

"You're whacked," said Max.

"He deliberately set off that alarm before we could find anything," said Nikki. "He's a mole; he's only here to spy on and sabotage us."

Max clenched his fists, but before he could speak, Cinnabar got into Nikki's face.

"You're barking mad," she said levelly, staring up at the bigger girl. "Max didn't trip the alarm, Wyatt did. And Max saved Wyatt's life."

"*Hontou ka?*" asked the director. "This true?"

Wyatt stared at the carpet. "Too right," he said, voice hoarse. "All my fault. If it wasn't for Max, I wouldn't even be here."

Max felt his face grow warm. Why was everyone speaking up for him even after he'd tried to run off? Didn't they know?

"And as for being a mole," Cinnabar continued, "he's no more a mole than Nikki is."

Two crimson spots appeared on the redhead's cheeks, and her eyes narrowed to slits. "You calling me a dirty mole?" Her voice simmered with danger, like dynamite stew.

"Right, that's enough," said Stones, stepping between them. "Stand down, sweet cakes."

Nikki's jaw set, but she said no more—unless you counted the volumes her eyes spoke to Max and Cinnabar. Once more, Max wondered why the beefy girl had it in for him. *Because she's a raging psycho nutter,* was his first thought.

"Anybody learn something useful?" The director's bright, birdlike gaze swept the room. She spotted the red notebook, which Max was holding across his stomach. "*Nanda?* What is that?"

He dropped it to his side. "Uh, nothing."

"Max lifted it from the office," Wyatt said admiringly. "Even with all that craziness going on."

Hantai Annie held out her hand. Briefly, Max regretted not having stuffed the book under his shirt when he'd had the chance, but it was too late now. He passed it over. The director flipped through a few pages.

"Code, *ka*? Maybe valuable. Good work, Max." She addressed the other orphans. "Anyone else?"

The spiky-haired girl stepped forward. "I took pictures of something that looked interesting." She handed her camera pen to the director, who jacked it into the computer, called up some images, and scanned through them.

"Good, Shan, very good," she mused.

"What is it?" asked Styx from his post by the door.

Hantai Annie frowned. "*Nanto iu ka?* How you say in English—shipping paper?"

"Bill of lading," said Mr. Stones.

She grunted. "Shows shipments going to museum in capital. *Yoku yatta*, Shan—good job!"

Shan nodded, suppressing a smile.

"Okay, everybody out!" said Hantai Annie. *"Hayaku!"* When the students hesitated, she stood. *"Hayaku* means *fast*—I have work to do."

The two men ushered the orphans from the room, but Max lagged behind.

"Still here?" asked the director. "You speak English? I said go!"

Max folded his arms. "A school for spies?"

"Ah, you figure it out on first day. Bright boy." Hantai Annie's attention returned to the bill of lading images on her computer screen.

Max moved closer. "You can't just take a pack of orphans and turn them into secret agents."

"Doushite da?" said the director. "Why not?"

"Because it's, I don't know . . . *illegal.*"

Hantai Annie waved Max's words aside. "Government wants orphanage to educate orphans. We teach useful skills."

"Lock picking? Code breaking?"

Hantai Annie nodded. "Espionage is old, noble profession, always in demand. Good job for when you grow up."

"But . . . you're trying to force me to become a spy," said Max.

"Force? Never." Hantai Annie looked up from the screen

and considered him. "We give you tryout. If you fit, you stay; if not, you go."

"What if I want to go *now*, to join my father?"

She shook her head. "Too dangerous. I am responsible for you safety. Cannot let orphans run off, chasing rumors."

"And what if I find my father and he wants me to live with him. What then?" Max stood right up against the desk, staring at the director. She met his gaze for a long moment.

"Then," said Hantai Annie mildly, "we let you go. Blood is blood. But until that day, *we* are your family."

Max's eyes dropped to the red notebook on her desk. "You know, I could work on cracking that code for you." *And find out why my father is in that book.*

"This?" The director rested a hand on the notebook. "This for professionals. Now, go. Practice your skills."

Max gave her a tight-lipped smile and left. He would practice his skills, all right. He would break out of this orphanage prison and find his father—then she'd *have* to let him go.

Since he'd already combed the first floor for weaknesses, he headed up to the second, prowling through back hallways and classrooms, alcoves and bedrooms. He interrupted a couple of study groups and one make-out session. But his search was as fruitless as an all-beef buffet. Every window was barred.

He climbed to the third floor, half thinking he might hang a bedsheet out a window and climb down it like Rapunzel's hair. Making his way along a smooth stretch of hallway unbroken by doors, Max noticed something odd. There, in the wall itself, was a narrow vertical gap—maybe three or four inches' worth—that stretched from floor to ceiling.

On closer inspection, he realized that a section of the wall had pivoted inward, like a secret panel, revealing a glimpse of a hidden room. Muffled voices carried from inside.

". . . must have the element." It was a creaky voice, like an older man. "Without it, the Process is crippled, nearly worthless."

Drawn by curiosity, Max crept nearer.

"Bien sur," came Madame Chiffre's familiar tones. Now Max could see the Maths and Puzzles teacher in profile through the gap, tinkering with something on a table. "But ze Nullthium eez rare, and illegal to import, *n'est-ce pas*?"

"They can't have bought up all of it," said the older man. A white lab coat and the back of a silver-haired head moved into view as he joined her. The man's body partly blocked a worktable, which was crowded with all sorts of tools. At the center, on a metal frame, sat an object that seemed to be a cross between an operator's headset and an old-fashioned American football helmet.

Max brought his eye to the gap for a closer look.

Madame Chiffre spotted the movement. "You there!" She rushed to the entrance, blocking the room from sight. "This eez off-limits for students. Why are you here?"

"Taking the grand tour," said Max lightly. "Aren't the peacock cages on this floor?"

The teacher's face didn't crack a smile; her nose jutted toward him like an accusing finger. "Stay on ze second floor or below, unless you're in class. Now, scoot!" She shut the wall panel in his face. A hidden latch clicked.

Interesting, thought Max. What's so secret about their little project? Did our field trip have something to do with it?

But as this mystery didn't promise to help his escape, he dismissed the encounter for the moment and finished inspecting the third and fourth floors. Still no unbarred windows. This was a maximum-security orphanage to end all maximum-security orphanages.

Temporarily stymied, Max returned to his room to plan his next move and found Wyatt sitting on his bed, chewing gum and holding the framed photo of his mother. When he entered, the blond boy jumped to his feet.

"Is this your mum?" asked Wyatt.

Max took the photo from his hands. "Yeah." He placed it carefully back on the nightstand beside the gold lighter and his lucky stone.

"She's pretty."

"She was," said Max.

Wyatt dug at the carpet with the toe of his shoe. "I, uh, don't have any pictures of my folks. My first foster took all that away, said I needed to 'adjust to reality.'"

Max gave a sympathetic wince. "Fosters."

"Too right, mate," said Wyatt. He cleared his throat nervously and gazed at Max. The silence stretched like a slingshot rubber band.

"Look," said Max. "I need to—"

"You saved my life," Wyatt blurted.

Max waved him off and busied himself straightening his bedspread. "Ah, you would've moved in time."

Wyatt shook his head, blond curls bouncing like springs. "I'd be cactus."

"Cactus?"

"Shark bait—dead or maimed, a mangled chunk of bloody flesh dangling from a steel . . ." His voice trailed off, and he shivered. "But you saved me."

"Anyone would have—"

"No. *You* did it." The blond boy stood uncomfortably close, his blue eyes boring into Max's. "I'm in your debt. If there's ever anything I can do for you, mate—*anything*—just ask."

Max started to object, and then paused as a thought struck him. He cocked his head, considered, and drew in a breath. "There *is* one thing. . . ."

"Name it," said Wyatt.

"Help me find my father."

A frown creased Wyatt's forehead. "But I thought he was dead. You're an orphan, right?"

Max sat down on the bed. "Can you keep a secret?"

Wyatt perched next to him. "Like the grave." He mimed zipping his lips, but the effect was diluted by his vigorous gum chewing.

"My dad is still alive," said Max. "I got a coded message."

"Far out," said Wyatt. "What's our move?"

"Read through my file, and that red notebook, for any clues on where he might be."

Wyatt nodded. "And where's your file?"

"Under lock and key," said Max, "in Hantai Annie's office."

"In—?" Wyatt swallowed his gum.

TEA AND BIKKIES AND BREAK-INS

AT DINNER THAT NIGHT, just as the orphans were tucking into a gut-busting Indian feast, the director and Styx strode into the dining room. Styx tugged at the collar of a black suit, which fit him about as well as a wet suit fits a grizzly bear. And Hantai Annie sported not her usual practical yoga clothes, but black silk pants and a high-necked blouse with a crimson plum-blossom pattern. Her hair was pulled into an elegant twist.

Clearly, something was up. The students paused at the sight, forks halfway to mouths. Speculation traveled along the table.

"Shut your pieholes, you lot!" Styx barked. "Director?"

Hantai Annie Wong stalked to the head of the table and surveyed the orphans for a long moment, hands clasped behind her back. At last she spoke. "This is dangerous time for our school. Our enemies are strong, so we must be smarter.

And quicker. In two days, I sending four students on special mission. *Toppu himitsu*—very secret."

Excitement rippled through the group. Max set down his half-eaten samosa and shifted in his chair to face Hantai Annie. He doubted he'd be eligible, but still—any opportunity to get out of this prison had his full attention. After only a night and a day at the orphanage, he was feeling as restless as a bald eagle in a birdcage.

"What's the mission?" asked Cinnabar.

"Who's going?" said Nikki.

The director sent her a challenging look. "Depends on you—all of you. Team will go to capital. If you make team, you learn mission."

"Ace!" crowed Wyatt. "How do we get on the team, then?"

"Be good."

"That's it?" said Nikki. "Just be good?"

Tremaine laughed. "That eliminates you, Nikki Knucks." She scowled and began to rise from her chair. Dermot laid a hand on her arm.

"Chotto mate!" Hantai Annie held up her palms in a *settle down* gesture. "Whoever does best in class goes on mission."

"Is everyone eligible?" asked Max.

"Everyone," said the director. Max felt a tingle spread through his limbs, like a slow-building fire. He just might win a chance to use his growing spy skills—while tracking down his father.

Nikki spluttered, "But, but that's not fair! Some of us have been here for years, while little Maxi-Pad just arrived."

"Yeah," Dermot seconded.

"So," said Hantai Annie, black eyes twinkling, "then you have unfair advantage." She spoke over Nikki's protest. "Do your best, everyone. This mission very important to your future—to *our* future. *Gambatta!*"

"*Gambatta*?" muttered Max.

"Go for it," said Rashid. He shrugged. "You pick it up after a while."

The director pivoted on her heel and marched from the room like a drill sergeant. Styx lumbered after her.

When the door shut behind them, the dining room erupted in chatter. Dessert lay momentarily forgotten on a tray at the center of the table—by all save Wyatt, that is. He grabbed a fistful of cookies, saying, "Shame to waste good biscuits," and sat down by Max.

"I'm stoked, mate!" Wyatt grinned widely. "Guess who's going on that mission?"

"Me," said Max. "But you can come as well."

Wyatt frowned. "Hey, but what about our little . . . you know, *project*?"

Max glanced around at the other kids jabbering away. He lowered his voice. "We'll do it tonight. And if I get any leads . . ."

"On your d-a-d?"

"I'll slip away and check them out in the city when we're on the mission."

Cinnabar eased into the chair on Max's other side. "What's all this about nipping off to find your dad?"

Max started at her intrusion. "Private conversation," he said, recovering and turning his shoulder on her. "Not your concern."

She held up an index finger. "First, you're in a spy school, so nothing is private. And second"—her middle finger joined the first—"Hantai Annie said I'm responsible for getting you settled, so yes, it *is* my concern."

"Don't you have someone else to annoy?" said Max.

Cinnabar pulled her hair back and into a scrunchie. "If you're planning to make the team so you can run off, I'll tell you right now you've got some big problems."

"Oh, yeah?"

"Yeah. Like, where will you sleep, and what will you live on?" she said. "You're only what, twelve?"

"Thirteen," Max said defensively.

Cinnabar's eyes flicked over him. "You're short for your age."

"But plucky. What's the other big problem? You're gonna tell on me?"

"No, you'll have to beat *me* for a spot. 'Cause I'm one of the best students here, and I am *definitely* going on that mission."

☼ ☼ ☼

Much later that night, Max and Wyatt sat in the downstairs library, flipping through *Survival Skills for the Modern Spy* and waiting for midnight to roll around. As far as Max was concerned, it couldn't come soon enough.

"And you're positive Mr. Stones won't be watching the monitors?" he asked.

"No worries," said Wyatt, turning a page. "Old Stonesy is like clockwork. Bloke's got to have his midnight tea and bikkie every night. Trust me, I've prowled this place before."

"Okay." Max had his doubts, but he didn't push it.

"Ooh, check this out!" said Wyatt. He pointed at a photo in the book. "Do you know how to survive falling into a shark tank?"

"Funny, but that never came up in my other foster homes."

Wyatt read, "'When the shark attacks, strike it repeatedly in the eyes or gills. If it senses you're not an easy meal, it will back off.'"

"Right," said Max. "And when are we ever going to fall into a shark tank?"

The blond boy looked up solemnly. "Really, Max. I thought you knew."

"Knew what?"

"All the best spy headquarters have shark tanks."

Max rolled his eyes. He checked his watch: Eleven fifty— ten minutes to go. For the twentieth time he inspected the lock picks and mentally reviewed their plan. It was as good as it would ever be.

Still, he fidgeted, flicking his gold-plated lighter on and off. A lot could go wrong, and he couldn't even be sure that they'd find something to help him locate his father. It was a risk, a long shot. But then, what foster kid's life wasn't?

"So, what do you really know about Hantai Annie Wong?" he asked, to kill time.

Wyatt shrugged. "She runs the school, she's a crackerjack spy, she mangles English. What else is there to know?"

"It doesn't bother you?" Max leaned his elbows on the oak table.

"What?"

"I mean . . ." He groped for the words. "Here she is, training a bunch of kids to be spies. Why kids? Why *us*?"

"Who cares?" Wyatt grinned. "We get to learn a lot of cool stuff. Mate, I'm praised for things I got thrown out of foster homes for. That's a step up."

"But we don't even know what side she's on."

"Side?" Wyatt reached into his canvas pouch and removed half a sandwich. The tang of tuna fish and spicy mustard drifted across the table.

"You know, the good guys or the bad guys?" said Max. "I mean, she could have us working for the worst scum of the earth."

"Ms. Annie?" Wyatt scrunched up his face as he bit into

the sandwich. "She's not like that. She's got heart."

Max spread his hands. "But how do you know? I bet she's not even from Hantai. I *know* that's not Chinese she's speaking."

A surf guitar riff rang from Wyatt's pouch, loud in the quiet room.

"Oops," he said. "Thought I had it on vibrate."

"Turn it off!" Max hissed.

Wyatt fumbled for his smartphone and silenced the alarm with a flourish. "There. It's go-time!" He stuffed the rest of the sandwich back into his pouch and stood.

"Luck," said Max, holding out his hand.

"Luck," said Wyatt, slapping it.

Cautiously, Max eased open the door and peeked into the entryway. All clear. He checked his watch. "Five . . . four . . . three . . . two . . . one. Easy Cheezy." Max held out his hand.

"Easy Cheezy." Wyatt passed him a can of processed cheese spray and then squeezed through the doorway and along the wall, stopping directly beneath the security camera. He squatted down and cupped his hands.

Max stepped into the makeshift stirrup, and Wyatt boosted him up. Two spritzes later, the camera lens was coated with a delicious, impenetrable cheese product. They made a beeline for the office door. Max opened his kit and removed a tension wrench and pick; but before he could begin, a low rumbling froze him in his tracks.

Grrrr . . .

A massive black-and-brown head out of nightmares emerged from the shadows by the stairs, followed by an enormous furry body. Gooseflesh rose all over Max's skin. His brain fired: Fight or flight? Then he recognized the monstrous creature.

It was the dog.

"Easy, Pinkerton," Wyatt whispered.

The beast growled even louder, sounding like a motorcycle gang revving up next door. Its hackles rose, and its lip curled to reveal a set of fangs like ivory steak knives. Pinkerton's dark eyes were fixed on Max.

"Easy, boy," said Max. "Sit! Relax! Chill!"

Stiff-legged, the huge dog stalked forward, great shoulder muscles bunching and unbunching, intent on its prey. Now the growls sounded like a jet aircraft.

Max edged back. "He'll wake up the whole house. Give him something!"

"What?"

"A toy. Your sandwich. Anything!"

Wyatt pouted. "But that's my snackie."

Pinkerton's growl rose another notch. Max's back bumped the front door.

"Wyatt!" he hissed. "Now!"

The blond boy fished the sandwich fragment from his pouch and held it out. "Here, Pinkerton!" The dog's nostrils twitched. His cinder-block head swung toward the food while a pink tongue the size of a hand towel licked its chops.

Three steps and a gulp, and the snack was history.

Max approached the office door. But once again, the dog began to growl.

"Oh, give me a break," Max muttered. He crossed to Wyatt, pulled the other half of the sandwich from his pouch, and flung it up onto the stairs. The monster dog padded off in pursuit.

"My sanger." The corners of Wyatt's mouth turned down.

"We'll make you another one. Come on."

They converged on the office door, and Max went to work. "You know what I like best about the classes here at Merry Sunshine?" he said, anchoring the tension wrench and probing the lock's inner structure.

"No, what?"

"They teach you something"—Max grinned as the tumblers snicked into place, the knob turned, and the door swung open—"you can actually use."

They switched on two LED flashlights Wyatt had been kind enough to filch from the equipment cabinet. Following their shielded beams, Max and Wyatt eased into the darkened office and shut the door behind them. The room felt different by night, spookier somehow. Shadows loomed, the samurai masks on the wall seemed to leer down at them, and the warm, stuffy air smelled of onions and incense.

Wyatt made straight for the computer, plopping himself down in the black leather desk chair. "Tell me your secrets, Sheila," he crooned, hitting the power button. A start-up chord boomed in the stillness. "Holy Dooley! Is she deaf?" He tapped a function key to lower the volume.

"Wait," said Max. "Don't change anything. She can't know we were here."

"Ah. Too right." Wyatt restored the original setting, then danced his fingers over the keyboard like a concert pianist.

Max hovered over his shoulder. "Well?"

The blond boy bit his lip. "Hmm . . . it won't let me in as the admin. Maybe if I try . . ." Another furious round of clacking keys. A frown. "Bummer."

"I thought you could hack this," said Max, gripping the chair back.

"You kidding? I am Wyatt, the Great and Powerful. All I need is time, mate."

Max shone the flashlight on his watch face. "Which we don't have. Stones returns from his break in eight minutes, and we need to be long gone by then."

Wyatt popped a hard candy into his mouth and cracked his knuckles. "She'll be apples."

"What?"

"No worries. I've hacked into tougher systems than this one."

Max sighed. Feeling as useless as a square-wheeled

bicycle, he decided to search for the red notebook he'd lifted from the warehouse. The desk had only one drawer, which contained pens, papers, and the usual bits and bobs you find in a desk—but no red notebook.

A blank sheet of stationery caught his eye. Max looked closer.

"'S-P-I-E-S,'" he read.

"How's that?"

"Systematic Protection, Intelligence, and Espionage Services—what it says on the school stationery. That's us." He smirked. "Subtle name."

"We're intelligent?" Wyatt said, gaze still fixed on the computer. "That's good news."

Max closed the drawer and paced around the office. The bookshelf held an assortment of books in different languages, a fat English dictionary, some plants, and a foot-high Buddha statue with an incense holder.

But no notebook.

His gaze landed on the sleek gray filing cabinet. *Hmm* . . .

In a heartbeat, the picks were in his hands and the flashlight was in his mouth, shining on the wafer lock. A few twists and turns, a little jimmying, and . . .

Click. The lock surrendered. Max slid the top drawer open and began flipping through the neat ranks of file folders.

"Did you hear something?" Wyatt asked.

"Squeaky drawer."

"Oh, good," said Wyatt. "Just as long as it wasn't . . ."

The office door swung open and the overhead lights switched on.

". . . the door."

TROUBLE WITH SHEILAS

MAX GAVE a guilty start and jerked away from the filing cabinet. "It's not what it looks like," he blurted. "We were—" He broke off when he saw who stood in the doorway. *"Cinnabar?"*

The girl's expression switched from stunned to accusing in the flick of a hummingbird's eyelash. "What are you doing here?"

The boys exchanged a look. "No," said Max. "What are *you* doing here?" Had she been spying on them?

"And why don't you close the door," said Wyatt. "And turn off the bloody lights."

Cinnabar seemed to recall where she was. She shut the door behind her and doused the lights. Then she switched on her flashlight. "Well, this is awkward."

"Not half as awkward as it would be if we told Hantai Annie you broke into her office," said Max.

"Fair point." Cinnabar pursed her lips. "Of course, then you'd have to tell her *how* you knew I'd broken into her office."

Max cocked his head. "Fair point."

"So, we have a standoff," said Wyatt.

They stared at each other some more, in silence.

The corners of Cinnabar's mouth tugged in the faintest suggestion of a smile. "I won't tell if you won't."

"Maybe," said Max.

"*Maybe?* You git, we're after the same thing."

Wyatt frowned. "You want to learn about Max's father too?"

Max kept his eyes on Cinnabar. "She means information. Now you know why *we're* here," he told her. "But what are *you* looking for?"

Cinnabar crossed to the computer. "Snoop while we talk?"

"Why not?" said Max. "I reckon we've only got about five minutes left."

She patted her hair. "Maybe a *little* longer. I created a diversion."

"Beauty," said Wyatt. "What kind?" He settled back into the chair and resumed his tapping on the keyboard.

"The trash bin fire in the courtyard kind."

"A classic." Max went back to rifling through file folders. "So . . . about your reason?"

Cinnabar inserted a flash drive into the computer. "It's my sister."

"Jazz?" said Wyatt. "Isn't she out on assignment?"

"She was. My older sister lives here as well," she told Max, "but she hasn't checked in with me for two days. I'm worried." She leaned across Wyatt, reaching for the keyboard. "Have you tried a backdoor?"

Wyatt elbowed her hand away. "*Yes*, I've tried. I'm not a complete grommet. Butt out and let me work."

"Touchy, touchy," she said.

Max finished searching the first file drawer and opened the second, paging through household bills, class records, and reams of duplicate reports to Child Welfare Services. Still no sign of his own file or the notebook.

The *tick-tick-tick* of the wall clock began to sound like the *tsk-tsk-tsk* of a disapproving foster parent. Time was running short.

What if I find no leads at all? What if I have to stay in this orphanage forever? To distract himself from these cheerful thoughts, Max asked Cinnabar, "Couldn't your sister be undercover or something? Maybe that's why she's out of touch."

Cinnabar looked up with a woeful expression. "You don't understand. She *always* calls. Jazz and I . . . Do you have a brother or sister?"

Max shook his head.

"After our folks died, Jazz made sure we always got placed together. She's stayed here with me even though she's old enough to leave." Cinnabar's golden eyes glistened. "If she hasn't called, it's because . . ." Her lips clamped together, and her gaze returned to the screen.

Max felt the urge to pat her shoulder, to tell her everything would be all right. But he didn't, partly because he'd never touched a girl that way, and partly because, in his experience, everything *wouldn't* be all right.

"Ha!" crowed Wyatt. "I'm a bloody genius."

"You're in?" asked Max.

"Cowabunga—in the tube!" Wyatt's fingers beat out a tattoo on the keyboard. "Let's just do a quick search for your dad." Cinnabar's fingers gripped his shoulder. *"And Jazz."*

Max glanced at his watch. Only a minute or two left, at most. He redoubled his efforts, and in the third drawer, wedged between two folders, he found it: the red notebook. He pulled it out, ready to lock up, until a file label caught his eye.

KNOWN OPERATIVES—INACTIVE

Operatives were spies, right?

Setting the notebook on top of the cabinet, Max lifted out the file and flipped through the reports. Each contained a brief summary of an agent's vital statistics and activities—many included photographs—and near the back of the folder he found a slim sheet on Simon Segredo.

Max stared. No photo, but there it was, his dad's life in black and white.

A buzzing distracted him. When he looked up, Cinnabar was fishing a phone from her pocket.

She checked the text message. "That's Shan," she said. "Time to go! Mr. Stones is on the move."

"Almost done," said Wyatt.

"Hey," Max asked her, "does that thing take pictures?"

Cinnabar joined him, snapping photos of Simon's file and several intriguing pages of the red notebook. Then Max stuffed the items back into their drawer and locked the cabinet. Pocketing the flash drive, Wyatt powered down the computer.

"All clear," Cinnabar whispered, one eye at the crack in the door.

Silently, the three orphans slipped out of the office, making sure to lock it behind them. From the dining room came a clatter and a grumbling voice.

"Stones," hissed Max. "Quick!" He dashed across the entryway to the library, with the others hard on his heels. When everyone was safe inside, Max flipped on the overhead lights.

"Are you barking mad?" Cinnabar whispered. "He'll see the light under the door."

"Exactly," said Max. "Now, sit at the computer or grab a book."

"How's that?" said Wyatt.

"Trust me."

The two orphans exchanged an *is-this-guy-mental?* look and took a seat at one of the sturdy oak tables. Wyatt roused the computer from sleep mode, while Cinnabar lifted a book on code breaking from the bookshelf.

"What are you—" Cinnabar began.

"I really don't get that other code," Max whined loudly. "It's *hard*. Could you guys go over it one more time?"

The other two stared at him in disbelief. Just then, the door swung open and Mr. Stones burst into the room.

"What's all this, then?" he growled.

"Oh, hi, Mr. Stones," said Max. "We're having a study session."

"*Study session?* In the bleeding middle of the bleeding night?" The burly teacher's eyes narrowed. "What are you lot up to?"

"Studying," said Cinnabar. "Max asked us to help him with codes." She held up the book and smiled. "He's a bit slow."

Max shot her a sharp look, but played along. "Yeah, my, uh, first day was kind of . . . intense."

Mr. Stones's gaze swept the room, drinking in every detail. Max was glad he'd left the red notebook in the filing cabinet. "Sure you weren't out in the courtyard just now, getting up to some mischief?" said Stones.

"Courtyard?" said Wyatt, his baby face all innocence.

"We've been here over an hour," said Max.

The bullet-headed man grunted. He searched their faces one more time, suspicious as a cat on a car ride to the vet's office.

"Is something wrong?" asked Cinnabar.

"You could say that, peaches," said Mr. Stones. "Some plonker lit a fire in the courtyard trash can."

Max held up his palms. "Just because I burned a few things doesn't make me a pyro. I didn't set that fire at the Bumburgers, and I didn't set this one."

"No one says you did, cupcake. But you lot should be in bed."

"We'll go soon," said Cinnabar.

Stones folded his arms. "Now."

"Okay," said Max. "Thanks for the help, guys."

Wyatt favored him with a genuine smile. "My pleasure, mate. And if you need some more . . . help tomorrow?"

"That'd be super," said Max. "In the morning, between classes."

Mr. Stones watched while the three orphans tidied up the library and turned off the computer, and then he escorted them upstairs to their rooms. Max's chamber came first.

" 'Night, all," he said.

The burly teacher clapped Max's shoulder. "Get your beauty rest. You'll need it for tomorrow."

"Tomorrow?"

"The contest to go on the away-team," said Stones, with

a sudden suspicious squint. "I thought that's why you were studying."

"Oh, that," said Max, yawning. "I'm totally knackered."

He eased into his darkened bedroom and shut the door. After getting ready for bed and slipping under the covers, Max picked up the photo of his mother. He gazed at her face in the dim glow of the night-light—forever smiling, forever young and beautiful.

Not bad for a first day, he told her. *Not bad at all.*

The next morning dawned as gray and brooding as a sulking statue. The air crackled with the promise of another storm, but that was nothing compared to the charged atmosphere at Merry Sunshine. Everyone was edgy. Everyone was ratcheting it up a notch—students tackling bigger challenges, and teachers giving tougher assignments.

Whereas Max's first Morning Warm-ups class had been demanding, today's was downright punishing. Rashid and Annie hurled balls like it was the final game of the World Series. Students dodged, dove, and twisted like circus acrobats to avoid being hit.

In Maths and Puzzles, Madame Chiffre introduced the Playfair cipher, a wicked-tricky code that didn't feel at all like play and was anything but fair. Even Max, with his superior deciphering skills, left the room headachy and muddled. Still, he corralled Cinnabar and Wyatt in the library for a quick meeting.

"So?" he asked them. "What did we learn last night?"

"Bring an extra snackie for the dog?" said Wyatt.

"Hilarious. Seriously, what did you find out?"

Wyatt flopped into a chair. The dark smudges under his eyes spoke of a night where sleep was in short supply. His "Well . . ." turned into a wide yawn.

Cinnabar leaned against an oak table, clutching a spiral notebook and looking as fresh as a spearmint kiss. "I learned that Jazz was in the capital on a mission—something called Operation Null." She gnawed on a thumbnail. "But I still don't know where she is now."

"No worries," said Wyatt. "I'll hack into the phone company's system, try to get a fix on her cell phone."

Cinnabar shot him a grateful look. "Thanks. I—"

"But what about my dad?" Max cut in. "What did you find on him?"

"So glad you care about my sister," snapped Cinnabar.

"I *don't* care," blurted Max before he could think. He winced and tried to soften things. "I mean, I don't know her. I hope you find Jazz, but what I really want to know is, where's my father?"

Stung, Cinnabar whipped a small sheaf of papers from her notebook and flung them at his chest. "Here! I printed these out from the photos I took. I hope you choke on them!"

The pages fluttered to the floor. Lips clamped tight, Cinnabar fled the room.

"Cinnabar!" Max cried. He took a couple of steps after her and faltered.

"You're a smooth one with the sheilas, mate," said Wyatt.

Distracted, Max frowned. "Sheilas?"

"You know—ladies?"

Max raked a hand through his hair, watching the door close behind Cinnabar. "I was just being honest." He bent to pick up the papers. "All I want is to find my father and get out of here."

"Yeah, but the *wahine* probably didn't need to hear that," said Wyatt. He pronounced the word *wah-hee-nay.*

"*Wahine?*"

"Girl," said Wyatt. "Surfer talk for *girl.*"

"I thought a girl was a sheila."

"It is," said Wyatt helpfully. "It's both."

Max shook his head to clear it. "Look, forget the *wahine.* Let's talk about Simon Segredo."

The blond boy lifted a shoulder. "I didn't get much from the computer files. A month ago, someone e-mailed Hantai Annie saying that your dad had resurfaced. And his name also turned up on an old list of agents and their aliases."

"Like, their code names?"

"Yeah. Maybe Cinnabar's stuff can tell us more."

Max spread the sheets on the tabletop, and they leaned over to read them. The coded pages from the red notebook weren't much help, so Max set them aside. But the known operatives report on Simon Segredo was another story.

"He graduated from Cambridge." Wyatt whistled. "Posh school."

Max ran a finger down the page, scanning nuggets of information. *Married . . . one son . . . worked for British government . . . many successful missions . . . missing, presumed dead.* Surely there must be an old contact number or favorite hangout?

He stopped at a short list of names and pointed to the heading. "What's this mean—'K.A.'?"

"Kangaroo Ambush?" Wyatt joked.

"Ha-ha. You should do stand-up."

"Actually, I'm guessing Known Associates," said Wyatt. "That's who he used to hang and work with." His expression brightened. "Hey, think one of them might know where your dad is now?"

"It's worth a shot," said Max. "But there're no phone numbers."

"Allow me." Wyatt carried the list over to the nearest computer, booted up a program, and began entering the names one by one.

"Dead . . . and dead," he said of the first and second. "No record," he said of the third. Then . . . "Ripper!"

"What?" Max leaned over his shoulder.

Wyatt's finger stabbed the monitor. "Alexander Plato—lives right here in town. And there's his number." He handed Max his phone.

Suddenly, Max felt as jittery as the first time he drank a cup of coffee. His insides twitched and his finger quivered slightly as he punched in the numbers. Again and again, the phone rang.

Then, just when Max was thinking that Mr. Alexander Plato had moved, a scratchy voice answered, "What?"

ASKING FAVORS OF THE ENEMY

CHAPTER 9

"MR. PLATO?" said Max, gripping the phone tight enough to crack it.

"Who is this?" The raspy voice seemed oddly familiar. "I don't know you."

Max cleared his throat. "Max Segredo, sir. I want to talk to you about my father, Simon Segredo."

Plato hung up.

For a moment, Max just stared at the phone in his hand.

"Well?" said Wyatt.

"He hung up," said Max. He pressed redial, but the phone just rang and rang. Two more tries and still Mr. Plato wouldn't answer.

Wyatt consulted the list. "Next known associate: Svetlana Remizov. Five-five-one—"

"No. Plato knows something; that's why he hung up. If I

could just see him, I bet I could get him to tell me."

Wyatt's eyebrows rose. "You're talking about breaking out of the orphanage?"

"Yeah," said Max. "Is there a problem?"

The blond boy leaned back in his chair. "Um . . . it's impossible?"

"You're just saying that because nobody's ever done it."

"Oh, heaps of people have tried," said Wyatt. "Nikki Knucks even got as far as copying one of the card keys, and that's not easy."

"But?"

Wyatt swiveled his chair to face Max and held up a thumb. "But you also need to have the right thumbprint to open the lock, and nobody's been able to fake that."

Max's eyes took on a faraway look. He laced his fingers together on top of his head and began to pace between the tables, back and forth, back and forth. *If all you need is a thumbprint . . .*

"Uh, Max? Shouldn't we be going to class?"

"Who has access?" he asked. "Who can open the lock?"

Wyatt grimaced. "I dunno. The director, the staff?"

Max nodded to himself. *It could work.* He went to the computer, searched through some Web sites, and found what he was after. "If I'm going to go meet Mr. Plato, first I need to get my hands on double-stick tape, glue, a pencil, and some scissors. Can you help?"

"Help, mate?" Wyatt smiled. "I'm bloody well going with you."

They waited until lunch was nearly over to put Max's plan into effect. A few kids lingered over dessert (a particularly moist lemon cake), but otherwise the room was empty—save for a Big Ben–sized stack of dirty dishes and a weary-looking Styx leaning against the wall, waiting to supervise the cleanup.

Max carefully filled a mug with fresh coffee and topped it with cream. Then, as Wyatt shielded him from view, he added half a bottle of Mr. Bing's Four-Alarm Hot Sauce from the condiments shelf. They had already smeared most of the cup with the graphite of several pencils, creating a powdery gray surface. Max set the mug on Wyatt's tray, together with some other cups and glasses. Together, they approached the bearlike man.

"Mr. Styx?" said Max.

"Just Styx," said the man. "Like Sting."

"Who?" said Wyatt.

Max picked up the doctored cup by its handle and offered it. "Looks like you could use some coffee."

"Too right." Styx lifted the mug and took a long sip. A moment later, his eyes widened, he spat out the coffee and spluttered, "Aagh! What the—?"

"Oh, I'm so sorry!" Max cried. "Wrong cup. Wyatt, some water!"

Balancing his tray on one hand, Wyatt lifted a water glass by its rim and passed it to Styx, whose pasty face displayed more shades of red than a Valentine's Day card rack. The big man grabbed the glass and chugged its contents down.

He coughed. "It still burns!" Then he peered at the empty glass. "And why's this sticky?"

"Jam, most likely," said Max, deftly retrieving the glass and passing it to Wyatt, who disappeared into the kitchen. He pretended to think. "Now, what do you eat if something's too spicy? Of course—rice!"

"Bloody, bleeding, burning *hot*!" moaned Styx, fanning at his mouth, to no effect.

At the dining table, Max scooped some leftover rice into a bowl as the lunch stragglers gaped. "Here." He handed the bowl and spoon to Styx, who immediately filled his mouth with the fluffy white grain.

Judging by the man's quieter moans, the rice seemed to be helping. Wyatt emerged from the kitchen and flashed a discreet thumbs-up, so Max apologized once more and followed him into the entryway.

"Beauty," whispered Wyatt. "The double-sticky on the glass picked up a perfect thumbprint."

Max felt a thrill of accomplishment. He was actually getting pretty good at this spy stuff. He patted Wyatt on the back. "All right. You get started on that."

"Where are you going?"

Max squared his shoulders and took a deep breath. "To ask a favor from my worst enemy."

Max found Nikki Knucks in her room, slouched in a chair with her feet on the bed, playing some sort of death-and-destruction video game on her phone. He stood in the open doorway as she ignored him, jabbing buttons with her thumbs and grunting, "Die! Die!" at her tiny display screen.

"Nikki," said Max.

Still not looking up, she wrinkled her nose and sniffed. "Smells like desperation, with just a hint of loserdom. Hmm . . . must be Maxi-Pad."

"Funny."

"What's funny is you at my door," said Nikki. Her close-set eyes, blue as the heart of a glacier, finally zeroed in on Max. "You've got nothing I want, we've got nothing in common, and you've got nothing to say that I want to hear. Get stuffed, you grotty wazzock."

Max clenched his jaw and took a calming breath. This was turning out to be just about exactly as much fun as he'd expected.

"Look, I'm not going to butter you up and act all nice—" he said.

"Oh, shock and horrors, what a surprise. Close the door when you go."

"—but I've got a proposition for you."

Nikki cupped one hand behind her head, flexing her biceps. "Does it involve my pounding your face?"

"It involves," said Max, "a favor asked and a favor owed."

For a few moments, the girl's tough shell cracked, and she laughed a full-throated, genuine laugh. "Oh, that's rich," she said. "You've got guts for a dimwat, I'll give you that."

Max plunged ahead. "Loan me your card key for one night—tonight—and I will owe you an equal favor."

Nikki's smile vanished from her face as if it had been vaporized. Her combat boots clomped onto the floor, and she strode over to Max, staring down at him from inches away. "Who told you I had a card key?" she whispered.

"A little bird," said Max, standing his ground.

"Rumors like that could get a little bird's neck broken." She reached past him to shut the door, and her breath smelled, oddly enough, like mint chocolate. "Even if I had a key, what makes you think, in that warped little brain of yours, that I would ever loan it to you?"

"You hate me for some reason."

Nikki sneered. "Three points for Captain Obvious."

"Why?"

Her eyes glittered. "*So* many reasons, Maxi-Pad. Your famous father, your smug little face. I don't know, maybe it's chemical." Nikki's fists clenched, and the potential for violence was sudden and real.

Max spoke quickly. "My owing you a favor will give you

power over me. In my warped little brain I'm thinking you might like that."

Nikki scoffed and gave his shoulder a shove. "I don't need a favor to have power over you, spazzmo." She swaggered toward her bed, but when she turned back, her face was thoughtful. "Why do you fancy a key, to go report to your masters?"

Max stifled a surge of irritation. "You *know* I'm not a double agent."

"That's what *all* moles say." She crossed her arms. "Anyway, even if I *had* a card key—not saying I do—you can't leave without the right thumbprint. So you're basically stuck."

"That's *my* problem, not yours," said Max. "So, do we have a deal?"

In a flash, Nikki lunged over to him and ran rough hands down his chest and stomach. Her eyes were as flat and cold as a snake's belly.

"Hey, hey!" Max said. "Not on the first date."

"Empty your pockets," snarled Nikki.

"Why should I?"

She held up a threatening finger. "If you're wired—if you're trying to tape me confessing to making a key, I'm gonna pound you all the way into next Thursday."

Max removed his lucky stone, some loose change, and a pencil stub from his jeans, placing them on a nearby desk. He then turned his pockets inside out. After examining the objects carefully, Nikki handed them back, keeping the coins for herself.

"How much money you got?" she asked.

"Almost five pounds, but not on me."

Nikki sneered. "Keep it, loser. All right, here's how it works. I loan you the key, one night only. You lose it, and I own your skinny bum. Forever."

"And your favor?" said Max.

Nikki's smile promised more unpleasantness than a day at the dentist's. "Oh, it'll be a whole *bunch* of favors."

"That's not the deal," said Max.

"That's *my* deal, if you want the key."

Max studied her, weighing his options. He *could* steal the card. Of course, if he did, guess who would be Nikki's number-one suspect? However you sliced it, if he wanted to get out and find his father, he'd have to tangle with Nikki in one way or another.

When Max didn't speak, she nodded. "We start with this: If, by some weird chance, you get picked for the mission and I don't, you give me your spot."

"Right." Max snorted. "Like they'd let me name a replacement."

"Doesn't matter," said Nikki. "If you're picked and I'm not, you step down. Got it?"

Max glanced away. It would be a calculated risk. If he could find his dad quickly, he might not need to go on that mission. If not . . .

At last he nodded and shook her hand. Nikki gripped his like a python with a grudge, but her palm was warm and sweaty. For the first time, Max had an inkling that she wasn't quite as tough as she pretended.

Nikki lifted the framed poster from the wall—her room had the blue SOMEONE IS ALWAYS WATCHING print with the spooky eyes—and laid it facedown on the desk. Prying up a corner of the backing, she slipped out a plain envelope and drew from it an electronic card key.

"If you get caught, you do *not* give me up, even under pain of torture. I've got a black belt. You know what that means?"

"Your brown belt is at the cleaners?"

"It means," she snarled, "I can cause a whole encyclopedia of pain."

Max smiled inwardly as he took the card. "I'll bear that in mind." He'd had a glimpse under her facade at her insecurities. Despite her experience and superior strength, he made her uneasy. Something to remember.

When Max returned to his room, he stashed the card key behind the framed LOOSE LIPS SINK SHIPS poster and was about to head to class, when something askew caught his eye. He examined the nightstand more closely. His mother's photo was still in place, but a slip of paper peeked out from beneath it.

Max scanned the room. No other signs of intrusion. His roommates—Jensen, a beefy, unremarkable boy with wheat-colored bangs, and Hans, a dark, moody type—were elsewhere. He reached down and slid out the paper. It was another note, encoded like the first and on the same stiff cardstock. In identical blocky capitals, it read:

SIOL XUX HYYXM SIOL BYFJ.

"This is getting ridiculous," he muttered. Didn't anyone send normal messages? And who was behind this, anyway? In the mad whirl of his first day, Max had lost track of that thought. And then something else struck him: Based on the e-mail Wyatt had hacked, Hantai Annie knew his dad was alive when Max confronted her, but she'd said nothing.

Why?

These questions faded into the background as Max sank onto his bed and got down to cracking the code. It looked like another Caesar cipher, but the shift was different. Not a three-letter shift, or even a four . . .

It took a minute, but Max finally recognized the six-letter shift. He didn't even need to jot down the two alphabets to crack it. Like last time, the message emerged in a flash:

YOUR DAD NEEDS YOUR HELP.

His gut tightened. Although Max had no idea how reliable his secret correspondent was, the message held a ring of truth. His lips curled in a smile. How perfect would it be, after all these years, if their meeting not only reunited their family but also got his dad out of a jam?

Max pocketed the note and savored the image of himself as a hero. Tonight's adventure might prove to be a big step in that direction. But one question nagged at him: Despite his assurances to Wyatt, would Mr. Plato really talk?

CHAPTER 10

LAUGHING PAST JOHNNY HOPPER

AFTER ALL the challenge and intrigue of securing the card key and fingerprint, the actual escape from Merry Sunshine Orphanage was almost a letdown.

But a *good* letdown.

As on the previous night, Max and Wyatt waited for Mr. Stones's midnight tea break. They tossed Pinkerton the dog a meaty bone salvaged from the kitchen trash. With the copy of Styx's thumbprint glued to his right thumb, Max tricked the biometric scanner while Wyatt slid the key card through its reader.

Click. The lock opened, and they entered the holding corridor between the inner and outer doors. The second lock yielded just as easily, and Max and Wyatt stepped out into the cold night air.

Wyatt gave a huge grin. "Freedom!" he whispered.

Max raised his arms in victory and did a silent, but nonetheless funky, butt dance all the way down the footpath and out onto the street. The night smelled of diesel fumes and wet concrete, and the city lights bathed the clouds' underbelly in sulfur yellow.

Not the most beautiful night, perhaps, but Max felt a thrill of excitement. Their plan was working!

Using the map feature on Wyatt's phone, they located Mr. Plato's address on Harrowby Lane and sorted out the quickest route. The grimy streets lay quiet after midnight, as few pedestrians ventured into this mostly commercial neighborhood. Silent as sentinels, parked cars glistened under streetlights.

Only the occasional vehicle rumbled past, splashing the two boys with headlamps and then returning them to shadow. Max and Wyatt tramped briskly along, hands jammed into pockets for warmth, eyes alert for police cars.

Three blocks from the orphanage, they turned down a busier street, this one boasting a few pubs and a small movie theater. Traffic flowed heavier here, and they did their best to look like they belonged, walking with purpose. The tube station waited only a block away.

"Cop!" Max hissed.

Up ahead, between the movie theater and the underground access, a shiny police cruiser waited at the curb. A bulky man in blue leaned against it, chatting with another man and idly watching the street.

Max and Wyatt traded worried looks. The last thing they needed was attention from Johnny Hopper.

"Do we find another entrance?" whispered Wyatt.

Max bit his lip. "Dunno." He dawdled by the theater doors to consider their options.

Just then, two couples exited the movie house, droning loudly about the film's "visual metaphor," "*mise-en-scène*," and "bleak worldview" as they strolled toward the underground. The policeman turned his head toward them.

Without missing a beat, Max grabbed Wyatt's arm and fell in behind the second couple. As they drew even with the cruiser, the blue-uniformed constable casually pushed to standing, shrewd eyes tracking them.

Max faked a laugh. "Wasn't that the lamest, um, visual metaphor, ever?"

Wyatt looked blank until Max nudged him. "Oh. Uh, too right."

"And the . . . measly scene?"

The cop scrutinized them closely.

"Measly . . . ?" Wyatt repeated, before the light dawned. "Oh! The measliest. Dry as a dead dingo's doughnut."

"Next time," Max yawned, "we pick the movie."

A few car lengths down the street, he pretended to check something on the phone, but tuned his ear for a word from Johnny Hopper. None came. He glanced back and saw that the policeman had returned to his conversation.

Relieved, the boys followed the moviegoers down the worn steps to the underground. A gust of warm air rose to meet them, carrying the distinctive subway perfume of diesel fuel and stale urine. At the wall-mounted vending machine they bought tickets for Harrowby Lane.

The device spat out his receipt, and Max gazed at the stub in his hand. For the first time in forever, he was free—away from the orphanage, away from Mr. Darny his caseworker, away from past and future foster parents. He could go anywhere, do anything he pleased. True, he only had four pounds in his pocket, but still. Freedom tasted sweet.

"Uh, Max? I think that's our train."

Coming back to himself, Max registered the rumbling from the tracks and the squeal of metal on metal. He tagged after Wyatt, through the turnstile and down some stairs.

Together, they raced for the platform, reaching it to find the train doors already open.

"Platform Four: Willoughby, Harrowby, Frankham, and Fewell," came the conductor's echoey voice. "All aboard!"

Max and Wyatt hurried inside, the doors sliding closed behind them. With a groan, the train jerked to life, and they grabbed a silver pole to steady themselves. In moments, a night-black tunnel swallowed the train. Their images floated like ghosts on the window glass: Wyatt's face pale and big-eyed; Max's long and sallow.

The glass also held the reflections of a handful of other

passengers farther down the car. A glazed-looking Pakistani businessman with his tie askew. A beefy, copper-skinned homeless woman muttering to herself and rummaging through a raggedy rucksack. And two youngish white men in scuffed black leather jackets, whispering and watching Max and Wyatt with hard eyes.

The train whipped around a few turns, causing all the passengers to sway in unison like a bobble-head-doll collection. It emerged from the darkness and pulled into the light of another station. "Willoughby, this stop. All out for Willoughby," the conductor's voice buzzed through the loudspeaker.

As the train rolled to a halt, the businessman leaned forward. He planted his hands on his knees and lurched to his feet, wobbling his way with great care onto the platform. The black-leather guys snickered.

Nobody new boarded the car. Soon the doors closed, and the train jerked forward into another gloomy tunnel.

"Oi, kiddies!" a sharp voice called.

Max raised his gaze to the glass and met the reflected stare of the taller man. He wore a sad, rather wispy goatee and an expression like he'd smelled something bad. Max and Wyatt ignored him.

"Oi!" called the other man, who was remarkably skinny but with a perfectly round potbelly, like a pregnant walking stick. "Don't ignore my mate, you plonkers. He wants to know if you gots any bees and honey."

Wyatt frowned and checked with Max.

"You know, *money*?" said Sad Goatee. "Me and my mate fancy a pint, and we're a bit short."

The two men rose to their feet and sauntered over, predatory sneers on their faces. Max scanned the car. Aside from the homeless woman still mumbling to herself, they were alone with these two lovely specimens.

His hand slipped into his pocket, brushing past his good-luck stone and folding around the few lonely bills. Without them, he had no return fare.

"What do we do?" Wyatt muttered, edging closer to Max.

"We're a bit short as well," Max called out. "All our cash is tied up in foreign investments."

"Oh, ha-ha," said Sad Goatee. But he didn't look amused.

"Right comical," said Potbelly. "Now, give us your honey, little bees, and no one gets hurt." He closed in on Max and Wyatt, holding out one grubby palm faceup.

Max tried to picture calling Hantai Annie for train fare back to the orphanage, and he shook his head. "Sorry. Banking hours are over."

The potbellied man scowled. He made a grab at Max, who hopped backward and caught Wyatt's arm.

"Come on!"

They spun and dashed for the passage to the next compartment, realizing too late that they were on the wrong end of the train's last car. Max and Wyatt skidded to a halt. The only way out led past the leather-jacketed thugs. And still the train barreled through the darkness.

Wyatt gulped.

"Don't rush off now, me Rob Roy," said Sad Goatee to Max.

"My name's not Rob," said Max. He advanced warily between the two rows of seats, Wyatt beside him.

"Rob Roy . . . *boy*," said Potbelly, drawing closer. "Tch, Jimmy. Kids these days . . ." The men spread out, blocking their way.

"The old rhymin' slang is dyin' out. A cryin' shame, really." Goateed Jimmy cracked his knuckles and grinned, revealing a mouthful of mossy-looking teeth. "Now, where was we?"

"Maybe we should give it to them?" Wyatt said, face white as a fresh marshmallow.

Max's hand slipped back into his pocket, closing around his good-luck stone. He thumbed its sharp edge. "Maybe we should," he said.

Looking past the men, Max could see that the train was emerging into a lighted area. He let his shoulders slump and shuffled toward Jimmy, dragging his feet to eat up time.

"That's more like it, bin lids."

"Let me guess," said Wyatt with a nervous titter. "Kids?" He fumbled in his jacket pockets for his wallet.

"Got it in one," chuckled Potbelly. His eyes were avid, focused on Wyatt's actions.

Max slowly drew his hand from his pocket, concealing the rock, sharp edge down.

"Harrowby," the conductor's voice boomed from the tinny speakers. "Harrowby, this stop." The station came into view.

"Give 'er here," said Jimmy, sticking out his hand.

"It's all yours," said Max. And with a sudden slash, he raked the stone's edge across the man's palm.

"You little git!" Jimmy cursed and staggered back, clutching his injured hand.

Max feinted at Potbelly's eyes, and the man backpedaled. "Go, Wyatt!"

The blond boy darted past them, making for the next compartment. Brakes squealed; everyone staggered. The platform was nearly at hand.

Max evaded Potbelly, but goateed Jimmy shot out a hand and snagged the back of his jacket. "Gotcha!"

"Max!" cried Wyatt.

Without pausing, Max shrugged his shoulders and rushed forward, letting the man strip the garment from his back. As the train lurched to a halt, Max and Wyatt slipped into the next car. The sliding doors opened.

Glancing back, Max saw the men closing in, sore as boils. He turned just in time to avoid a man-monster twice the size of Styx who was entering the train car.

"Oi!" the giant boomed as Max and Wyatt squeaked past him out the door.

117

But the black-leather guys weren't so nimble. They smacked head-on into Man-Monster and bounced off his massive chest. The big bruiser growled.

As the doors closed, Max saw gnarled hands the size of dinner plates catch Jimmy and Potbelly by the necks and thump their heads together, easy as clapping erasers. Max gave a relieved chuckle.

The boys rushed through a turnstile and up the worn concrete steps.

"I'm such a shark biscuit," Wyatt said.

"Why?" said Max.

Wyatt trudged upward. "I couldn't think of a single move. Some spy I am."

"I'm just glad I brought my stone." Max patted his pocket. "Maybe it's lucky after all."

When they reached street level, Max and Wyatt entered a neighborhood that brought new meaning to the word *dodgy*. The run-down block of flats across the street looked like its landlord hadn't shown it any love in a very long time. Feral cats yowled and hissed in an alleyway.

Four or five rough men talked in the shadows of a boarded-up storefront a few doors down. Their laughter was as hard and brittle as stale pizza crusts.

Wyatt consulted his phone for the address, sighing in relief when it led them the other way down the street. Two blocks later, they reached their destination.

Like a grande dame fallen on hard times, this ramshackle building had once been stylish and elegant, the toast of the neighborhood, no doubt. But now its steep roof was patched, its walkways cracked and weedy, and its wrought-iron railings splashed with graffiti.

Max straightened his shirt, glancing over at Wyatt. "Lovely spot."

"Charming."

"No big deal, right? After all, what's the worst that could happen?"

"He says no, and we go." Wyatt offered a tentative smile, and they slowly approached the house together.

Unit D claimed the back-left corner of the upstairs. As they climbed the creaky wooden steps, Max was relieved to observe that a dim light shone behind the flat's curtained window. It had only just occurred to him that Mr. Plato might not be awake after midnight.

His throat felt as dry as the heart of a haystack. His stomach fluttered. He tried peering through the crack between curtain and window frame as he stretched out his hand and knocked on the door.

"Mr. Plato?"

Bam! Bam!

Two shots boomed out, punching ragged holes in the front door at about eye level. Max staggered back, stung by splinters. His heart raced. *Too close.* If he and Wyatt had been standing in front of the door, they would now be ex-orphans.

"Holy Dooley!" Wyatt squeaked, dropping to a crouch.

"Don't shoot!" cried Max. "We're friendly!"

"Plus, we're just kids!" called Wyatt.

A hacking cough rattled inside the flat. "*Eejit* kids, I'd say." It was the same raspy voice Max had heard over the phone. "Didn't your ma and da teach you not to come knocking after midnight?"

"Please," said Max. "Can we come in?"

"Clear off!"

"It's Max Segredo."

A pause. "Max?" More coughing. "Aw, Jayus, Mary, and Joseph. For the love of . . ."

Max exchanged a look with Wyatt. "Mr. Plato?"

A long moment passed. Three hard clicks from the door, and it swung inward with a creak. Cautiously, Max poked his head around the door frame.

"Hello, Max Segredo."

Just inside stood a gaunt old man loosely holding a pistol at his side. He wore a frayed brown bathrobe and pink slippers, and his paper-pale features were bathed in blue TV screen light.

When Max saw who it was, his mouth fell open. "Mr. *Quinn*?"

GUNFIRE AT A GET-TOGETHER

Chapter 11

WYATT GAWKED, his blue eyes round as teacups. "You *know* each other?"

Max stared at the haggard man, at his white cotton-candy hair and sunken cheeks, at his blue NOBODY EXPECTS THE SPANISH INQUISITION T-shirt and wrinkled pajama bottoms. He spoke in a wondering tone. "But you're dead."

"Not entirely," said Plato/Quinn. "Get inside."

"*How* do you know each other?" asked Wyatt.

Max murmured, "Mr. Quinn was my second foster father."

"Wait, what?" said Wyatt.

"We're too exposed out here. In, now!" The old man dragged the boys inside, never releasing his chunky, ash-gray handgun. He snagged a makeshift periscope from an end table and poked it out the door, peering at the street. "Did you spot any long black cars?"

"Not here," said Max. But he flashed on the vehicles he'd seen at the Bumburgers' fire and later near the orphanage. He frowned. "What—?"

"Maybe they didn't see you."

Max blinked. "But you were executed by Gurlukh warlords," he said. "You and Mrs. Quinn. That's why they sent me to another foster home."

"Cor, you *really* know each other," said Wyatt.

Plato/Quinn shut and locked the door. Ruefully, he poked a finger into one of the bullet holes. "Holey door, not a good thing," he muttered.

"Mr. Quinn!" said Max. "What's going on?"

"Sorry, boyo." The old man gave Max his full attention, a sad smile softening his ravaged face. "So sorry. The real name is Plato, Alexander Plato. Sweet baby Moses, but you've grown! And you look so much like your ma."

Max chopped a hand through the air. "Skip the sweet talk. You owe me an explanation!"

"You're right, you're right." Plato held up his palms in a mollifying gesture, pistol still gripped in his hand. "And explanations go better with tea. I was just making some. Fancy a cuppa?"

"Beauty!" chirped Wyatt. "With heaps of sugar."

Max rolled his eyes.

Mr. Plato shuffled into the kitchen, calling over his shoulder, "Sit, sit! I'll root out some biscuits to go with it." The kettle whistled, cups clattered, and cupboards opened and shut.

Max surveyed the dingy flat. The walls were stained tobacco brown, and the wallpaper hung in sad strips here and there. A great old dinosaur of a TV set squatted opposite a couch that, had it been a horse, would have been sent to the glue factory long ago. A pair of mismatched tattered armchairs completed the picture of charity shop leftovers.

Max joined Wyatt on the sofa. On the TV, a black-and-white movie played with the sound on low, men in big hats and trench coats talking tough. The couch smelled of mold and cough syrup.

"Mr. Plato was your foster?" said the blond boy. "How is that even possible?"

"Max's da arranged it, actually," said the old man, reentering the room. He carried a tray, which held a teapot, some cups and saucers, a plate of cookies, and his pistol. "And believe you me, that wasn't easy."

Max leaned forward, galvanized. "My father did it? How?"

As Mr. Plato set the tray on a scarred coffee table, Max noticed how his knobby, veined hands shook. Another cough racked his skinny body. The vital, middle-aged man who had taken him into his home only six years earlier had melted away, leaving this scarecrow in his place.

"Your da . . . landed in a wee bit of trouble at work," said Plato.

"Yeah, we know," said Max. "He was a spy."

"Oh." The old man drew an armchair up to the table and sank into it. "Yes, well. We were spies together, your da and I. He made some fierce enemies, and so he had to leave the country or die an ugly death. Milk? Sugar?"

"What?" said Max distractedly. "Whatever."

Plato poured the tea, then added sugar and milk to all three cups. "Help yourself to biscuits." Wyatt scooped up a handful of the cookies and began munching away.

"So, my father?" Max prompted.

"Right," said Mr. Plato. "After your dear ma passed, rest her soul, your da pulled some strings long-distance. He arranged for our associates, the Lees, to foster you."

"Until they were eaten by crocodiles," said Max.

"Gnarlacious," breathed Wyatt. He blew on his tea and slurped it, watching the other two like they were a particularly riveting soap opera.

Mr. Plato winced. "Pity, that. A mission gone bollixed. Then Simon called in some favors and lined up Agnes and me as your next foster parents."

Max's throat felt tight. "And you did such a bang-up job of that."

"Ah, boyo . . ." The old man sighed, and his sunken eyes glistened. "We tried. We taught you codes and all, but we didn't know how the whole kid thing worked, you see. We didn't know what a youngling needed."

"So you left me with a babysitter and went off to central Asia?" Max snapped.

Plato shrugged wearily. "Sorry. Spies make rubbish parents."

"You don't say."

The old man studied his teacup. "Agnes was executed. I escaped but . . . well, I never came back for you. Your da would've been so disappointed in me, rest his soul."

"He's not dead," said Max.

Mr. Plato's head rose. "Wise up, lad. He's gone."

"I got a coded message—"

"*Two* coded messages," Wyatt added.

"—saying he's still alive, and he needs my help," Max finished.

The old man's teacup clattered onto the saucer. "Not possible."

"Deeply possible," said Wyatt, crunching into another cookie. "We found an e-mail at the orphanage confirming it."

"But then"—Mr. Plato pushed himself up, eyes widening—"he's in danger, terrible danger. You, too!"

Max rose to his feet. "What do you mean?"

"His old enemies. They're up to something big, and they're out to settle scores. Even with me—that's why I shot first when you knocked." His gaze drifted to the front door, and he clucked his tongue at the damage. "*Tch*. That's coming out of my security deposit."

Max gripped his former foster dad's arms. "Mr. Qu—er, Plato. I need to find my father. Where do I look?"

"Tully Oxenfree."

"Where's that?" said Max.

The old man's eyebrows lifted. "Not where, *who*. The top intel broker in the capital. If anyone's heard something, Tully would know."

A sharp knock rattled the front door, making them jump. Mr. Plato reached for his pistol. "Who's there?"

"Police," a gruff voice barked. "Open up."

"Hold on. I'm not decent." Mr. Plato backed away toward the hall, keeping his gun trained on the door and beckoning to Max and Wyatt.

"Into the closet with you," he whispered. The old man opened a hallway door to reveal a narrow space packed with threadbare coats and winter gear. He kicked aside some old boots and a scrap of carpet to reveal a ring set into the floor. "My bolt-hole."

"What's a bolt-hole?" asked Max.

Plato frowned. "A hole through which you bolt, of course. No good spy is ever without one. The trapdoor leads downstairs—just in case."

A fist pounded against wood. "Sir, open the door *now*!"

"Coming!" called Mr. Plato, one eye on the entrance.

Wyatt stepped into the closet. Max balked. "Where can I find Tully?" he whispered.

Mr. Plato turned to face him. "Max, don't go to the capital. It's far too dangerous. You—"

Bam! Bam! Bam!

Three shots echoed. The old man cried out and spun half around, clapping a hand to his side. "Scram!" he grunted. "I'll hold them off." He ducked behind the corner and fired at the front door. The gunshots boomed in the cramped hallway, and the tang of gunpowder hung sharp and acrid in the air.

"But—you're wounded." Max hesitated, torn.

"Go now!" hissed Plato. Blood oozed between his fingers, but his smile was fierce and wolfish. "After all these years, let me do something right by you."

The police—or whoever stood outside—returned Plato's fire. Bullets zinged through the air. Wyatt yanked on the ring, but the trapdoor wouldn't budge. "Aah! We're stuck!"

"Don't be ridiculous," said Max.

He ducked down to help. Together they hauled on it again and again, but the escape hatch still wouldn't open.

"You're right," said Max. "We're stuck."

Wyatt's eyes were round as snow globes. "What now?"

"Plan B."

Gunshots and shouts reverberated through the apartment. The intruders were blasting through both the front and kitchen windows, but curtains hampered their view. Plato kept up a lively return fire.

"Give up yet, you Millies?" he shouted during a brief lull. More gunfire answered him.

The front entrance was out, so Max turned the other way, ducking into the bedroom. A quick glance took in a sagging unmade bed, a banged-up chest of drawers, and dirty clothes carpeting the floor.

"Cozy," said Max. "But I'd fire the housekeeper." He hurried over to the windows and looked outside. Directly below, an open Dumpster yawned.

Max threw up the sash and hammered at the screen until it popped out. "Come on."

Wyatt joined him and peered dubiously out the window. "Down there?"

Just then, a long barrage of shots popped like lethal popcorn, followed by the crunch of a door being kicked in.

"Down there," said Wyatt. He wriggled through the opening, hung by his hands, and dropped.

Footsteps pounded in the front room. Max hated to leave Mr. Plato, but this was no time for regrets. He climbed through the window and jumped, landing with a squish.

The rank aroma of rancid pizza and rotting vegetables enfolded him. His head rested on a spoiled cabbage, and his elbow had ended up in a gooey mess that smelled like something from a vulture's lunch box. No time to be finicky. Trailing garbage, Wyatt and Max scrambled over the edge of the rubbish bin and into the muddy alleyway.

With a last glance behind, Max led the way, moving as quickly and quietly as possible, back toward the train station. A rough voice called from the window—indistinct, but whoever it was didn't pursue them.

"They—they were shooting at us." Wyatt looked positively green. "I, we, could've been killed." Max hustled him along the alley without a word.

Not until they were sitting on the next train home did Max feel able to speak. He pulled at a loose thread where the bench seat fabric had split. "Remember you asked me yesterday about the worst fosters I ever had?"

"Yeah," said Wyatt.

"The Quinns weren't it," said Max. "Except for the way it all ended, they were the best." But will I ever get the chance to tell Mr. Quinn that? he wondered.

By the time Max and Wyatt were trudging down the empty, echoing streets to the orphanage, a light drizzle had begun to fall. They said little, each lost in his own thoughts. But when they reached the wrought-iron gate to Merry Sunshine, Max paused.

"Now I've *got* to find my dad," he said. "No matter what happens, I'm going on that mission."

"Too right," said Wyatt. His face was still pale, but now it was resolute. "We'll track down that Tully, no worries."

Max felt a warm rush of gratitude for Wyatt.

They crept up the walkway, using the card key and fake thumbprint to unlock the outer door. The holding corridor was as quiet as an unspoken regret. But when they opened the inner door, a surprise awaited them.

Hantai Annie Wong stood in the center of the entryway, fists on hips and ebony eyes glinting. *"Kusai."* She sniffed. "You stink."

Max and Wyatt exchanged a look. They sure did.

"You have a nice night?" she asked.

"Uh, I guess," said Max warily.

"Not anymore," said Hantai Annie.

CHAPTER 12

ATTACK ME LIKE YOU MEAN IT

AFTER AN EXCRUCIATING ten minutes of grilling in her office, and an assortment of what Max assumed were curse words in several languages, the director dismissed Wyatt. When Max rose from the overstuffed sofa to follow, she said, *"Chotto mate.* You stay."

He sank back down, arms folded and face carefully neutral. This was it. Hantai Annie would pack him off to juvenile hall, and his best chance at finding his father would go up in smoke. If they let me keep my lock picks, he thought, maybe I could break out of juvie. But that wasn't much consolation.

Hantai Annie stood at the barred window, watching the rain. Silence pooled, broken only by the ticking of a clock. At last she spoke. "You a terrible, terrible orphan. But you a good spy."

"Well, that's something," he heard himself saying. "At least I won't have to get by on just my charm."

"Baka yarou!" she snapped. "Don't talk smart."

Max winced, sucked it up, and apologized.

Mollified, the director grunted and then sank into her leather chair. "What I do with you, Max Segredo?"

"Send me to live with my father."

Hantai Annie shook her head. "I hear rumors that your father came back."

"But it's—"

"So far, just rumors."

Max leaned forward, elbows on knees. "Then let me get out there and learn the truth."

The director gave a snort. "You try, and look what happens. Shakedown from bad men, getting shot at. *Dame da*," she scolded. "You could have died."

Max mentally cursed Wyatt for spilling the whole truth about their escapades. "Look, it wasn't as bad as it sounds," he said. "I could try again."

"No." Her voice softened but held its intensity. "Max-*kun*, you want to be with your father. That is normal. But you are still *kodomo*, a child. I am responsible for you safety. You stay here."

Max threw up his hands. "Then how am I meant to find him?"

"You're not. *I* will ask my contacts, see what they know."

Hantai Annie cast him a stare that made the scowling samurai masks on the wall look like pussycats.

He crossed his arms. "I've been in the foster system for seven years. I know how it works. Nobody looks out for you, so you've gotta look out for yourself."

The director's face was troubled. "*Family* looks out for you, Max."

"Exactly." Max spread his hands. "That's why I was trying to find mine."

"No. *We* are your family now."

"Yeah, right." He stood, full of restless energy. "All us orphans, we're just your junior spies. You'd never let us get adopted. You're using us—admit it."

To his surprise, Hantai Annie didn't bark at him. She didn't argue. She merely shook her head. "You have tough life, Max-*kun*. You don't know Merry Sunshine, don't trust us. So I teach you one thing about family: family forgives."

"Yeah, right."

Uncomfortable with her steady gaze, Max scuffed over to the bookshelf and picked up a jade turtle, idly turning it over in his hands. On impulse, he hurled the little figurine at the heavy iron heater by the wall. Its head and front legs chipped off. "Forgive that!"

Hantai Annie's eyes flashed briefly, then her soft expression returned.

"I forgive more than that. I forgive you breaking into my

office, and I forgive you little . . . mission tonight."

She knew about the break-in, too? Max's face flushed, and it felt like bees were swarming in his chest. He didn't know how to take her words. "So, just like that, I'm forgiven?"

"Yes."

"What's the catch? I can't go on the away-team, right?"

"No," said the director. "If you qualify, you can join team."

His hands felt heavy and awkward, so he thrust them into his pockets and nodded curtly, afraid to trust his own voice.

"We forgive, but Merry Sunshine has rules," she said. "You broke rule, so tomorrow you clean breakfast dishes."

"Of course." Max sulked. "I *knew* there was a catch."

"Now, go sleep," said Hantai Annie. "Class starts in four hours."

Max shuffled over to the door, yawning in relief. As he reached it, a thought hit him, and he turned. "Hey, how'd you know we broke out tonight?"

"A little bug told me," said Hantai Annie.

"Don't you mean a little *bird*?"

She raised her eyebrows. "No, bug. You live in house of spies, Max-*kun*. You should know, everything is bugged."

Max's mouth formed a silent *oh*. He flashed on some of the less-than-flattering things he'd said about her when he was alone with Wyatt. *Oops.* Too late to take them back now.

Hantai Annie's mouth twitched. "And one more thing."

"Yeah?" Max said warily.

"If you ever try to crack biometric lock again," she said, "make sure fake thumbprint matches card key."

He winced. "I'll try to remember."

When morning rolled around, Max's head felt packed with wool. His eyeballs itched, and he couldn't stop yawning. But his teachers and fellow students were, if anything, more intense than they'd been the previous day.

One of the younger kids sprained an ankle during warm-ups, Puzzles class devolved into a shouting match between Nikki and Cinnabar, and the competition in Lock Picking class grew so fierce, the weasel-faced Dermot ended up in tears.

All in all, a busy morning.

To top it off, Cinnabar seemed to be avoiding Max, getting up and changing seats every time they ended up near each other. He wasn't sure what to make of this. On the one hand, he didn't feel like apologizing, because he'd done nothing wrong, just told the truth. But on the other hand, her sister *was* missing. Maybe he should reach out or something.

Nikki, however, was another matter entirely.

He *knew* he didn't want to talk to her, as the subject of his getting her key card confiscated would undoubtedly come up, and he didn't see how that could possibly end well. But, as with many things in life, he didn't have much choice in the matter. Just before Mixed Martial Arts, she caught him in the entry hall.

"All right then, barmpot?" Clad in a white karate *gi* with a black belt, Nikki leaned against the doorway, blocking the entrance. Her small blue eyes glimmered with a dangerous light.

"Yeah, I'm peachy," said Max. "You?"

Somehow, Nikki made raising an eyebrow look like cocking a pistol. "I don't think you're so peachy, Maxi-Pad. I heard Hantai Annie took away someone's fake card key last night. Tell me it wasn't mine."

"It was yours."

Her brows lowered, and her meaty face reminded him of a particularly nasty bull he'd seen on a TV special about bullfighting. As he recalled, things hadn't ended well for the matador. "What did I tell you?" she growled.

"We got caught," said Max. "There was nothing I could do, but I kept your name out of it."

He tried to brush past her and enter the room, but Nikki stopped him with a hard hand to the chest. "That's not gonna cut it."

Just then, someone cleared her throat behind him. "Well?"

Max turned to see the Indian woman who'd nearly skewered him with knives his first day at the orphanage. Her long raven hair was neatly pinned back, and she wore a sparkling white *gi* like Nikki's—only on this woman it looked like high fashion.

"Where you come from, is it customary to prevent the

137

teacher from entering the classroom?" she asked.

Sullenly, Nikki replied, "No, Miss Moorthy."

"So?"

"Sorry, *sensei*," Nikki mumbled. She made the briefest of bows, then pivoted on a heel and stalked into the room, raking Max with her gaze as she did so. Clearly, this was far from over.

"New boy," said the teacher.

"Max," said Max.

"Have you had any martial arts training?"

He shrugged. "Not really. Unless you count attack play."

"I don't." Chandrika Moorthy laid a hand on his shoulder and propelled him into the room before her. "Take it slowly. Watch and learn."

The space was empty of furniture, the floor covered with thick brown mats. A dozen or so students—some clad in outfits like Nikki's, some in sweatpants and T-shirts—stood facing their teacher.

"Good morning, class," said Miss Moorthy.

"Good morning, *sensei*," the group chorused. Max found a vacant spot and joined the rest.

After leading them through some warm-up stretches, practice kicks, and punches, the teacher called on Tremaine.

"Let's show them *kubi nage*."

The Jamaican teen strolled up to the front of the room and bowed to her. "All right, *sensei*."

In a lightning move he rushed Miss Moorthy with one hand out like he intended to throttle her. The teacher dodged, grabbing his wrist and the back of his head. A quick spin and Tremaine hit the mat, flat on his back. They demonstrated it again, more slowly, with Moorthy describing her actions as they went.

To Max's surprise, the moves reminded him strongly of the attack-play training that Foster Parents #3, the Dickensons, had given him. Had they, too, been spies, friends of his father? Max wondered. How much of his life had been influenced by the dad he never knew?

"Thank you, Tremaine," said Miss Moorthy, clapping her hands. "Now, everyone find a partner and practice."

The students near Max quickly paired up. He cut between them, searching for Wyatt, but the blond boy had already chosen Cinnabar.

A hand tapped Max's shoulder. "Ready, partner?" said Nikki. Her smile would've made a Komodo dragon flinch.

Everyone else was spoken for. Max's number was up. Time to face a black belt with a grudge.

"Partner A, attack!" said Moorthy.

Max and Nikki faced off. She bowed and grinned again, showing teeth as small and square as Chiclets. "Attack me," she said, "like you mean it."

Max sighed. He approached her as he'd seen Tremaine do, and almost before he could blink, he found himself sailing through the air and landing on his back with a *whump*.

"Again!" the teacher called.

Twice more, Nikki dumped Max onto the mat. But the third time she followed him down, bracing her forearm over his throat and giving his nose a thump with her fist.

Stars exploded before his eyes. Something wet ran down Max's lip. He struggled, but Nikki held him down.

"Your scrawny bum is mine," she hissed. "I *own* you now."

"Own me?" he choked out. "You couldn't afford the payments."

Miss Moorthy strolled past them and tapped Nikki's side. "Partner B, your turn!"

Max rose, wiping his face on his T-shirt. It came away bloody. He scowled and braced himself for Nikki's assault.

The red-haired girl struck like a supercaffeinated snake, slipping past his guard and giving him a good throttle before he broke her grip. They separated. Max rubbed his sore neck and braced for the second attack.

This time, he thought, we'll play it *my* way. Rather than try the defensive move they'd learned, he drew on his attack-play training, grabbing Nikki's arm, spinning, and flipping her over his hip.

She crashed to the mat. Instantly, Nikki sprang up at him, red-faced and snarling. And once again, Max followed his instincts, gripping the front of her *gi* and planting a foot in her stomach. He straightened his leg as he fell backward, sending the beefy girl flying over his head and onto her back, landing hard.

Max rolled to his feet. Nikki was a little slower to rise, but judging by her murderous expression, she was no less intent on mopping the floor with him.

Miss Moorthy stepped between them. "Excellent! That wasn't *kubi nage*, but it was effective. Class, did you see how the new boy used *tomonage* when attacked from a different angle?"

Taking a moment to look around, Max noticed that most of the students had stopped their own practice to gape at him and Nikki. She glowered at him over the teacher's shoulder.

"Are you sure you haven't studied judo?" asked Miss Moorthy.

"I think I'd know if I had," said Max.

She clapped his shoulder. "High marks, new boy. Remember, class, in a real fight, you must always stay flexible, follow your instincts. The *dojo* is nothing like the real world."

Wyatt raised his eyebrows, impressed, and Max grinned back, feeling a surge of pride.

Everyone changed partners, and the lesson proceeded. But even from across the room, Max could feel Nikki's glare burning through the back of his head. His buoyant mood deflated. This problem was not going away any time soon.

After class, he headed up to his room to change his bloody, sweaty T-shirt before lunch. Cinnabar fell in beside him.

"You sure know how to drive a girl crazy," she said.

"It's a gift." Max glanced over, then away. "Not that she needed much help. I think Nikki is—what's the technical term—mad as a box of frogs?"

Cinnabar lifted the sweaty hair off her neck. "She's had it tougher than most. I heard something about a foster who used to burn her with lit cigarettes."

"Ugh."

"But yes," said Cinnabar, "she is a wee bit psycho."

As they climbed the stairs, Max stole another glance at her. "So, uh, are we talking again?"

She lifted a shoulder. "I guess. Seeing you get a bloody nose somehow cheered me up."

"Gee, thanks." He gave his upper lip another swipe with the T-shirt sleeve.

"Max, you're an idiot. But maybe, somewhere deep underneath, you mean well."

"Um, okay."

"You just need to take other people's feelings into account. It's not all about *you*, you know."

"I know that." But even to himself, his tone sounded defensive.

They reached the second-floor landing. Up ahead, a silver-haired man was climbing the steps to the third floor. His tweed jacket seemed in danger of splitting across his broad back, and he proceeded slowly, as if unfamiliar with the concept of exercise.

"Who's that?" Max asked Cinnabar.

Her eyes narrowed. "Never seen him before. But here's a hot tip: When a girl offers you a chance to say you're sorry, don't pass it up." Head high, she flounced past him, making for her room down the hall.

"Sorry!" he called after her, and grimaced. Girls were complicated.

Inside Max's room, Wyatt sat on one of the beds, tinkering with his laptop computer. His face lit up when Max entered. "Stellar news, mate!"

"That's great," said Max. "Um, don't you have your own room?"

Wyatt frowned. "This is it. I swapped with Hans; I'm your new roommate."

"Oh. Some spy I am." Max peeled off his T-shirt, mopped his face with it, and dug a fresh one out of his footlocker. "So, what's up?"

"I had one of my ace programs do a search for your father's aliases."

"And?"

Wyatt waggled his eyebrows. "Just got a hit on one of them: Kevin Whitehead." He swiveled the laptop around to show the screen.

"What am I looking at?" Max squinted at the display.

"Only this morning, someone used Mr. Whitehead's debit card at a coffee shop called Human Beans."

"So?"

"Human Beans is a ten-minute walk from here."

A smile, incredulous and slow, spread across Max's features. "Do you mean . . . ?"

"Either someone swiped his card," said Wyatt, "or your long-gone dad was just in our neighborhood."

HOW TO TAIL
AN ALBANIAN

A THOUSAND escape plans raced through Max's mind—faking an illness so the paramedics would carry him outside; hiding in the rubbish bin; doing something so incredibly vile that the school would kick him out right away—but Wyatt shot them down one by one.

"Ms. Annie's got her eye on you," he said. "She's just waiting for you to try another walkabout."

Max kicked his bed in frustration. "There must be *something* I can do."

As it turned out, there was.

The first class after lunch was Surveillance Techniques, which Roger Stones conducted in the garage—not the most comfy of classrooms. Chilly and cramped, the room smelled of paraffin oil and wood shavings, though neither was in evidence. Metal folding chairs faced a wheeled chalkboard.

Max and Wyatt shuffled in with the rest of the students and found their seats.

"Listen up, you pillocks," said Mr. Stones, rapping the chalkboard frame to get their attention. "Today we practice the toughest kind of surveillance: tailing."

Tremaine and Rashid snickered and elbowed each other.

The bullet-headed man scowled. "Minds out of the gutter, cupcakes. Tailing means surveillance on the hoof, and what's the first rule of tailing?"

Several hands shot up. Mr. Stones called on Shan, whose spiky hair sported stripes of purple and green.

"Rule number one: Don't get spotted," said Shan.

"Bang on target," said Stones. "And that calls for blending into the background—which in your case would mean only shadowing someone at the circus."

A few students chuckled. Shan self-consciously touched her tri-tone hair, then straightened and leveled a defiant look at them.

"No bright colors." Stones indicated Wyatt's fluorescent green GOT SURF? T-shirt. "And no flashy togs." He raised an eyebrow at Tremaine's shiny multi-zippered jacket. His gaze landed on Max. "In fact, you should look like this kid. Average as a brick."

Max didn't know whether to be insulted or pleased.

"You mean *thick* as a brick," sneered Nikki.

He decided on insulted.

Mr. Stones paced at the blackboard, hands clasped behind his back. "Only the best agents can pull off solo tailing—"

"*I* could do it," said Nikki. Dermot offered a weasely smile and bumped fists with her.

"In your dreams, sunshine," Stones said pleasantly. "Today, you lot will have a go at tag-team tailing. Two partners, one subject."

"Who do we follow?" asked Cinnabar.

"Civilians," said the teacher. "Now, watch closely." He spent several minutes scribbling on the blackboard, detailing various methods of double-teaming a subject. True, his scrawls resembled football plays drawn by an orangutan with arthritis, but they got the point across. When he was done, Mr. Stones summoned the glum-faced Styx into the room.

"Me and Styxie will take you out two-by-two to practice."

"Don't call me Styxie," muttered the big man.

"And remember," said Stones, "one of us will always be tailing *you*, so don't get cute."

Wyatt looked over at Max, deadpan. Max suppressed a smile. Didn't they know? Foster kids wrote the book on getting cute. He felt in his pocket for the scrap of paper on which he'd written the coffee shop's address.

For twenty long minutes, Max waited as two pairs of students went out to practice their shadowing. Then it was his turn. Although he would have preferred Wyatt, Max drew Shan as a partner. On their way out of the garage, Cinnabar caught his eye and mouthed, *No funny business.*

He gave her his blandest *Who, me?* expression.

Outside, the wind had picked up. A chilly breeze lanced through Max's thin borrowed jacket and blew his hair back across his forehead. Just shy of the street, Mr. Stones stopped them for final instructions.

"Here." He handed Max a blue baseball cap and a pair of glasses.

"Sorry, blue's not my color," said Max.

"This ain't a fashion show, peaches. It's trade craft," Stones growled. "After you switch lead position, use these to change your appearance. That way, the mark doesn't make you. Clear as beer?"

Max shrugged. "Clear enough."

For Shan, Mr. Stones provided a cloche cap that covered her tricolor hair. "Now all we need is a likely victim." He watched the street for a minute. Foot traffic was moderate, with workers returning from their lunch break, housewives out shopping, and college students headed for the underground or nearby university.

"Dead perfect." The burly teacher indicated a grandmotherly type with curly Brillo-pad hair and an oversized purple handbag. "There's your subject: Mabel Grockenspeel, Albanian double agent."

"You know her?" asked Shan.

"My ex-wife," said Mr. Stones. When the girl's mouth

dropped open in surprise, he rolled his eyes. "'Course I don't know her, cupcake. It's an exercise. *Pretend.*"

Shan gave a disgusted snort.

"Right then," said the teacher. "Max, take A position; Shan, you're B. Follow Mabel for a few minutes, then switch."

Max waited until their subject had established a half-block lead. Then he tucked the glasses into a pocket, popped the cap onto his head, and strolled after her, sticking to the opposite side of the road. "Mabel" forged steadily ahead, a little bounce in her step. She appeared to have no idea she was being followed.

At the corner, Max glanced behind. Shan dawdled down the other side of the street, head bent over her smartphone, texting away. Stones and Styx were nowhere to be seen.

A few minutes later, Max turned and signaled to Shan. He knelt and retied his shoelaces while the girl picked up her pace, moving into the A position a half block behind Mabel. After they had a fair lead on him, Max then crossed the street and strolled after Shan.

At the next corner, he paused, as if unsure about his direction, then slid the cap inside his jacket and pulled out the plain-glass spectacles. As he polished them with his T-shirt, he idly scanned the damp streets.

No Stones, No Styx. No Hantai Annie. Just a bunch of normals, out for a walk, as peaceful as you please. At the thought of the director, Max felt a stab of guilt, followed by a rush of anxious energy. He needed to move. And it seemed like he was free to do so.

Max stifled a smile. Could it be this easy? He checked the street, where Mabel window-shopped and Shan perched on a bus bench, seemingly focused on her phone. Surely Styx and Stones lurked somewhere nearby, watching them? If so, they were extremely well hidden.

On impulse, Max set off along the side street, head down, shoulders hunched. He walked a dozen steps . . . twenty . . . thirty. A giddy feeling bubbled up from his gut, like the aftereffects of chugging too much Coke. He was doing it; he was getting away! And the café where someone had used his father's debit card waited only four streets over, a five-minute walk.

Max chuckled and quickened his pace. Things were definitely looking up.

He maintained this sunny disposition until, just as he passed the next building, a tall man in a blue uniform stepped from an alcove and clutched his arm.

"Here now, lad," the man said in a voice like steel wrapped in suede. "Where do you think you're going?"

BAD COP, WORSE COP

CHAPTER 14

SNARED in the policeman's grip like a trout in a net, Max struggled. "Let me go! I didn't do anything!"

"Hush, boy," said the cop, tightening his grasp. His thumb pressed a nerve, and a twinge of pain lanced up toward Max's shoulder.

"Ow!"

"You want to settle down and listen, or you want to be cuffed? Your choice."

Max sized up the officer. The lean, pale-skinned man loomed over him, as tall as Styx, sheathed in an immaculate blue uniform that looked like it had been tailored on Savile Row. His thin lips and long jaw had a wolflike cast, but his large brown eyes turned down at the outer corners, lending the man a look of distant sadness. He seemed like someone who meant business.

Max checked around, but didn't see Styx or Stones yet. "I'll listen," he said.

"Good." The cop released his arm, and Max worked it around a little, coaxing feeling back into it. "I'd hate to Tase you, but I will if you run." He patted a blocky-looking black-and-yellow pistol on his hip.

"You'd Tase a kid just for running away," said Max.

"If I must," said the officer. His gaze flicked around the street, and he motioned Max closer to the building. "But I'd rather talk like civilized people. You live at that orphanage, yes?"

"Yeah."

"For how long?"

"Only a few days."

The policeman's gaze kept roving over their surroundings. "Ever see anything . . . unusual going on there?"

Max frowned and edged back. "What's this about? Aren't you busting me for being a truant?"

The man's eyebrows rose, and his hand rested on the butt of his Taser. "Why, no. Should I?"

"Uh, no. Don't trouble yourself." Max warily surveyed him. "But if you don't want to bust me, what *do* you want?"

"Information." The tall officer bent his knees a little, bringing his face closer to Max's level. "For starters, what's your name?"

"Max."

"Max, the people I work with want to know what goes on inside your orphanage."

Max cocked his head. "The people? You mean, the police?"

The man smiled one of those movie star smiles, all perfect teeth and megawatt sunniness. "Not exactly." He plucked at the blue fabric of his tunic. "This is borrowed."

"Then who do you work for?" asked Max.

"Let's just say, a very powerful organization with very powerful friends." The fake cop touched his hat brim in salute to a young woman strolling by, then resumed when she'd passed out of earshot. "Max, what do you want?"

"A smartphone that can read minds, a slice of lasagna as big as a house, and for Burundi to win the World Cup." Max grimaced. "What do you mean, what do I want?"

The man spread his hands. "How would you fancy a real, permanent home, with people who love you, a room of your own, and all the games, treats, and electronic gadgets you can possibly imagine?"

"You mean, like an adopted family?" The officer nodded, and Max fought to keep his face blank. "I'm listening."

"You could have all that and more, in exchange for a little information."

"What kind?"

"Reports on any unusual projects taking place inside the orphanage, or any mentions of *Eisenheimer*."

"That's it?" said Max. A mental image of that secret

chamber on the third floor flashed through his mind.

The tall man made an elegant movement with his shoulders that might have been a shrug. "The information would need to be of use, but in essence, that's it."

Max glanced across the street, where an old dog on a leash was leading an older lady, both tottering along. He bit his lip. If this man's group had the kind of influence he claimed, maybe they could help him get what he *really* wanted. The idea of revealing Merry Sunshine's operations gave him a squirmy feeling, but maybe he could feed the man enough nonessential information to satisfy him.

Things just might work out if he played this right. And besides, it wasn't like he'd be hurting Hantai Annie directly. . . . "I *might* do it," said Max.

"Excellent decision."

He held up a hand. "But if I do, I don't want to be placed with an adopted family."

"No?" The fake cop arched an eyebrow. "Then what *do* you want?"

"Find my father, Simon Segredo," said Max.

The man frowned, as if troubled. "Your . . . father?"

Max crossed his arms. "If this group is as all-powerful as you say, that shouldn't be a problem. So, Mr. . . . ?"

"Taylor. With a *Y*." The phony policeman's gaze flicked past Max's shoulder.

"How do I get in touch when I—"

Suddenly, Mr. Taylor reached out and gripped Max's wrist, snapping handcuffs onto it. "You expect me to swallow that, you little beggar?" he snarled. "Eh? I'll take you downtown and sweat the truth out of you!" He cuffed the other wrist.

Thrown, Max stammered, "W-why are you—"

"What seems to be the problem, officer?" boomed a deep voice from behind him. Craning his neck around, Max spotted a grim-faced Roger Stones.

"Caught me a truant," said Mr. Taylor in a coarse, working-class accent. "The brat claims he's not, but he's talkin' rubbish. You know him?"

"This one?" Mr. Stones caught Max by the shoulder and turned him around. "He's one of ours—ain't you, cupcake? From the orphanage down the road."

Max hung his head, pretending to be ashamed. "Yeah."

"All right, then," said the phony cop. "Take him, and good riddance. It'll save me a trip back to HQ. C'mere, you."

He spun Max back around and bent to unlock his cuffs. Shielded from Stones's view, he slipped a small card into Max's hand. Max palmed it, transferring the message to his pocket as soon as his hand was free.

"Remember this next time you fancy doing somethin' naughty." Mr. Taylor gave Max a steady gaze. "Someone is always watchin'."

"Cheers, officer," said Mr. Stones. "I've got the little git from here."

The fake cop touched the brim of his cap, then turned and strode off.

Stones's thick fingers clamped onto Max's shoulder like a demolition claw onto a tumbledown shack. "You're in for it now, sunshine. You have royally put your foot in the goo this time."

Max winced and feigned remorse. "Sorry, I don't know what got into me."

"I do." Mr. Stones barked a laugh. "You thought you'd do a rabbit, didn't you? Run off and find a better life, eh?"

Max tried a shrug—not an easy task with the man's eagle-talon grip on him.

Lifting a palm-sized, matte-black communications device, Mr. Stones said, "Show yourself." Then he pointed down the block at the fake policeman's receding figure. From an alleyway Taylor had just passed, a bearlike figure emerged and lumbered toward them. Styx.

"We knew you'd do a runner," said Mr. Stones.

Max's eyes widened. "How . . . ?"

"Please. Almost every third orphan tries it their first time out."

Max didn't think this called for a comment, so he didn't make any. Moments later, Styx joined them, wearing a shabby brown sports coat, a crooked orange tie, and his usual glum expression.

"Just as predicted," said Mr. Stones. "Young Max here isn't happy with our accommodations."

"That so?" said Styx.

"It's no Ritz-Carlton," said Max.

Mr. Stones smirked. "We'll have to tell the director about this one, won't we, Styxie?"

"Don't call me Styxie," the big man mumbled.

"Mind taking him to Miz Annie? I've got a tailing exercise to run."

"I suppose," said Styx. "Come along, you." And he led Max back down the streets to the orphanage, stone-faced.

The man's silence weighed on Max, and after a minute of it, he asked, "So, this sort of thing happens a lot, then?"

Styx said nothing.

Another minute passed. Max asked, "How much trouble you reckon I'm in?"

The big man glanced at him, grunted, "Loads," and faced front again.

Max gulped. He wondered whether the price he'd pay for running off would be worth it. The mysterious Mr. Taylor had better deliver on his promise.

Not surprisingly, Hantai Annie was less than thrilled with Max's latest stunt. When Styx told her the news, she paced up and down in front of her desk, ranting in whatever language she favored. Styx slipped out the door.

"Dame jya nai ka! Baka yarou!" she barked. "You stupid boy, Max-*kun*, very, very stupid!"

Max sat slumped on the familiar overstuffed couch in her office, elbows on knees. He didn't think childcare workers were supposed to talk to kids like that, but he didn't see much point in mentioning it just then.

"You betray my trust," the director snapped. *"Dame da!"*

"Sorry," he said. "I didn't think it'd be a big deal."

"You both ears broken?" said Hantai Annie. "You hear what I say last night? Going outside alone is very, very dangerous."

"But it's daylight," said Max. "And I was only going a few blocks. What could happen?"

At that moment, the director resembled a frizzy-haired Guy Fawkes Day sparkler. Her dark eyes sizzled. Heat radiated from her in waves. All that was missing was multi-colored sparks.

"Day, night, doesn't matter," she said. "And not just dangerous for you—dangerous for *us*. School has enemies, and you helping them."

Guilt wriggled like a tapeworm in his guts. Hantai Annie's words were truer than she knew.

She rattled off another rapid-fire phrase in Korean or Mongolian, Max wasn't sure which. "I take some time and come up with perfect punishment for you. Count on it."

His mouth set in a tight line. So much for Hantai Annie's noble words about family forgiveness. Before he could learn exactly which diabolical punishment the director had planned, Mr. Stones burst through the office door, eyes wide.

"They're gone!" he cried. "Someone's snatched two of our best."

As if a switch had been thrown, the director's anger evaporated. She grew as still and focused as a hunting panther. "*Dare da?* Who is gone?"

"Rashid and Tremaine."

Max sat up straight, alarmed despite himself. Serious Rashid, who'd given him a clue about his dad, and smiling Tremaine, the martial arts whiz—both gone? A cold whisper of fear snaked up his spine.

"Who did this?" asked Hantai Annie.

The burly teacher ran a hand over his bald scalp. His sarcastic patter and cool attitude were gone, swept away by worry. "I don't know; I couldn't ID them."

The director grimaced. "Tell me."

"The boys are out practicing their shadowing, when a van stops in the road," said Mr. Stones. "Men in black pour out. I'm a block behind, and as I run up, they toss the lads into the back of the van and speed off."

"You didn't follow?"

"I was four blocks from my car. They were gone in a blink."

"*Imaimashii.*" Hantai Annie's fists clenched. "We must find them. Did you see license plate?"

"It was blacked out."

"They leave no clues?"

Stones shook his head, and the office lights gleamed off his bald dome. He fished in a jacket pocket and brought out his hand. "Just this." On his broad palm rested a many-petaled white flower with a yellow center. "I found it in the gutter, right behind where the van stopped."

At the sight of the bloom, Hantai Annie's face crumpled and went gray as a November Tuesday. She sank blindly into the nearest chair, muttering something.

Mr. Stones frowned and stepped closer. "Director?"

"What is it?" asked Max, thoroughly confused.

"LOTUS," said Hantai Annie. "They found me at last. We are lost."

THIS FLOWER
SPELLS DANGER

MAX'S GAZE traveled from Hantai Annie to Mr. Stones, to Styx, who'd just poked his head through the open doorway. "We're lost because of a *flower*?" Max asked. "You realize that makes absolutely no sense."

Mr. Stones looked like he'd been punched in the stomach with brass knuckles. He leaned against the desk for support.

"What?" asked Styx.

"LOTUS," said Stones.

"Oh?"

"They snatched two kids."

"Ohhh," said the big man. He shambled into the room, slack-faced, and sank onto the other end of the couch. The cushion lifted under Max.

"Will someone tell me what's going on?" said Max.

"LOTUS found us," grunted Styx.

"Someone else?"

Hantai Annie stared out the office door, but Max suspected she wasn't seeing anything in the here and now. "My past . . . catch up with me."

Max rolled his eyes. No one was making sense, but something had happened that affected the school, two kids he knew—and by extension, he himself. That much was clear. As he shifted his feet to get up and search for a coherent adult, the director spoke again.

"When I was young person, I work in national security for my country." Her voice was soft, thready, not at all her usual gruff bark. "A—*nanto iu no ka?—independent* agency recruited me. They said their goal was world peace."

Mr. Stones snorted.

"I was young," said Hantai Annie. "Foolish."

"So they weren't into the whole peace thing?" Max guessed.

"Not hardly," said Stones. "Money, power, bloody revolution—that's more their line."

The director's voice grew stronger. "They hide truth from me. But after one year, I discover who was behind agency, what their real mission was."

"And then?" said Max.

"I confront my boss. He laughed, called me *soboku dana*."

"Daft?" said Mr. Stones.

"Naive," said the director. Her fists clenched. "I quit agency, ran away. They send people after me, skilled agents, but I was more skilled. I vanish."

Max looked down at the carpet and pursed his lips. He'd had some experience with hoping things would be one way and having them turn out another.

The director continued. "After many years, I come here. I start this school to make up for the bad I did, to fight against LOTUS."

Max frowned. "But why train kids? Why not work with grown-ups?"

"LOTUS spread lies through spy community. No government, no agents would work with me." Hantai Annie stood and ran a hand along the surface of her desk, looking around the room. "They underestimate Annie, just like they underestimate *kodomotachi*. Children."

"But why would LOTUS snatch two students?" Mr. Stones mused, rubbing his jaw. "Why not simply attack the school?"

Hantai Annie folded her arms and held her elbows, as if she felt a chill. "I have idea. . . ."

Max's brow furrowed. Something about students going missing rang a distant bell. What *was* it . . . ?

At that moment, the fax line jangled, making them all jump. Hantai Annie stared at the old machine as if a rattlesnake had just materialized on her credenza. It buzzed and made whining fax-machine sounds, and soon a sheet of paper began emerging from the printer.

Max checked the room: all the adults were focused on the

chattering device. The paper twitched its way out, and finally it dropped into the tray. Face grim, Hantai Annie picked it up and scanned the message.

"Well?" asked Mr. Stones.

Wordlessly, Hantai Annie turned the sheet to face him.

"'If you want to see your orphans alive again, deliver the Process,'" he read aloud. "Do they mean—?"

"Get Chiffre and Vazquez," she told Styx. "*Hayaku!*" The big man rose and lumbered out the door.

"What's the Process?" asked Max.

Hantai Annie turned to him. "We talk later about your punishment. I did not forget."

"Well, that's a relief," said Max. "I'm in danger of being kidnapped by a bunch of evil flower lovers, and you won't even tell me why."

"You in danger because you stubborn and foolish," snapped the director. "*Baka yarou!* Now, go."

Stung, Max rose and stalked to the door. He couldn't *wait* to find his father and go live with him. Hantai Annie Wong was exactly like every other foster parent and group home administrator. It was her way or the highway.

Out of sight, Max lingered in the entryway, waiting to hear what was said. Secrets could be valuable, especially to someone like Agent Taylor.

"How do they bloody well know we have it?" That was Mr. Stones's voice, deep and resonant.

"Someone talked," said the director. "Or else we have mole. Either way . . ."

"We're up a tree without a ladder," said Stones. "Let's call off the mission to the capital."

"No. *Tondemonai*."

"It's dangerous for the brats."

"More dangerous if we don't stop LOTUS."

Max bristled. Two kids—or *brats*, as Stones called them—get kidnapped, and all these people can think about is their stupid Process? Some family this was.

He wanted to walk right in there and tell them off. But he kept his mouth shut because he'd just realized something: He was going to take Agent Taylor up on his offer. And he knew precisely where to start.

After all the fuss, it took another hour or so for the orphanage to return to its normal operations—if you could call what went on at Merry Sunshine *normal*. But at last the teachers emerged from their secret meeting. Younger students went off to Beginning Martial Arts with Chandrika; Max, with the rest of the older kids, trooped upstairs with Victor Vazquez for Electronic Surveillance. A few students noticed that Rashid and Tremaine were missing, and speculations flew concerning their whereabouts. Max stuck to his purpose, saying nothing.

Mr. Vazquez looked more like a tango instructor than an

electronics nerd. He was tall and lean, with piercing dark eyes and slicked-down black hair, and his burgundy leather jacket creaked faintly whenever he moved his arms. As he prowled past Max's chair, the scent of gardenias trailed in his wake.

"I ask you, my friends," said Mr. Vazquez, gesturing to a table at the front of the room, "which of these seemingly innocuous items is a listening device?"

Max eagerly turned his eyes to the table. On it sat a USB cable, a pen, an electrical outlet adapter plug, a computer mouse, a credit card case, a calculator, a vase, a teddy bear, and a coffee mug. His fellow orphans blurted out answers.

"The mouse and pen!" said Wyatt.

"No way," sneered Nikki. "It's the plug, the calculator, and the pen."

"Everything but the mouse and the calculator," said Cinnabar.

"The teddy!" cried Dermot. When Nikki scowled at him, he said, "What?"

"All of them," said Max quietly.

Victor Vazquez pivoted smoothly and pointed at Max. "Very close, young man," he purred. "This"—he picked up the mug and took a slurp—"is my coffee. Brazilian blend; *mmm.* The rest . . . all designed to pick up sounds and transmit them up to three hundred meters." He smiled, a full movie-star twinkle. "Impressive, yes?"

"I'll say," muttered Nikki Knucks, tracking his movements like a lovesick puppy.

Max snorted.

"These devices come in two flavors," said Mr. Vazquez, turning up the twinkle. "Mocha and raspberry." He scanned the room. "A little joke."

All the girls tittered. "Oh, Mr. V., you're so funny," said Shan.

Wyatt looked over at Max and rolled his eyes. Max noticed Cinnabar mooning over the teacher, and he felt an unfamiliar stab of jealousy.

"Actually, it's radio transmission mode and recording mode," said Vazquez with a smirk. "The transmitters send to a receiver equipped with a memory"—he indicated a row of small black boxes with antennas—"while the recorders have their own flash memory."

Over the next hour, Vazquez went on to detail how to plant and monitor the listening devices. Max listened closely, eyes glued to the items on the table. Somehow, he had to get his hands on one of them. What he needed was a diversion. . . .

The end of the session arrived without Max having devised a way to distract attention. He felt in his pockets for something helpful, but they only yielded Taylor's card, his own good-luck stone, and the lighter. Somehow, he didn't think that tossing a rock through the window or lighting the room on fire would prove the most effective distractions.

Maybe Wyatt would help? He looked around, but his friend was just leaving.

Max lingered in his seat, doodling while the last students packed up. Over by the door, Cinnabar, Shan, and an older girl Max hadn't met yet ringed around the teacher, chattering, giggling, and flipping their hair. Max glanced about the room. Nearly everyone else had gone.

Perhaps he could just pocket one of the devices while Mr. Vazquez was busy with the girls?

He eased out of his chair and strolled over to the bookshelf where the receivers lay on display. One of them was a little smaller than his hand. Perfect. He reached for it, and a voice from behind sneered, "Planning some extra-credit spying for your overlords?"

Max turned. Nikki loomed close, crowding him against the shelf. "Just taking a closer look," he said.

A wave of giggles from the other girls drew Nikki's attention that way. Her expression was both sour and wistful, like a withered lemon dreaming of its days on the tree.

Max had a flash of inspiration. "You know, he's never going to notice you."

"What?" Nikki scowled.

"Mr. Vazquez. You'll never be his favorite—not with all that competition."

"You're daft, barmpot," said Nikki. But her eyes revealed doubt.

Max pressed harder, letting his hand with the receiver casually drop to his side. "Forget about him recommending you for the mission."

Two spots of color appeared on the redhead's cheeks. "I wasn't—"

"No? Oh, so then you have a *crush* on him?" Max slipped the receiver into his pocket and turned away from the table.

"Get *stuffed*!" The beefy girl thrust her palms at Max's chest in a stiff shove.

He didn't fight it. The impact sent him into and over the table, scattering the listening devices willy-nilly onto the floor. Max landed with a thump. His attack-play training had helped him avoid serious injury, but his left hip ached where it hit the edge, and his head rested on a teddy bear.

Nikki strode around the table, fists clenched. "You take that back!" she cried.

From below, she looked like a goddess of war—if the goddess of war had wild red hair, eyes like blue BBs, and a zit in the crease of her nose. Max propped himself up on his elbows and hoped that Mr. Vazquez would stop her before she jumped on him and squashed him like a bug.

Sure enough, the teacher appeared behind Nikki. "Hey, hey, hey!" he said. "Settle down. The equipment is delicate." He placed a restraining hand on her shoulder.

At his touch, Nikki's rage evaporated. The girl folded in on herself, mortified. "I'm so sorry," she mumbled.

Max felt a twinge of guilt at playing on her insecurities, but when he discovered the pen transmitter by his elbow and slipped it into his jeans pocket, that guilt quickly evaporated. It was every orphan for himself.

He helped set the table upright and glided out the door past Cinnabar.

"What was that all about?" she asked, giving him a curious look.

"Anger management training." Striding down the hall, Max patted the receiver and pen in his pockets. Now he had the bug. All that remained was to plant it and reel in the secrets.

FALLING ON DEFT EARS

MAX WAITED until dinnertime, when he hoped the staff would be busy elsewhere. After wolfing down his pizza, he sauntered up to the third floor, pen bug tucked in a pocket. The hallway was warm and stuffy but deserted, smelling faintly of mildew, carpet cleaner, and a wet-dog odor from the furnace vents (or possibly from Pinkerton the dog).

Easy as spilling a secret, Max found the stretch of wall where he'd seen the hidden panel on his first day at the orphanage. He laid an ear to it, listening for voices inside. Silence. Running his hands over the smooth surface, Max felt for a crack or some kind of hidden trigger. Nothing. He scowled. Twice he walked the length of the hall, probing high and low.

Maybe the panel operated on a spring release? He pressed the wall in several places, but no trick door popped open. Max eyed the brass sconces. Perhaps the trigger was concealed in a lighting fixture? He reached for the nearest one.

A tuneless humming reached his ears. From around the corner, not ten feet away, stepped a portly silver-haired man in a tweed jacket, his nose buried in a sheaf of papers.

Too late to flee. Max would have to brazen it out.

"Oh, hi," Max said. "I didn't think anyone else was up here."

"Eh?" The man glanced up and waddled to a stop just in front of Max. He tapped the top sheet. "Look here, did you know that although copper is nine point five percent less conductive than silver, it's also approximately ten times less expensive per ounce?"

"Really," said Max.

"Of course," said the old man. His gray eyes twinkled behind round spectacles. "And since this operation isn't exactly made of money, it should save us a pretty penny, while not sacrificing—" He broke off, blinked, and seemed to really notice Max for the first time. "I say, isn't this floor off-limits for children?"

Max faked a grin. "Aw, the director lets me walk up here sometimes for exercise. But I haven't seen you before. Are you one of the teachers?"

The man chuckled. "Well, not as such. You might say I'm a consultant." He placed a hand on his ample gut. "Dr. Jacob Eisenheimer. And you are . . . ?"

Max fought to keep his face neutral. *Eisenheimer* was the

one Agent Taylor had been asking about. Maybe he could learn something here without resorting to bugging. "Uh, Max Segredo. So are you here helping with the project?"

When Dr. Eisenheimer laughed, his eyes practically disappeared behind rosy apple cheeks, giving him the look of a beardless Santa Claus with a bad home perm. "Oh, my word. You might say that. It's *my* project."

"Really?" said Max, surreptitiously activating the pen in his pocket. "Tell me more."

The doctor beamed. "Well, it's quite fascinating, actually." He flipped a sheet of paper over to its blank side and patted his pockets. "The principle is easier to explain with diagrams, but I don't seem to have a blasted—" Dr. Eisenheimer spotted Max's listening device. "Ah. Borrow your pen?"

"Uh," said Max. But by then, the old man had already lifted the gizmo from his shirt pocket, uncapped it, and begun sketching.

"You see, neural oscillation, or as you might say, brain waves, can be mapped quite precisely using the Kuramoto model. In fact . . ." He doodled some more, and Max was glad that the listening device contained an actual working pen.

"Alors," said a woman's voice. "What eez this?"

Max turned to see Madame Chiffre bearing down on him, nose leading the way like a battering ram. "Uh, I was just having a nice talk with Dr. Eisenheimer," he said.

"After I specifically told you to stay off ze third floor."

The teacher's eyes narrowed. "Do you think you are special?"

"Um, yes," said Max. "But doesn't everybody?"

"Do you think ze rules don't apply to you?"

He tried for a charming smile. *"Rules?* I thought they were more like guidelines."

Madame Chiffre clutched his upper arm and began walking him back toward the stairs. For a slender woman, she had a grip like a badger's jaws. "This eez your last warning. You will observe ze rules or I will talk to ze director. *Vous comprenez?"*

"I got it," said Max, pulling his arm free. "And your nails could use a trimming."

Farther down the hall, Dr. Eisenheimer held up Max's listening device. "Young man, your pen!"

"Keep it," said Max, scarcely believing his luck. "I have a feeling it'll do more good with you."

Three minutes later, Max sat cross-legged on his bed, earbuds plugged into the receiver. His roommates, Wyatt and Jensen, were still at dinner or off studying somewhere. The hallway lay deserted. He was all alone, listening to the forbidden sounds of the Secret Room Show.

"But that's not ze worst of it," Madame Chiffre was saying. "LOTUS has taken two of our students hostage, to trade for ze Process."

"Never!" said Dr. Eisenheimer. "They must not possess the invention, no matter what."

"But ze students . . ."

"Regrettable, I grant you. But you know full well what would happen if we let this fall into enemy hands."

Max's lip curled. This man was worse than Stones and the director. But at the same time, he couldn't help appreciating the listening device. Its sound came through so clearly, it was as if the speakers stood there in the room with him. Then, after a hollow creak and the scuff of footsteps, two more voices joined the show.

"I borrowed some time." It was Hantai Annie's voice. "They think I consider their offer."

"But what good will that do?" Madame Chiffre said. "We don't even know where their headquarters eez."

"Stones and I will locate it and rescue the boys," came a smooth tenor voice—Victor Vazquez. "And even if we fail, perhaps the students' mission will succeed."

"Good point," said the doctor. "Hijack the Nullthium-Ninety and they've got nothing—even if they somehow steal the plans. Without the element, the Process won't work."

"Victor, you and Roger-san must not fail," said Hantai Annie. "Rescue those boys, and Jazz, too. LOTUS cannot have Process, but we cannot let children die."

Max felt absurdly pleased at her caring. Maybe he'd misjudged the director. And what was all this about Jazz—had LOTUS captured her as well? He listened closely, but Hantai Annie made no more mention of Cinnabar's sister.

"You may count on us," said Vazquez. The conversation

then turned to the logistics of assembling a rescue team.

Max rested his chin on his hands. *What in the world is this Process, and why is it worth so much?* He stared down at the faint diamond pattern on the blue bedspread, pondering. He could almost picture the four adults in the secret room, standing around the table.

Paper crinkled. "Now, shall we focus on the business at hand?" roared Dr. Eisenheimer. Max flinched. The man must have been speaking directly into the pen. "We have a device to complete, and we're running low on polyimide substrate, dielectric fluid, and these other elements. Any ideas?"

"If ze lab would stock these things, perhaps I could do a little after-hours 'shopping' later tonight," said Madame Chiffre. They all chuckled.

"Okay," said the director. *"Sou shiyou."*

"Alors, I have nothing to write with," said Madame Chiffre. "Anyone, a pen?"

Two thumps like someone being brained by a log were followed by a rustling like truck-sized rolls of fabric being unspooled. The doctor must be patting his pockets, thought Max, pulling his earbuds partway out. Not good.

"Here, use mine," said Dr. Eisenheimer's tinny voice.

No!

More thumps, bumps, and rustling blasted through the miniature headphones. Max held his breath. Would they notice that the pen was actually a listening device?

He cautiously replaced the earbuds. A shooshing like someone skiing down a paper mountain at warp speed filled his ears.

"Nice pen," boomed Madame Chiffre.

Max bit his lip. But all the doctor said was, "Thanks."

He missed the next bit, thanks to deafening rustles and thuds. Was the doctor returning the pen to his pocket or playing drum major with it? At last the voices returned to their former clarity.

"—if she does," Dr. Eisenheimer was saying, "I must still return home for the last piece."

"Not tonight," said Hantai Annie. *Abunai.* Tomorrow, after team leaves—then you go."

"But what happens if—" Madame Chiffre began.

A shadow rippled across Max's bedspread. He didn't hear what the teacher said next, because his mini-headphones were suddenly yanked away.

"Gotcha." There stood Nikki Knucks, an evil grin on her face and Max's earbuds dangling from her fist. "I knew you were a mole," she said. "I *knew* it. And now I've got the proof."

CHAPTER 17

WALTZES WITH BUFFALOES

"YOU'RE LOONY," said Max. "I was just listening to Cinnabar and Shan gossip."

"Oh, yeah?" said Nikki. "Let's check it out."

"No!"

Max lunged for the earbud cord, but Nikki jerked it away, pulling the receiver off the bed with it. He caught the device before it could hit the floor, and the earbud jack popped right out.

"Give it here," said Nikki.

Max bounced off of the bed and backed away, holding the receiver behind him. "I don't think so."

The big girl sprang like a tiger, swiping an arm around his right side for the receiver. He twisted away and hopped onto Jensen's bed.

"You're a stinking double agent," she growled.

"Am not," said Max. Brilliant comeback, he thought. For a second grader.

Nikki flushed red to the roots of her hair, making her look rather like an angry tomato with a crimson wig. She leapt at Max, but he jumped off the bed.

"You're spying for that fake cop," she snarled. "Admit it!"

Max circled, keeping Jensen's bed between them. "Fake cop? And how do *you* know about him?"

The girl's eyes widened as she realized her mistake. "I, uh . . ."

"He asked you to spy on this place, didn't he?" *And how many other kids had Agent Taylor talked to?*

"No!" cried Nikki. "I turned him down."

"Couldn't find any info to trade, more likely," said Max. "*You're* the mole—you're just rubbish at it."

"That's a filthy lie!" Abandoning her martial arts finesse, Nikki rushed him like a maddened buffalo. She was *fast*. Max danced back to avoid her, and his heel caught the edge of his own footlocker.

He stumbled. That was all the opening Nikki needed. She plowed into him, and he toppled, receiver still held behind him.

Crunch. Their combined weight proved too much for the sensitive device. It was squashed flatter than a beetle under a boot.

Nikki's hands drove at Max's throat. He caught her wrists. They rolled, grappling.

"Fight! Fight!" someone yelled from the hallway. Footsteps pounded.

Max could spare no attention for their audience. He thrashed about with Nikki, keeping her wrists in a death grip as she strove to choke him senseless.

"I don't . . . want to fight . . . a girl," Max grunted.

"You'd better, wimp," she said. "This one's fighting *you*."

They collided, hard, with someone's bed frame. Max's head struck wood, white spots danced before his eyes, and they tumbled apart.

Dizzy, he shook his head to clear it. If he let her pin him down she would surely punch his ticket with her karate fists of doom. Max tried lurching to his feet, but Nikki's shoulder drove into his gut, sending his air out with a *whoosh*.

Down they went again. This time, Nikki scrambled up first, planting herself on his chest. It was déjà vu all over again. A triumphantly mad light shone in her eyes as she drew back her right fist. Her T-shirt pulled up, exposing a stretch of bare midriff.

Something clicked in Max's mind. He couldn't beat her with brute strength, but there might be another way. . . .

His hands lanced out at that pale belly and began vigorously, and ferociously, tickling her.

"No-ho-ho-*ho*!" Nikki cried, writhing. "Sto-ha-ha-hop it!"

She twisted and squirmed like a two-year-old at bath time, trying to evade Max's merciless fingers. But he showed no pity. Finally she tumbled off him, curling into the fetal position.

Elated by the turnabout, Max rolled up onto one knee and pressed his advantage. Nikki's hands flailed weakly; her elbows were locked to her sides in self-defense.

"Oh, I'm sorry," Max said. "Are you ticklish?"

"Oi!" a voice bellowed, somewhere above him. "Knock it off." A hand the approximate size and softness of a cast-iron skillet gripped Max's arm, dragging him up to his feet.

Panting, he glanced around. Faces crowded the doorway: Wyatt, Jensen, Shan, and others. The bearlike figure of Styx loomed beside him.

"You are *dead*," snarled Nikki. Fists clenched, she rose off the floor into a fighting crouch.

Styx stepped in front of her. "I said, knock it *off*. What's this all about?"

"He's a mole," said Nikki.

"No, *she's* the mole," said Max.

The big man held up a warning finger. "Ladies first."

Max snorted. Nikki Knucks was a lot of things, but not, so far as he could tell, a lady.

"This prat planted a bug and was spying on someone," said Nikki. "I caught him at it."

"Where's the proof?" asked Styx.

Nikki indicated the smashed receiver and earbuds lying nearby. "There, see?"

"I was just practicing for class," Max lied smoothly.

The big man scowled and picked up the pieces. "Who broke it?"

"He did," said Nikki.

"She did," said Max. "When she attacked me."

Styx turned to the girl. "Nikki?"

"Okay, technically that's true, but that's not the point," she said. "The point is, he's a double agent. He was *spying*."

Styx wearily rubbed his face with one of those huge hands. "In a school for spies, I should bloody well *hope* he was spying."

"But you don't—" Nikki blustered.

"Put a sock in it." Styx sounded like a grizzly waking up hungry from his winter nap. "Both of you, toilet duty. Nine o'clock tonight!"

"But she—" Max began.

"*Gerroutofit,*" Styx growled. He glared at the students filling the doorway. "Show's over. Scat!" They melted back into the corridor, and he switched his attention to Nikki. "You too, Miss Knucks."

With one last murderous glower at Max, she sauntered out the door, Styx close behind. "Let that be a lesson," he said on the way out. What kind of lesson, he didn't mention.

Max seethed at the unfairness of it. Here he was, drawing toilet duty simply because he'd been attacked by that nutcase Nikki. Never mind that he *had* been spying; it was the principle that mattered—the breakage wasn't his fault.

He thought about exposing her dealings with Taylor, then realized something: whichever mole slipped the agent good intel first would get what they desired.

Max pawed through the drawers of the room's only desk and hunted up a sheet of notepaper. Then he began crafting a note in Caesar's code, detailing a few choice bits of what he'd learned about Eisenheimer and his Process. Later, he'd slip it into an empty soda can and drop it out a window on the orphanage's blind side, following the instructions on Agent Taylor's card.

He wiped his palms on his jeans, not quite able to suppress a twinge. He was walking a fine line here. But there was no turning back now.

Nikki Knucks was right: he *was* a double agent.

CHAPTER 18

THE GO-TEAM GOES FOR BROKE

AT BREAKFAST the next morning, the dining-room atmosphere was thick with suspense, nervousness, and the aroma of frying bacon. The orphans' chatter seemed forced and overloud, their occasional laughter brittle and phony. Concern about the missing students alternated with excitement over the coming mission.

"Today's the day," said Wyatt, sitting down with a second helping of ham and eggs.

Max pushed his own half-full plate away. "How can you eat?" His stomach was tied in some kind of complicated sailor's knot. The greasy ham smell made him queasy.

"Brekkie's my favorite meal," said Wyatt. "Besides, I have a feeling we're going on that mission. And that means I need to keep my strength up."

"Maybe *you're* going," said Max, "but Hantai Annie

wouldn't trust me to spit on her head if her hair was on fire—never mind going to the capital."

Across the table, Cinnabar was putting up a good front. Max had told her what he suspected about LOTUS capturing her sister Jazz, and it had only made her determination that much fiercer. "We'll give you a full report," she said, with a carefully studied tinge of boredom. But Max noticed that she'd shredded her paper napkin and was toying with the pieces.

When Hantai Annie marched into the room, conversations stopped. She stood at the head of the table, hands clasped behind her, feet apart, surveying the orphans like a general reviewing her troops.

"Most of you know that, yesterday, our enemy kidnapped two students," she said. Murmurs greeted this announcement. "And many of you ask if the mission is *kyanseru*. Canceled."

At that, nervous chatter swelled.

Hantai Annie's voice cut through it like a chain saw through butter. "I say the mission is more important than before. The mission stands."

"But what about Rashid and Tremaine?" Shan asked. Worry lines creased her forehead.

"Mr. Stones and Mr. Vazquez will rescue them," said the director. "Never fear. And Hans and Catarina going along for help." The two older students nodded with grim-faced satisfaction, and a smattering of applause broke out. *"Demo,"*

Hantai Annie continued, "today, other team goes to capital. I talk with all teachers, and they recommend four students for mission." She stared down the length of the table.

"Here goes," muttered Wyatt, laying down his fork and crossing his fingers. Cinnabar sat up straight and smiled tightly, as if she were a beauty pageant contestant waiting to be crowned.

Max crossed his arms. No way would he be picked, but part of him couldn't help hoping.

"Number one, Cinnabar Jones."

Cinnabar gasped in relief. Shan, on her left, patted her shoulder, while Nikki shot her a dirty look.

Max knew how much this meant to Cinnabar. "Nice one," he murmured. She flashed him a quick blinding smile and turned to whisper to Shan. He felt an odd tingle, like that smile had kindled something in his chest.

"Next," said the director. "Jensen Swensen."

"Yeah!" crowed Jensen, clenching his fist and bopping it on the table. Max's stomach tied another knot.

"Nikki Knucks."

At the sound of her name, an expression very much like relief washed over Nikki's features, followed quickly by a truculent smile. She nodded at Max with a *told you so* smirk. He looked away in disgust. He was halfway glad he wouldn't be going along.

"And last team member . . ."

Wyatt leaned forward, mouth hanging open.

". . . Max Segredo."

Max sat back in his chair, utterly and thoroughly gobsmacked.

A clamor of voices burst out in the room. Nikki's complaining whine rose above the racket—something about "dirty sneak" and "no experience," so Max assumed she was talking about him. But he didn't care. A goofy grin stretched across his face. The day suddenly felt full of possibility, and Max was one step closer to finding his father.

He turned to Wyatt. The blond boy's mouth tugged down at the edges, but when he noticed Max's gaze, he forced a smile.

"Ace," he said, giving Max a weak thumbs-up. "Yeah. Good on ya."

"Sorry you didn't get picked," said Max.

Wyatt lifted a shoulder. "No worries. I'm happy as a dog in a hubcap factory." But his grin was a little wobbly.

Cinnabar leaned across the table and patted his arm. "You're better than Jensen, everybody knows that."

"Too right. Jensen's probably the world's only living brain donor." Wyatt cocked his head as a thought hit him. "And that's meant to make me feel *better*?"

Max raised his eyebrows and looked at Cinnabar. She winced.

"Damare!" Once more, Hantai Annie's command sliced

through the noise. "Everybody shut you mouth!" Voices quieted, and faces turned her way. "Better. Go-team, my office in ten minutes. Everyone else, eat up; go to class." She spun on her heel and marched from the dining room, back straighter than a steel ruler.

Without another word, Wyatt picked up his plate, scraped the leftovers into the trash bin, and left his dish on the dirty stack. Max watched as the blond boy shuffled out the door.

"He really wanted it," he said.

"I know," said Cinnabar. "It's a shame. But we've got to stay focused on the mission." She stood. "See you in ten."

But *whose* mission? Max mused. Hers, mine, or Hantai Annie's?

Four mysterious indigo book bags rested beside the filing cabinet in the director's office. Max's attention kept returning to them as Hantai Annie Wong sat the team members down for their briefing.

"Our enemy, LOTUS, is working with smugglers," she said.

Max raised a hand. "Um, what does LOTUS stand for?"

"Stand for?" She scowled. "*Nanda?* Anything that brings profit or power."

"No, the name. What does it—" Max broke off as Hantai Annie's scowl deepened. "Never mind."

"LOTUS smuggling illegal materials into country for

very dangerous project," Hantai Annie continued. "Show them, Styx."

The bearlike man mashed a few keys on a laptop computer, then held it up so the four orphans could see. The screen displayed two photos: one of a good-sized industrial barrel, and the other of its contents—some unimpressive purplish-gray powder.

"This," said the director, "is Nullthium-Ninety. Dangerous stuff."

"Not much to look at," said Jensen.

Hantai Annie shot him a glare. "Danger not in *looks*. Danger is in what it *does*."

"What's it do, then?" asked Jensen, brow furrowing. "This . . . Nolte-Ninety?"

"That's on a need-to-know basis," growled Styx.

"Do *you* know?" asked Max.

"No." Styx glowered.

"*I* need to know," said Jensen.

"No, you don't," said Hantai Annie. "All *you* need to know is stop this shipment."

"But if I don't know what it does—" Jensen broke off as Nikki elbowed him in the ribs.

"Go on," said Cinnabar. "We're listening." She shot Max a glance, her golden eyes sparkling with excitement. He felt a tug at his heart.

The director paced in front of her desk. "Smugglers deliver

shipment to museum. Somehow they pass it off as . . . *nanto iu ka*? Article facts?"

"Artifacts?" Styx suggested.

Hantai Annie blew out some air and tucked a stray curl behind her ear. "Crazy language. *Artifacts*, yes. And your mission is—"

"To burn it?" Max offered.

"To blow it up?" said Nikki eagerly.

The director grimaced. "No. First, confirm shipment, then stop it."

The orphans exchanged glances. "Not that I doubt our wicked macho spy skills"—Max quirked an eyebrow—"but four kids are supposed to stop an evil organization full of trained professionals?"

Unexpectedly, Hantai Annie Wong smiled. *"Kichigai gimi da?* Crazy?"

"Uh, yeah," said Max.

"But you not alone. Two veteran agents—Styx and Chandrika Moorthy—will help you."

"Do we get guns?" asked Jensen.

The director scoffed and tapped her head. *"This* is spy's best weapon."

"Hair?" asked Jensen.

Styx cleared his throat. "Shall I go find a replacement, director?"

"I'll be good," said the beefy boy, holding up his palms

in surrender. "I'm just nervous. I babble when I'm nervous, that's all."

Hantai Annie gazed at him steadily until Jensen blushed and fell silent. She retrieved some papers from her desktop and passed a sheet to each student. "Read, memorize, and burn."

Max smiled at the instructions. No problem with the burning.

"What's this?" asked Nikki Knucks.

"Your cover," said the director.

Max looked up from the dossier. "But it says I'm using my real name. How is that a cover identity?"

Cinnabar leaned over and tapped the sheet. "Read the rest."

"I'm a *Catholic school student*?" Nikki jeered. "In what parallel universe?"

Max and Cinnabar shared a glance rich with amusement.

"You all private-school students, *ne*?" said Hantai Annie, striding to the door. "On field trip. Styx, make sure they burn papers after, then hand out book bags." She paused on the threshold. "You have half hour to get ready."

The big man lumbered over to a small fireplace and lit some crumpled newspaper under a stack of fresh logs. "Right, you lot. Get crackin'."

CHAPTER 19

ONE WAY TO TELL IF YOU'RE BEING TAILED

UP IN HIS ROOM after the briefing, Max slung his book bag onto the bed and removed its contents: his Catholic school uniform and sturdy black shoes, miscellaneous school supplies, a travel pack of toiletries, a pen recorder, a smartphone, two smoke bombs disguised as erasers, and a coiled length of ultrathin high-tension line.

He surveyed the spartan room. Depending on how things went during this mission, he might not be seeing it again. If so, it wouldn't be his shortest stay at a group home.

He tucked a change of clothes into the bag and stowed his mother's photo in the zippered pocket, just in case. Would she have been proud of his spy abilities, or disappointed that he was following in his father's footsteps? He'd never know. Peeling off his jeans and T-shirt, Max began donning his disguise: white shirt, gray slacks, blue blazer, and striped tie. He snorted. *Some disguise.*

"You look like an usher at the wedding of Mr. and Mrs. Sidney J. Boring." It was Wyatt, leaning on the door.

"You're telling me." Max slipped into his jacket, looped the tie around his neck, and stared at the ends of it, bemused. "Somehow when I heard 'disguise,' I thought of something cooler. Fake mustaches and funny hats, at least."

"*That's* funny," said Wyatt, nodding at Max's outfit. "Here, let me help. Flip up your collar."

"You know how to tie a tie?"

Wyatt tugged on one end until it hung lower than the other and began looping the long side around into a knot. "My gran always said a proper bloke's gotta know how to do three things: tie a tie, catch a wave, and dance the cha-cha-cha."

"Interesting woman, your gran."

Wyatt made a wry face. "Yeah. Well, at least I managed one out of three." His tongue tip poked from his mouth as he did some more looping and knotting. His breath smelled like butterscotch and chocolate.

"Listen, Wyatt," Max said. "About the mission . . ."

The blond boy brushed it aside. "I'm over it. Ms. Annie knows I'm about as handy as mud flaps on a speedboat."

"That's not true."

"I'm a rubbish spy. I'd freeze under pressure and endanger the mission. Everyone knows it."

"You're a good spy," said Max. "You'll get your chance."

Wyatt grimaced, focusing his gaze on the knot. He gave

it a couple of tugs, then slid it up to Max's neck and flipped the shirt collar down. "Close enough."

"Cool."

The blond boy took something from his pocket and pinned it to Max's lapel. "For luck," he said. "Used to be my gran's." The yellow button read: LIFE'S A BEACH.

"Um, thanks?" Max stepped over to the nightstand and scooped up his lighter and stone, tucking each into a pocket.

"I know you're planning to slip off and find that info broker," said Wyatt.

"Tully."

"And I want to help." Wyatt handed him a scrap of paper with a phone number and e-mail address on it. "Ring or text me if you need anything. I've got your back."

Max's throat felt tight. He'd met plenty of kids in group homes, most of whom would sell him out for a warm Coke and a candy bar. Wyatt was different—he actually went out of his way to help. "But why?" asked Max.

The blond boy gave a lopsided smile. "We're mates, mate. Ain't we?"

Max nodded. Feeling awkward, he reached out and clapped Wyatt's shoulder. For a moment, he couldn't speak. "Look," he finally managed, "if I don't come back—"

"Don't say it!" Wyatt's blue eyes went as round as saucers. "It's bad luck."

"I don't mean if I get *killed*, you git. I'm talking about . . . you know, if I find him."

Wyatt's face lost its worried look. "Ah."

"You can have my stuff," said Max. "Whatever's left."

Fweet! Fweet-fweeeet!

Three piercing whistle blasts echoed up the hallway. "Get a move on, Segredo!" Styx bellowed from the staircase.

Max smirked. "Ah, the voice of an angel." He hooked an arm into his book bag strap, swung it onto his shoulder, and sketched a rough salute to his friend. "Cheers, then."

"Cowabunga, mate," said Wyatt. "And if you make it to enemy headquarters, watch out for shark tanks!"

"Riiight." Max favored him with a skeptical look.

When he trotted downstairs, the other three team members were already waiting in the entryway with their packed bags. Jensen Swensen wore his school uniform with the same enthusiasm as Max; the girls were dressed much like the boys, but with gray skirts and long gray socks.

Nikki cackled. "Aww, Maxi-Pad wooks wike a widdow-bitty baby banker."

"And you . . ." Cinnabar's glance raked her up and down. "You look like third runner-up for the Miss Teen Dweeb contest. Whereas, I"—she twirled like a supermodel—"rock this outfit."

Max had to admit, Cinnabar wore her uniform with flair—the shirt collar flipped up, the tie loosened. Her dark curls glistened, and her legs—this was the first time he'd noticed her legs. They were toned and shapely. He ran a finger under his own stiff collar, suddenly needing some air.

The front door opened, and the martial arts teacher looked in. Max almost wouldn't have recognized her with the horn-rimmed glasses and no-nonsense bun. "Well?" asked Miss Moorthy. "Waiting for an engraved invitation?"

The four orphans shouldered their bags and trooped past her into the narrow hall that led to the outer door. "Wait!" The teacher held up a hand to stop them. "From here on out, you'll refer to me as Miss Mundy, and to Styx as Mr. Glumsteen. Clear?"

"Hold up," said Jensen. "You get aliases and we don't?"

"Precisely," she said. "Clear?"

Four nods answered her.

"Stay close," said Miss Moorthy. She looped her shiny black handbag over her forearm and reached inside, extracting a serious-looking pistol with a charcoal-gray finish.

"That's the stuff!" crowed Jensen. "Full-on firearms!"

Miss Moorthy cast him a withering gaze, and Jensen mimed zipping his lips. Max's nervous glance met Cinnabar's. This was no training mission. Deftly, the teacher flicked off the safety and worked the slide—*chook, chook*—before peering out the peephole. Then she scanned her card key and pressed her thumb into the touch screen.

"As soon as I open this, run to the car. Styx—rather, Mr. Glumsteen—will be waiting." Miss Moorthy pushed the door open and leveled her pistol at the street. "Now, go!"

Max hustled down the walkway, followed closely by the other three orphans. The Range Rover's doors hung open, and Styx crouched behind one of them, pistol in hand and eyes darting about. Tracking the man's gaze, Max noticed nothing but an overcast day and the usual street traffic. Still, he hurried over and slid into the backseat.

Cinnabar and Jensen piled in behind him, while Nikki and Miss Moorthy took the front seat. Doors slammed. Styx put the car into gear and moved smoothly onto the street.

"Shouldn't we be burning rubber?" said Nikki.

"Ooh, listen to Miss Expert," said Styx sourly.

Miss Moorthy shifted in her seat to check the road behind them. "For your information, Miss Knucks, we shouldn't. Since we haven't determined whether LOTUS knows our precise location, it's best not to call attention to ourselves with rash moves."

"You can bet they've got eyes in the area," said the big man. His restless gaze roved between the mirrors and the road ahead.

As they passed a side street, Max noticed a long black car launching itself from the curb and into the flow of traffic, two spots behind them. He wouldn't swear to it, but it might have been the same make and model he'd seen on the night he joined the orphanage.

"How can you tell if you're being followed?" he asked.

"Spotting a tail isn't as simple as one might think," said Miss Moorthy. "The good ones usually stay a few car lengths back."

The Range Rover turned left at a light. In the side mirror,

Max watched the black car drift along behind them. Was the passenger holding something like a phone up to his mouth? Hard to say.

"Of course, the best crews usually employ two or even three units for tailing," Miss Moorthy/Mundy continued. "That way, they can trade off the lead so you're not always seeing the same vehicle behind you."

A dark green Volvo pulled away from the curb and eased in front of the black car, which slowed to let it in. Max frowned.

"And if they're *really* tip-top," Mr. Glumsteen added, "they'll have someone on a parallel street."

Cinnabar nudged Max. When he turned, she pointed out of Jensen's window, down another cross street, where a second sleek black car was paralleling their course.

"It's been there awhile," she murmured.

At the next light, the Range Rover turned right. Watching the side mirror, Max noted that the black and green cars behind them followed suit.

One block later, Styx veered right again. And again the cars followed.

"Styx—uh, Mr. Glooms . . . bee," Max began.

"That's *Glums*bee," said Nikki.

"Glums*teen*," said Cinnabar tartly.

"What?" said Styx.

Max checked the mirror again. "We've got two cars tailing us: black and dark green."

"You don't say," said the big man, making yet another right.

"That's why he's taking evasive measures," said Jensen. Max, Cinnabar, and Miss Moorthy turned to stare at him in astonishment. "What? I can read. It was in *Survival Skills for the Modern Spy.*"

"Then perhaps you'll tell us what it means when one makes evasive actions and one's pursuers don't drop out to avoid detection?" said Miss Moorthy, taking another glimpse out the rear window.

"Uh," said Jensen.

"It means they don't care if we spot them," said Max. And indeed, the dark green Volvo was right on their tail.

"Got it in one," said Styx, pressing harder on the accelerator.

Cinnabar eyed the next intersection, which was approaching at an ever faster rate. "And *that* means . . . ?"

Tires squealed as the bearlike man floored it. He swung out, blew past the sedan waiting at the stop sign, whipped back into his own lane to avoid an oncoming SUV, and screeched around a pedestrian in the crosswalk. "Plan B," he growled.

Max spun in his seat to watch their pursuers. Horns blared as the green car tore into the intersection and narrowly missed two oncoming vehicles. The Range Rover had about a half-block lead, which widened when the Volvo swerved to avoid a woman with a stroller and slammed into several rubbish bins.

"Hah!" crowed Nikki.

The black cars were nowhere to be seen. Styx roared around a corner on two wheels, barreled down an alley, and hung a sharp left onto a main road—directly in front of a truck. The driver stood on his brakes, his grille mere inches from the Range Rover's rear. Cinnabar gasped. The smell of burning rubber filled the car's interior, and the truck's horn blared like a rogue elephant charging.

"Let's see 'em follow *that*," said Styx, accelerating smoothly into traffic.

Max looked back. The stalled truck blocked the Volvo's path. The green car tried to bull its way across the sidewalk but got wedged between a stately elm and a wrought-iron fence. By the time it backed up to find another way through, the Range Rover had turned left and passed out of sight.

Jensen blew out a gusty sigh. "That was close."

"What happened to the black car?" Max mused.

"We left it in the dust," said Nikki. "Duh."

Max didn't bother answering, but he kept an eye out as Styx whipped down the cross street and turned again.

"No worries, boy." Mr. Glumsteen slowed to just above the speed limit. "I'm a professional."

Just then, the long black car emerged from a side street and pulled right in ahead of them. "In the dust?" Max said. Nikki grunted.

"Um, how's it going to tail us from in front?" said Jensen.

"Maybe they don't *want* to tail us," said Cinnabar.

And with that, the black car's rear bumper swiveled upward, releasing a load of dark little objects onto the road.

"What in the—?" said Miss Moorthy.

Styx stomped on the brakes, too late. The Range Rover ran over the objects, and all four of its tires went instantly, and completely, flat.

CHAPTER 20

SECRET MESSAGES DOWN THE LOO

JENSEN YELPED. The heavy car skidded, its rear end slewing around to the right. The beefy boy fell against Cinnabar, who slid into Max. Even in the midst of all that, Max noticed the scent of her orange-blossom shampoo.

"Bloody tacks," snarled Styx. He fought for control, steering into the skid. They missed a parked car by a hair's breadth. Max heard the squeal of brakes and a thump, as the SUV behind them didn't.

"I think they want to capture us," said Cinnabar.

"Cheery thought," said Max. "Let's not."

One block back, the green Volvo drove into sight, with the second black car close behind. Styx wrestled the wounded Range Rover through a gap between two parked cars and plowed onto the sidewalk. A plump grandfather tumbled off his bicycle. Three girls screamed and dove into some bushes.

"Watch out!" cried Nikki.

"Don't have a thrombo," said the big man. The car rattled and juddered down the uneven pathway on its flat tires, making Max's teeth clatter like castanets.

"What are you doing?" he asked.

"Remember Plan B?" Styx inclined his head at the train station sitting on a low rise up ahead. "This is Plan B."

"In the front zippered pouch of your bags, you'll find train passes," said Chandrika Moorthy, as if she weren't being jounced up and down like a bobble-head doll. "If we run, we can just make the ten sixteen."

Max eyed the steps to the station fast approaching. Where on earth would they park the car?

"Hang on," grunted Styx. He stomped on the brakes and cranked the wheel. Max slid into Cinnabar, squishing her up against Jensen.

With a fierce shock, the Range Rover bounced directly up onto the steps. Everyone in the car was briefly airborne. They landed with a jolt, and Max bit his tongue. The car ground to a halt, two steps below a woman with a stroller.

Pfffff! Air bags inflated, slamming into the front seat's occupants.

Passersby gawked.

"Move smartly, children!" said Miss Moorthy/Mundy. She popped her airbag.

"Gerroutofit," growled Styx.

Max shoved at his door, half falling onto the steps. Cinnabar hopped out after him, and they followed Nikki and the rest up the stairway toward the ticket lobby. Behind them, the pursuing cars skidded to a stop in the middle of the road, a pair of black-suited men and women piling out of each vehicle.

At the top of the stairs, the go-team burst into a busy lobby. Travelers waited in line at ticket windows, said farewell to loved ones, bought snacks and magazines, or stared up at the electronic board where departures were listed.

"Track four!" cried Chandrika Moorthy. "Now!" Their group hustled over to the turnstiles.

Digging past erasers and pencils, Max groped in his bag for the train pass. Just as his fingers closed on the slick card, three dark-suited spies reached the vestibule. "Enemy agents, six o'clock!" he hissed.

Jensen stared up at the big station clock in confusion. "Where? I don't see 'em."

"Don't you ever watch movies? Six o'clock means— Oh, never mind!" Max thrust the tall boy ahead of him. "Swipe your card!"

Their pursuers barreled across the lobby, shoving people aside. The lead agent looked like a bad-tempered gorilla in a five-hundred-dollar suit, and the svelte, snarling woman behind him appeared to be the world's most ruthless supermodel.

Max checked his team. Miss Moorthy and the girls had already passed through, but Jensen was having trouble getting his train card to scan. The enemy agents were only forty feet off and closing rapidly. Styx reached under his jacket for his pistol.

"Wait!" Max caught his arm. "I've got a better idea." He plucked a smoke-bomb eraser from his zippered pouch. "Make this work."

Mr. Glumsteen pulled the two halves of the eraser apart and gave the device a twist. "Go!" he cried, hurling it at the ground before the oncoming spies.

A flash of light, and *foof!*—a thick cloud of bluish-gray smoke billowed up from the device.

"Fire!" yelled Max.

Jensen chuckled. "Trust the pyro to come up with that one."

Max scanned his pass and burst through the turnstile, with Styx hot on his heels. Panicked shouts echoed, as people milled about in fear, looking for the flames.

Dashing for the train, Max risked a glance back. Smoke filled the area beyond the turnstiles, a fire alarm clanged, and figures swirled about in the murk.

"Last call," a metallic voice boomed from the loudspeakers. "Capital City, track four. *Boooard!*"

Max and Styx trotted up the steps and into the passenger train car just before the doors snicked shut. For a moment,

Max clung to the cold steel pole and let his forehead drop against it. His heart was hammering like a carpenter on a deadline.

"Well," said Styx, "you're not totally useless." His thick paw thumped Max's shoulder. "Look there."

Max stared out the window behind him. The platform was slipping past as the train accelerated, and Gorilla Man and Ruthless Ruth ran alongside, angry faces twisted and mouths working. Max would have bet a pro athlete's paycheck that they weren't saying a prayer for his safe journey.

"Who were those guys?" Cinnabar murmured.

The jittery team had settled into two banks of facing seats. Shaken by their close call, the orphans eyed every passenger with suspicious glares.

"LOTUS agents," Miss Moorthy/Mundy said quietly. She tucked a stray lock of hair back into her bun and adjusted her glasses. "They must be very desperate indeed, if they're not even attempting to stay undercover."

"Or very confident," muttered Mr. Glumsteen. He stared out the window, face set in a frown.

"We've got five hours before we reach the capital," said Miss Moorthy. "Get some rest if you can." She drew her phone from her purse and began texting, presumably to Hantai Annie.

After a good half hour of sitting, Max got antsy. Every

now and then, he felt an itchy twitch between the shoulder blades, like someone was watching him. But each time he turned around, the same assortment of bored and distracted faces stared back. At last he stood.

"Where are you going?" Miss Moorthy looked up from her phone.

Max shrugged. "Stretch my legs. Back soon."

"Keep an eye out," said Cinnabar, glancing up from her novel. Max gave her a reassuring nod. Jensen and Nikki continued their card game without comment. Styx brooded.

Their seats were located midway along the train, close to the front of their car. Max ambled back toward the carriage behind them, idly tapping the tops of the brown leatherette seat backs and scanning the faces of his fellow passengers.

Most ignored him. One met his gaze—a sharp-faced businesswoman with fox-colored hair and a hunched posture. But as they traded stares, Max decided the woman was anti-teen rather than anti–Merry Sunshine. Just as he broke eye contact, someone bumped past him with a muttered, "Pardon."

Instantly alert, Max spun to check him out. But all he saw was the back of a camel-hair overcoat and a jaunty driving cap perched on the head of a tall man, who soon passed into the next carriage.

Max felt for his wallet and lucky stone. Both were still

in his pockets, but he also found a scrap of paper that hadn't been there before. Unfolding it, he read a coded message:

KCCR KC GL RFC BGLGLE AYP.
    -RYWJMP

Looking up, he noticed the sharp-faced woman still glaring at him. Max palmed the message, stuck out his tongue at her, and made his way to the back of the car, where he slipped into an unoccupied lavatory. He stared at the note, mentally substituting letters until the cipher yielded its secrets. The simple two-shift Caesar cipher read:

MEET ME IN THE DINING CAR.
    —TAYLOR

Max flicked on his lighter and held the paper over it until it caught fire. When the flames stung his fingers, he let go, flushed the burnt message down the loo, and ran the water in the sink. He caught his reflection in the mirror, and if he hadn't known himself better, he would've said he looked nervous.

What was Agent Taylor doing on the train? Did he already have news of Max's father?

The next few minutes would tell.

Max splashed water on his face and headed for the dining

car. Two compartments back, it was really more of a glorified snack car, offering tea, coffee, some prefabricated sandwiches, overpriced cookies, and overaged fruit. Only two of its half dozen café tables were occupied; Taylor sat at one of them.

As Max approached, the tall man offered a thin-lipped smile. But when Max started to join him, Agent Taylor said, "No. Sit at the next table, would you?"

"Why?" said Max. "I've got B.O.?"

Taylor shook his head. "In case your friends show up."

So Max climbed onto a high stool at the adjoining table, which put him beside, and slightly turned away from, Mr. Taylor. The conductor called out a city name, and the train slowed for its scheduled stop.

Taylor had ditched the cop disguise. Today he was clad in an impeccably tailored suit the gray-green of a stormy sea, a charcoal tie over a pale green shirt, and a pair of fine Italian loafers that looked like they cost more than a month's rent on a posh downtown apartment. His camel-hair overcoat and jaunty cap were draped over the second stool at his table.

He crossed his legs, adjusted the knife-sharp crease in his trousers, and poured a steaming hot cup of tea from his pot. As he did, his eyes scanned the room, from the jaded young woman behind the snack counter, to the older couple at a corner table. Satisfied, he leaned toward Max.

"I received your first message," he said. "Good show. What's the latest?"

Max leaned away. "Hang on. I've got some questions of my own first."

Taylor cocked his head, a faint look of amusement playing over his long face. "Well, I suppose you're entitled. Tit for tat, and all that. What did you want to know?"

Max glanced out the window at the travelers waiting on the platform. "Have you found my dad yet?"

Taylor frowned. "Ah, it hasn't been quite so easy as one would hope."

"Why not?"

"Well, the man's a trained spy, isn't he? My contacts have confirmed that he's in-country—possibly in the capital—and we're chasing down some leads. But consider this, Max."

"What?"

"He may not want to be found."

Max bit his lip and glanced out the window at the passengers boarding. "I don't care. That was our deal: Find him."

Taylor blew across his tea to cool it. "Our efforts continue. Now, what's the latest intel on Eisenheimer?"

"Not much." Max shrugged, considering what he felt comfortable revealing. "One thing I left out: he said he'd be returning to his house sometime today, to pick up something for their project."

The tall man's eyes sparkled. "Brilliant," he muttered. He drew a slim, elegant phone from an inside coat pocket and began texting away.

Max checked out the dining car. No sign of his team; no new café patrons. "Next question: Where can I find an information broker named Tully?"

Taylor stopped texting and arched an eyebrow. "Tully?" He considered. "Tully has an unofficial office at The Eye, but—"

"The Eye?"

"An all-night coffee shop in the capital. But that's no place for children."

"I'm not a child."

Agent Taylor's eyes narrowed. "Why do you want Tully?"

"That's my business," said Max. "Who do you work for?"

The agent actually chuckled. "Excellent question. But I don't believe I'll share that yet. Tell me, what is your ragtag band planning to accomplish in the capital?"

The answer sat right there on his tongue. It would be simplicity itself to spill their plans to the agent. But something kept Max from revealing them.

"I don't believe I'll share that." He checked the car again, suddenly worried that Styx or another team member might walk in on them. "One last question."

As the whistle blew and the train began to move, the tall agent leaned back on his stool and leveled his gaze on Max. "Very well."

"How did you know to catch this train? We outran everyone chasing us."

Taylor smiled. *"I'm* a professional. Those others—"

"Beg your pardon." Two burly men in dark-blue conductor's uniforms materialized beside the table.

"Yes?" said Taylor. He let his hands drift under the table to his lap.

"Oh, not you, sir," said the dyed-blond conductor, who looked like a Korean weight lifter. "The boy."

"Are you with the school tour group?" asked the black-haired conductor, a pale fellow with snaggle teeth.

"Uh, yeah," said Max. He glanced over at Taylor. "I am."

The blond one gestured. "You're to come with us. Right away."

"What's the matter?" Agent Taylor asked.

"None of your concern, sir," said the black-haired conductor, stepping between them and clutching Max by the arm. "Come along, boy."

Up close, the man reeked of onions and cheap cologne. His uniform was subtly different from the conductor's who had checked Max's train pass earlier, and it bore no company insignia.

"What's happened?" Max stood, feeling torn—concerned for his team yet somehow reluctant to accompany the men. He tried to free his arm, but Onion Breath's fingers clamped down.

"I'm sure they'll tell you all about it," said the muscular blond, with false cheer. "Hurry now, they're waiting."

Onion Breath tried to drag him away from the table.

"Let go," said Max, digging in his heels.

In one fluid movement Agent Taylor turned and leaned forward. "Release him."

Blondie blocked the agent's path. He was shorter by a few inches, but built like a refrigerator on steroids. He placed a meaty hand on Taylor's chest. "Back off, mister."

"You forgot to say *please*."

Agent Taylor calmly reached up with his left hand, took the man's pinkie, and twisted it back and down, forcing Blondie into an off-balance crouch. Then his right hand darted out like a striking cobra, stiff fingers driving into the other man's throat. Blondie gasped and collapsed in a heap.

Onion Breath stared, mouth agape. Max spotted Taylor's teapot within reach and snagged it by the handle. He swung his arm around, flinging scalding Earl Grey tea, and the heavy teapot, right into the man's face.

The girl behind the counter shrieked. Onion Breath swore and fell back a pace, releasing Max's arm. On the floor, Blondie was making sounds like a cat hawking up a hair ball.

"You've done it now, boy," growled the black-haired man. His once-pale face glowed red, like a molten-lava sunburn. Max ducked under his grab and sprang to one side, upsetting the corner table, sandwiches, and drinks into the lap of the older couple.

A woman's voice snapped, "What's all this?" and Max

looked up. Miss Moorthy stood in the café doorway, lean, lethal, and lovely—like a gunslinger dressed as a schoolteacher.

Just then, an earsplitting alarm shrilled, and the train jerked to a halt, spilling Max and the other passengers onto the floor.

"Oh dear, what's happening?" said the older woman, now wearing slices of luncheon meat and wilted lettuce like flowers in her hair. "Did we crash?"

"Emergency stop," said her companion, gruffly.

By the time Max regained his footing, Miss Moorthy/Mundy had joined him. "What in heaven's name were you doing?" she demanded.

"Those guys tried to drag me off," he said, indicating Onion Breath and Blondie. The scalded man was helping his partner to his feet. "They said the team was waiting for me."

"I've never seen them before," said Chandrika, and a compact black pistol appeared in her hand, as if by magic. She let Onion Breath see it. "Have a seat, gentlemen. Call security," she told the shaken woman behind the counter.

Max scanned the carriage for Taylor, wondering how to explain his involvement.

"Where's that man who was helping you?" asked Chandrika.

"What man?" said Max, for Agent Taylor had disappeared.

CHAPTER 21

MORE THAN MEETS THE EYE

DURING the rest of the train ride, as the others chatted, read, or played games, Max brooded. Was Agent Taylor working for LOTUS? If so, why had he attacked Blondie, who was clearly a LOTUS agent?

Was the man merely stringing him along to gain information, or would he really deliver the whereabouts of Simon Segredo? Despite Taylor's help with the phony conductors, Max trusted him about as far as he could spit, so he decided to proceed with his own plans to meet Tully as soon as possible.

The train made two more stops before the capital, but no other enemy agents popped out of the woodwork disguised as clerks, porters, or belly dancers. Shortly before reaching their destination, Miss Moorthy called a conference.

"Clearly, LOTUS knows we are on this train, so they'll have agents waiting at the station," she said quietly.

"Do we shoot our way out?" asked Jensen.

Styx snorted. "The day I hand you a firearm is the day I'm crowned Queen of the May."

Cinnabar smiled, and Nikki gave Jensen's shoulder a friendly punch.

"We slip away undetected," said Chandrika. "A simple diversion in the station, then a subway to a taxi to the hotel. Clear?"

Everyone nodded.

"What kind of diversion?" said Max.

Miss Moorthy smiled. "Oh, I've called in some friends to help."

The team that exited the train sported a rather different look from the one that had boarded it. Gone were the private-school uniforms; all the orphans wore casual street clothes. Styx had donned the false mustache and thick glasses he had worn on Max's first field trip. Chandrika had braided her hair into a long ponytail and garbed herself in a traditional Indian *salwar kameez* and scarf.

"You really think this will work?" Max asked Styx.

The big man grunted. "Dunno. But trickery trumps gunplay, most times."

"And when it doesn't?"

Styx patted the shoulder holster concealed under his jacket. "Time for a bit of the old bang-bang."

Following the crowd, they emerged into the grand concourse, a vast open area of shops, food vendors, ticket machines, and hundreds of bustling people, all under a vaulted ceiling of peacock-blue iron fretwork.

Max's eyes darted left and right. He felt as exposed as a cockroach on a kitchen floor. Then he heard the music.

The insistent *thump-thump-ba-thump-thump* of a popular dance tune blasting from some hidden place, the bass so heavy Max could feel it in his back molars. Out in the middle of the wide lobby, a woman began to bob her head and move to the music. Two businessmen joined her.

Max scanned the faces all around them. There—across the lobby, a pair of dark-suited figures stood watching the foot traffic like hawks on a high branch. Was that Gorilla Man and Ruthless Ruth?

As the team hurried onward, more and more people began joining the dance, moving in synchronization to the relentless beat—twenty people, then fifty, then a hundred.

"It's a flash mob!" Cinnabar clapped her hands in delight and began moving gracefully to the rhythm.

"A what?" said Max.

"You need to get out more often," said Jensen.

Max glanced back at the enemy agents and saw that the team had been spotted.

"Faster!" he shouted over the throbbing music. "They're on to us."

"Just watch," said Miss Moorthy. And sure enough, the LOTUS agents were unable to penetrate the highly rhythmic mob; in short order, they were entangled in the dancers, and the team made its getaway.

As they hustled down a tunnel to the underground, Miss Moorthy allowed herself a smug little smile. "It always pays to support the arts."

The rest of the trip was precisely as advertised: a subway to a taxi, and a taxi to their lodgings, a tidy but nondescript hotel in a quiet neighborhood. After an early dinner with the team, Max settled into the room he would share with Jensen. Right away, the beefy boy switched on the TV to a rugby match.

Max sat on the bed, feet jiggling with nervous energy, fiddling with his lighter. He had already used his phone to locate The Eye, the all-night coffee shop where Tully could be found, and map out a route to it. But the thought of waiting around for Jensen to fall asleep before slipping out made him want to burst like a cheap piñata.

Max swung his legs off the bed and snagged his jacket.

"Where you off to?" asked Jensen, glancing up from his game.

"I'm bored," said Max, pulling on his coat. "Think I'll check out the rest of the hotel."

The other boy frowned. "But Miss Moorthy—um, Mundy—said we're supposed to stick together. You know, the buddy system?" His gaze was still riveted to the game.

"Don't sweat it," said Max. "I'll be fine."

"No, no." Jensen stood. "I've got to go along or we'll both get in trouble." But like a bloodhound on a scent, his eyes were drawn back to the TV screen. "What? Aw, *no*! You're mental, ref!"

Max took advantage of the distraction to edge closer to the door. With a decent head start, he figured it wouldn't be too hard to give Jensen the slip. He reached for the knob.

"Hang on. I'm coming." Jensen grabbed his coat and joined Max at the door.

Max stifled a sigh.

As they started down the hallway, he had a sudden inspiration. "Hey, let's see what the girls are doing." He rapped on the door of the room beside theirs.

Cinnabar opened it. "What's up?" Past her, Max could see Nikki sitting on the edge of the bed watching a familiar game on TV.

"Oh, I just felt like taking a stroll," said Max with a significant look at Cinnabar. "And Jensen was going to—"

The tall boy pushed past him and into the room. "Hey, is that Uckfield versus Hornchurch?"

"Yeah, and Uckfield's gonna get their bums handed to them on a platter," Nikki sneered.

"Sure," said Jensen. "When chicken have teeth."

Cinnabar sized up the situation in a flash. "You know, I do fancy a walk—think I'll join you," she said. "Cheers, Nikki." But the redheaded girl was so immersed in the game, she barely even registered their departure. Jensen gave Max a thumbs-up and belly flopped onto the other bed.

"Thanks," said Max as they rode the elevator down to the lobby. "You don't really need to come with me. I was only trying to get rid of Jensen."

Cinnabar gave him a level gaze. "But I insist." They crossed the vestibule, pushed through the outer door, and stepped onto the sidewalk. It was full dark, and cold. Heavy clouds hung over the city, yellow-bellied from the reflected lights.

Max forced a chuckle. "I'm just going for a walk. You wouldn't enjoy it."

"On the contrary. It'll do me good to stretch my legs."

He rounded on her. "It'll be boring. Really, really boring."

"Boring?" Cinnabar's eyes widened innocently. "A visit to Tully, the famous intel broker? I doubt that very much." She laughed out loud at the expression on Max's face. "Wyatt told me. I couldn't resist stringing you along."

"Hilarious," said Max. He gritted his teeth. What *was* it with Cinnabar, always shadowing him on his extracurricular activities?

"I want to see if Tully knows anything about my sister."

Max scowled and made a last halfhearted attempt. "But I'm taking the underground, and who knows what kind of people hang out at The Eye. It could be dangerous."

Cinnabar arched an eyebrow. "Like being a foster kid and a spy isn't? Besides, I've got money for a cab." She patted her tiny handbag.

Max sighed.

They flagged down a taxi at the corner, and Max told the driver their destination. "The Eye?" said the driver, a round black man with a sleepy gaze. "So you're both spies, then?"

Max and Cinnabar traded a startled look. "Uh, of course," said Max. "I'm James Bond, and—"

"And I'm Mata Hari," finished Cinnabar.

The driver cackled and pulled away from the curb. "Used to be in the trade myself. Why, I recall one time, in Istanbul . . ."

Ten minutes and three stories later, he deposited them on a dark street in a grimy-looking neighborhood of row houses and apartments over shuttered-up shops. Cinnabar paid the man, and the taxi sped off. Down at the far end of the block, a noisy pub blasted its music into the night while two patrons argued outside.

Max and Cinnabar stood bathed in the pink-and-green neon lights of the all-night coffee shop. A faded mural covered the building's facade, depicting pyramids, a river, and what looked like a mess of ancient Egyptians going about their ancient Egyptian business. Smoked-glass windows reduced the patrons inside to blurred shapes. Above the red wooden door, green neon tubes formed an eye inside a pyramid, rays of light radiating from it with each blink.

Over that, tall pink letters spelled out THE EYE, and, in smaller script, ALWAYS OPEN.

Now that they were actually here, Max felt a curious buzz of energy running through his limbs. He wasn't nervous, exactly. But a lot was riding on this meeting. He shifted from foot to foot.

"Well?" said Cinnabar.

Max took a deep breath and reached for the doorknob. "Let's do it."

The rich, dark aroma of roasted coffee met them as soon as they crossed the threshold—as did an enormous white man with arms like tree trunks and a rumbling voice that would've made thunder jealous.

"Firearms," he growled.

"I—what?" said Max.

A hand the size of a phone book appeared in front of him, palm up. "No guns inside," said the man-mountain.

"Who needs guns?" Max joked nervously. "I hear the espresso is lethal."

The giant didn't crack a smile. He filled the better part of the cramped entryway, and Max wondered briefly whether it had been custom-built around him.

"We're not armed," said Cinnabar.

In answer, the man gave them both a quick patdown, then boomed, "Welcome."

They squeezed past him and into the coffee shop proper. The hum of muted conversations and a lazy sort of Italian hip-hop greeted their ears. The space was narrow but deep, with a high ceiling and decorations in that same faux-Egyptian style. Colorful rugs hung on the walls. A gently curving mahogany bar ran half the length of the room, and The Eye's patrons bellied up to it on stools or sat at various café tables scattered about.

Max surveyed the crowd. They were old and young, male and female, dressed mostly in dark colors, and with faces seemingly every hue of tan, brown, and beige. Their restless eyes continually scanned the room, aware of the slightest occurrence.

"Which one's Tully?" murmured Cinnabar.

"Probably some bald guy in a beret and sunglasses. Let's find out." Max stepped up to the coffee bar with a boldness he didn't feel. When the barista gave him a sidelong look, he asked, "Where can we find Tully?"

The cocoa-colored woman shrugged. "Who's Tully?"

Cinnabar laid a large-denomination note on the bar. "We'll have two hot chocolates . . . with Tully."

The barista took the money and turned to fill their order.

"*That's* how you do it," Cinnabar said with a little smirk.

Max rolled his eyes.

The woman filled two mugs from the spigot of a large, gleaming urn, squirted a dollop of whipped cream on top of each, and set them on the bar, along with the change.

"You don't understand," said Cinnabar. "That's for you. And you forgot Tully."

The barista gave her a flat, bored look. "Can't forget who you don't know," she said, and moved down the bar to another customer.

"Maybe you should've used a bigger bribe," said Max innocently. "Here, let me handle it." He sized up the other patrons at the bar and settled on a small man with dirty blond hair and a ferret face. Max took the stool next to him.

With elaborate casualness, he spun to face the room and muttered out of the side of his mouth, "Hey, mister. Know where I could find a guy named Tully?"

Ferret Face swiveled his head, leaned toward Max with a yellow-toothed smile, and said, "No."

"'No,' you don't know him, or 'no,' you don't know where he is?"

The smile dropped, and a switchblade appeared in the man's hand. "Just no."

"Okay." Max moved down the bar. He got the same result (but without the knife) from a Vietnamese couple, a surly Frenchman, and a whip-thin blond woman with an impenetrable accent that might have been Russian.

Cinnabar joined him. "No luck?"

Max shook his head. "But there *is* one more thing we could try." He stepped into the center of the room, took a deep breath, and shouted, "Hey, spies! Does anyone here know where to find Tully?"

Conversations stopped dead. Faces stared, hostile or curious.

A heavy paw landed on Max's shoulder. Man-Mountain rumbled, "Time for night-night."

Max squirmed, but his efforts had about as much effect

as kickboxing a granite cliff. The huge man steered Max and Cinnabar toward the exit.

"Please," said Max. "It's urgent. I've *got* to see him."

"It's life or death," said Cinnabar. *"Please."*

But Man-Mountain's iron grip didn't slacken. He pushed them ahead of him, back into the cramped entryway.

"I'll go to the Fair Trade Office," Max blustered. "Your service stinks."

And then a delicate brown hand drew aside a plush burgundy curtain Max hadn't noticed before, probably because it had been behind the giant's post.

"Wait, Skipper," said a voice like liquid taffy.

Max frowned. Man-Mountain's name was *Skipper*?

"Let them in," said the unseen voice.

Skipper grunted and gave the orphans a shove forward. Behind the curtain stood a generously curved woman with wide amber eyes, a strong nose, and a Bluetooth headset. She looked Middle Eastern and mysterious.

"You wanted to see Tully?" she said.

"Yes," said Max. "Take us to him."

The woman smiled. "Easily done. I'm Tully."

INTEL INSIDE

CHAPTER 22

"HUH?" said Max. "But I thought . . ."

Cinnabar swatted his arm. "Zip it, cabbage head."

Tully's smile broadened. "Roxana Tülay Ochsenfrei," she said, with a slight bow. "Welcome to my little corner of the world."

Her private nook was surprisingly spacious, furnished comfortably with soft couches and bright pillows. Computer monitors covered one wall, and empty espresso cups littered nearly every flat surface. Tully motioned them to sit on a cream-colored leather sofa, claiming the armchair to the left of it for herself.

"Mrs. Oxen, uh, Oxfeffer . . ." Max began.

"Please," she said. "Call me Tully."

"Tully, I'm trying to find my father, Simon Segredo. Have you heard anything? Do you know where he is?"

The woman's wine-colored silk pants rustled as she

crossed her legs. She leaned back in her chair, sipped from a cup, and gave Max an appraising stare. "Perhaps," she said. "What do you have to trade?"

"Trade?" Max repeated.

Tully's dimples deepened. "I'm an information broker. My services don't come free. Customers trade me—money, intel, or favors. Which do you bring?"

Max barked a laugh. "Well, my trust fund is all tied up, so I guess it's information or favors."

"Hmm." She eyed him with a doubtful expression. "I don't usually like to trade favors with minors. Is your intel valuable?"

Max flicked a glance at Cinnabar. What exactly would it be safe to tell?

Cinnabar crooked a finger, and when Max leaned closer, she whispered, "You can't tell her about our mission." Her lips tickled his ear, making him shiver involuntarily.

"I know that," Max whispered back. "I'm not a barking moron. I'll think of something."

"Just don't tell too much," hissed Cinnabar.

"Ah, lover's secrets," Tully said, fiddling with her headset. "Delightful."

Max and Cinnabar jerked apart. Max blushed. "I'm not—uh, we're not . . ."

The information broker held up a hand and spoke into her Bluetooth.

"*Pronto . . . Sì, sì . . . Dove si trova adesso? Ah, grazie.*" She turned her attention back to Max. "So? What can you tell me?"

"Hantai Annie Wong is running an orphanage that's actually a training school for spies," he blurted.

Cinnabar slapped his arm. "Max!"

Tully blew out some air in a dismissive way. "Old news. What else?" Her amber eyes wandered to the bank of monitors on the opposite wall.

Max bit his lip. Did he dare . . . ?

"Some of the teachers at school are working on a secret project."

Cinnabar's eyebrows shot up. "What?"

The woman leaned forward slightly. "Go on."

"It's uh, called the Eisenheimer Process," said Max. He shifted awkwardly on the sofa. What could he tell her that wouldn't endanger anyone? "I don't know what it does, but I can tell you this: LOTUS is very keen on getting their hands on it."

"Mmm." Tully lifted an ultra-slim laptop computer from her side table, hit a couple of keys, and typed rapidly, purple-painted fingernails dancing. At last she finished. "We have a trade. Your father, Simon Segredo, is . . ." She typed some more and read the screen. "Here in the capital, or somewhere nearby."

Max shot to his feet. "He's *here*?! Where?"

Tully tapped another key. "My little birds tell me he arrived last month and was captured by LOTUS."

"What!?" Max's face crumpled and he turned away, shuffling aimlessly toward the bank of monitors. How could that be possible—to find his father and lose him, in one stroke?

He was distantly aware of the information broker's voice continuing. "I don't have a precise location, but odds are good he's either at a safe house or at LOTUS headquarters."

Max spun to face her. "Where's that?"

Roxana Tülay Ochsenfrei showed him the palms of her hands. "That, my young friend, is the mother of all secrets. Not even *I* know that."

Max slumped. Tully leaned over to another side table for a small plate of treats and offered it to him, her voice softening. "Here, have an Oreo. They're imported."

He turned away. Cinnabar reached out for him, but Max avoided her, hugging his arms tightly. Had all of his efforts— breaking into the orphanage office, finding Plato, qualifying for this mission, and coming to see Tully—been for nothing?

Numbly, he stared up at the monitors, noticing that two of them showed different angles on The Eye's patrons. Ferret Face was paying his bill and leaving. The Vietnamese couple was deep in conversation. Max didn't care.

Behind him, he dimly heard Cinnabar asking for news of her sister, Jazz. She bartered back and forth, finally convincing the information broker to accept a future favor in trade. But her news was no better.

"Your sister also has been captured by LOTUS," said Tully, "while on a mission here in the capital. Where she is now, only Allah can say."

"Oh," said Cinnabar, in a small voice.

Max felt he should turn around and say something to comfort her, but just then, a familiar figure showed up on the monitor. He squinted at the image. "Is that Styx?"

Startled, Cinnabar jumped to her feet and joined him. "It is! We've got to get out of here."

Max felt empty, sluggish as a waterlogged canoe. But he supposed she was right. "What's he doing?"

"Looking for a hot date," Cinnabar snapped. "Look, I'd love to find out, but we've got to go before he sees us." She turned to Tully. "Is there a back exit?"

The information broker shook her head, hoop earrings swaying gently. "Only the way you came."

"Marvelous," said Cinnabar.

Max peered at the gray surveillance camera images. "And who's he talking to? It looks almost like Ruthless Ruth from the train station."

"*Who?*" Cinnabar looked at him like he'd sprouted a third eye. "Get a grip, Segredo. We're going. *Now.*" She trundled him toward the entrance. "Thanks for the news, Tully, even if it was bad."

The woman raised her espresso cup in salute. "A pleasure doing business with you. I'll have Skipper distract your friend." She tapped her Bluetooth and murmured something.

Cinnabar dragged Max to the curtain and peeked around the edge. They could just see Skipper's massive back migrating into the main part of the coffee shop, like a receding glacier. When he'd passed out of sight, she towed Max to the door. "Get a move on, slow coach."

"Might as well," he said, still numb from the shock. "Nothing better to do."

"Nothing *better*?" said Cinnabar, giving him a shake. "We've got to find LOTUS headquarters, break in, and rescue your dad and my sister. Oh, and maybe even disrupt a Nullthium-Ninety shipment along the way. You call that 'nothing better'?"

Max eyed her narrowly. "Stop trying to cheer me up."

"Stop being a total berk."

Max could feel a smile threatening to break out on his face. He nodded brusquely. "Okay, then."

And with that, they slipped out of The Eye and into the night.

"Tell me again why we're not breaking into this dump after hours?" Nikki Knucks grumbled.

It was the next morning. The go-team waited in line outside the Natural History Museum, back in their private-school disguises, looking like any other group of bored students and teachers out on a field trip. Max and Cinnabar had worked late into the night, trolling the Net for clues on the whereabouts of LOTUS HQ. Nothing had turned up. Tired and wired, they were hoping to find something helpful here—the only LOTUS hot spot they knew of.

Miss Moorthy shot Nikki a warning glare. "Keep your voice down, Miss Knucks. Remember your cover."

Nikki rolled her eyes. She didn't need to speak; her face spoke volumes.

"We're here now," the teacher said, "because when Mr. Glumsteen and I reconnoitered last night, we found the shipment hadn't arrived yet."

"Right," said Styx. Max cast him a furtive glance, then looked off down the street when the big man turned his way.

"Yeah," said Nikki. "So?"

"This will be a close thing. We must be on hand when it turns up. And the other reason we're here now is because in the daytime we can just"—she smiled at the docent as they passed through the doorway—"walk right in."

"I still think we should blow some stuff up," Nikki muttered. The docent gave her a strange look.

Styx bought their admission tickets, and the go-team joined the visitors streaming into the cavernous central hall. Max tried not to gape at the high, vaulted ceiling, the wickedly cool dinosaur skeletons, and the acres of black-and-ivory checkerboard marble floors. None of his fosters had ever taken him to a museum, and if his parents had ever done so, he couldn't recall.

"What's the matter, Maxie?" Nikki sneered. "Scared of some widow-bitty dinosaurs?"

"Nah." Max indicated the enormous apatosaurus skeleton

233

that stretched half the length of the hall. "Your relatives don't frighten me."

The redheaded girl growled and lunged at him, but Styx snatched her collar in one big hand and held her back like she was a frothing Rottweiler. "Cool it!" he hissed.

"*He* started—"

"Ah-ah-ah." Mr. Glumsteen pulled Nikki's collar so tight it cut off her protest. "I don't care. Behave or leave."

Sullenly, Nikki subsided.

Chandrika Moorthy drew them all into a tight huddle. "We suspect they're processing and repackaging the Nullthium in a workroom. It's just between the Hall of Birds and the Progress of Mammals."

Jensen raised a hand. "You *suspect*? You mean, we don't know for sure?"

"That's the mission, Einstein," rumbled Styx.

"Confirm and disrupt," Miss Moorthy/Mundy agreed. "Now, we'll have two-man teams in both halls, watching the workroom. Cinnabar and Jensen in the mammals hall; Nikki and Max in the bird hall."

Max and Nikki groaned simultaneously, marking the first time they had ever agreed on anything.

"But he's a bleeding mole," said Nikki. "He'll probably shop me to LOTUS."

"Look who's talking," said Max.

Miss Moorthy held up a hand. "Enough. Mr. Glumsteen and I will watch the loading docks, and we'll check on you from time to time. If you see something, come to us—do *not* act on your own. May luck favor us all."

Max traded a wistful look with Cinnabar as they headed for their stations. It would've been much easier to pursue their own mission if they were stationed together. Surveillance duty with Nikki Knucks was down at the bottom of his list of favorite things, along with walking on hot coals and French-kissing scorpions. But with luck, he might still learn something from that workroom that could help his father. A slim hope, true. But better than nothing.

In the Hall of Birds, Max and Nikki sat on opposite ends of a bench, as near as possible to the workroom. Its door stood just out of sight, at the end of a hall behind a roped-off archway marked EMPLOYEES ONLY.

For the first hour, they said nothing. Max studiously ignored his companion and sketched a raptor on his drawing pad. With mounting impatience he waited for Nikki to take a lavatory break so he could investigate the workroom on his own, but she sat there like a stump. Tour groups came and went. Docents occasionally passed by, but gave the pair no more than a cursory inspection.

At one point, Styx ambled past and raised a curious eyebrow. Max shook his head: *nothing*. Back at the orphanage in surveillance class, which felt like a year ago, Mr. Stones had failed to mention that stakeouts were *excruciating*.

Finally, a squeaky sound echoed from the hall behind the EMPLOYEES ONLY doorway. Max readied his pen camera to capture whatever was on its way. Nikki sat up straighter and pretended not to be watching.

Then a wheeled cart rolled into view, bearing a mop, a broom, and three gray plastic rubbish bins. It was followed by a plump brown woman in blue coveralls and a mass of dreadlocks, bobbing her head to the music piped in through her earbuds.

Max sighed. But he kept filming just in case, as she walked up to the workroom door, unlocked it, and wheeled her cart inside.

"Ooh, scary janitor." Nikki's voice startled him. "Think Hantai Annie will hand you a gold star for catching that?"

Max ignored her.

"You're giving me the silent treatment?" She clapped a hand to her chest. "Oh, Maxi-Pad, that really crushes my spirit." Nikki stood, tossing her notebook and pen aside. "This stakeout bites."

"Where are you off to?" said Max, trying to sound casual.

"The little girls' room," she said in a mocking tone. "Ta-ta."

At last. But of course he couldn't investigate the workroom until the janitor left.

Max sat jiggling his foot. *Come on, come on.* Five minutes later, the cleaner exited the workroom, pushing the cart and singing along to her music in a little-girl voice. Max stood.

Just then, Nikki returned and resumed her post. Max sat back down, clenching his jaw.

Shortly after that, Miss Moorthy/Mundy turned up wearing a worried look. "Have either of you seen Cinnabar Jones?"

Max shook his head. Had she found a lead and left to seek LOTUS headquarters without him? He gnawed his lip.

"Try the loo," said Nikki. "Or maybe she's gone off Max, and she's hunting a new boyfriend."

"I'm not her boyfriend," Max snapped.

"Who said you were?" Nikki scoffed.

Miss Moorthy scowled at them and hurried onward without further comment.

Fifteen minutes of unendurable waiting later, the squeaky noise was back. Another cart, with another three rubbish bins on it, appeared in the hallway, this time pushed by a painfully skinny white man hunched over like a question mark. From the corner of his eye, Max watched the second janitor wheel his cart into the workroom.

"That's gotta be the tidiest place in this dump." Nikki sneered. "What a lame mission. We're staking out a CleanerFest."

Max scratched his chin, the beginnings of a plan forming in his mind. "Why would two different janitors clean that room on the same morning?"

Nikki shrugged. "Maybe it's their break room, dimwat. Ever think of that?"

"Then why would they bring their carts inside?"

Nikki didn't have an answer to that, so she gave him a dirty look.

After a few minutes, the second janitor left. He glanced over at them, and Max let his gaze drift dully past the man, just another bored schoolkid. But inside he burned to take action. This was just the excuse he needed.

He waited to be sure the man had gone, and then he stood, checked the hall for docents, and strode toward the roped-off doorway.

"Hey," Nikki hissed. "Where are you going?"

Max fished his lock-picking kit from inside his blazer pocket and stepped over the rope, into the hall. "Taking a quick peek to see what all the fuss is about."

Nikki rose. "You can't do that. *I* should be the one doing that."

Max squatted in front of the workroom door and put an ear to it, listening for any inhabitants. Nothing. He took out a tension wrench and a pick. But before he could begin, a hard hip crashed into his side and bowled him over.

"*My* job," said Nikki. "You owe me a stonking great heap of favors, Segredo. Remember?"

She was deeply annoying, but she had a point. "Don't take all day," he snapped. "I'll keep watch."

Max retrieved his sketch pad and leaned in the doorway, blocking Nikki's actions from the other visitors in the Hall of Birds. Just then, two female docents passed through the gallery.

"I say," said the older of the two, in that slow, loud voice some people use for talking to foreigners. "You. Can't. Go. In there." She pointed at the sign. "Staff only. Speak English?"

Max flushed. This had happened before. People noticed his almond eyes and golden skin, and automatically assumed he was F.O.B.—fresh-off-the-boat from Asia. But this was no time to make a case out of it.

He forced a smile. "Not a problem, mum. I'm sketching this *Raphus cucullatus* for a school project." He indicated the nearby skeleton of a dodo bird. "I'll stay out of the hallway."

"Oh." The gray-haired woman blinked in surprise. The docents conferred in low tones, while Max kept the innocent smile glued to his face. *Hurry, Nikki*, he thought. Finally, the older woman said, "All right then, son. Mind that you do." They strolled into an adjoining hall, and Max breathed out a sigh of relief.

Whatever she lacked in personality (and she lacked a lot), Nikki Knucks possessed in tradecraft. A minute later she muttered, "There. One last tumbler, and . . ."

Snick-snuck.

The lock surrendered, the door swung open, and the secrets of the smugglers' workroom were theirs for the taking.

CHAPTER 23

LOCKED, STOCKED, AND BARRELED

"VOILÀ!" said Nikki. "That's French for 'I'm a genius lock picker, and you're not.'"

Max snorted and pushed past her into the room. The long wide chamber stood empty, lit by greenish fluorescent lights. Four worktables filled the center of the space, heaped with an assortment of bones, steel rods, pots of varnish, plaster of Paris, and a whole mess of unidentifiable odds and ends.

"You watch for the janitors," said Max.

"Yeah, right." Nikki bumped his shoulder hard as she swaggered by him.

"Fine. We'll both search." He shut and relocked the door, and they spread out, camera pens busily recording the room and its contents. Tools and aprons hung on hooks by the door; the rest of the walls were lined with racks of metal shelving, crowded with different-colored rocks, dinosaur and animal models, and all manner of reference materials. Beside the worktables stood a row of nine chest-high metal drums.

Max pawed through the papers, looking for anything that might indicate the location of LOTUS's base of operations, but most of the sheets seemed to concern museum business. Having explored along one wall to the far door, Nikki turned back and began prying the lid from a barrel with a screwdriver.

The electronic chirp of Max's phone was as startling as a thunderclap in the stillness.

"Turn it off, you git!" Nikki whispered.

He fumbled the offending phone out of his jacket pocket. The display name read *Agent W*. "Hello?"

"Max, it's Wyatt. How's the museum job, mate?"

"How do you know where I . . . ?" He glanced over at Nikki, who had removed the lid and was recording images of its contents. "Um, now's not a good time, Wyatt," he murmured.

"Oh." Wyatt sounded hurt. "Of course. I understand. Important mission and all. Need-to-know basis."

Max set his pen and sketch pad on the worktable and shielded his mouth and the phone with his free hand. "No, it's not that. It's just . . . I'm in the middle of something."

He edged around the table to the nearest in the line of drums and found it empty. From the far end, Nikki pumped a fist in triumph. "*Null*thium-*Nine*ty!" she sang in a taunting stage whisper.

Max felt a stab of jealousy that she'd been the first to find it, even though he was keener on pursuing his own mission. He awkwardly cradled the phone on his shoulder and forced a metal ruler under the lid of another barrel.

"Well, I wanted to say, sorry to hear about your dad," Wyatt said. "Cinn texted me."

"Thanks," said Max. "We're working on it."

"And I want you to know, I'm going flat-out like a lizard drinking, mate. I'll get you a location for LOTUS HQ, don't you worry."

"Thanks, Wyatt. You're—"

Just then, men's voices rumbled right outside the door. "You hear something?" said a high, scratchy voice, like a rat running across sandpaper.

Nikki and Max froze. With fumbling fingers, Max hit the phone's OFF switch and stuffed the device into a pocket.

"Just you gabbing," growled the deeper voice. "Let's pack up and hit the road."

Nikki's eyes went wide. As a key clattered in the door lock, she popped the lid back onto her barrel and dashed for the far door. Max dropped the ruler and scrambled after her.

Halfway out, Nikki turned and noticed something. "Your pen, spazzmo!"

Ugh. Stupid, stupid! Max thought. He wheeled, sprinted back to the table, and snatched up his camera pen and sketch pad.

The doorknob began to turn. Too late to follow Nikki. Pulse pounding, he scanned the room for a hiding place.

With no time to spare, Max vaulted into the empty barrel and pulled the lid on after himself.

"Could've sworn I heard something," said Scratchy Voice. From Max's perspective inside the drum, the man sounded a bit muffled.

"Don't be such a Nellie," said Deep Voice. "Help me load them barrels."

Max heard the squeak of wheels, men grunting, and heavy objects landing on a cart, over and over. He held perfectly still and thought invisible thoughts. With any luck, the men would take the full barrels and leave his behind.

The drum beside him scraped against his hiding place as it was lifted and loaded. Then a sudden thump on the lid of his barrel made Max jump.

"And what about this one?" said Scratchy Voice.

"Can't remember if we filled it."

Max held his breath. Would they remove the lid? He worked a hand into his pocket, feeling for his lucky stone; though whether he wanted to use it as a weapon or a charm, he couldn't have said.

Rough hands rocked the drum back and forth, and he had to brace himself to avoid bumping into the sides. His barrel was hoisted into the air.

"Feels full," said Deep Voice. He gave a rough chuckle.

"With this hangover, I'm lucky to remember me own address. Come on, let's roll. I'm knackered."

The sensation of movement—bumps and swaying. The cart squeaked its way out of the workroom, along some corridors, and into an elevator. Max lay as still as a shadow, scarcely daring to breathe. As they went, he was treated to a blow-by-blow account of Deep Voice's pub-crawling adventures the night before. He wasn't sure what "chundering" meant, but from the man's description, it didn't sound like anything he'd care to experience for himself.

At last they reached what must have been the loading docks. Even through the metal drum Max could hear the *beep-beep-beep* of a truck backing up and smell the faint odor of diesel fuel. He wondered if Miss Moorthy and Styx were watching him right now, tracking the shipment.

He sincerely hoped so.

The cart stopped with a jerk. After much grunting and some creative cursing, the two men wrestled the drums into an echoey space. A truck bed? Then came a loud metallic rattle followed by a *thunk*.

Very faintly, the sound of the men talking came to Max.

Scratchy Voice: "Lock 'em tight now. Lose this cargo and we lose our heads."

Deep Voice: "Worry, worry, worry. You're such a Nellie, Roy."

Max waited until the voices had faded and all was quiet.

Then, slowly and gingerly, he pushed against the lid of his barrel. No movement. He pushed again, harder, and when that didn't work, struck a series of small quiet blows near the edges with his lucky stone.

Finally, the top lifted. Max shifted it, carefully taking hold of an edge, and peeked out. Darkness. He stood, setting the lid atop a nearby drum, and with extreme care, he extracted himself from his hiding place.

Hands out, he explored. Max banged his shin on something hard and bit his lip to keep from crying out. A little farther on, his hands encountered a cool metal surface—the inside wall of the truck. He groped his way around, edging past barrels, until he reached a surface with horizontal metal ridges, what he assumed was the truck's pull-down rear door.

An engine turned over. The floor began to vibrate.

Hurrying now, Max felt all around, searching for a latch or a lever, something that would open the door. Nothing. He was stuck in a big steel box.

With a grinding of gears, the truck rolled forward. Max lost his balance and bonked his head against the metal door.

Great. Just great. Whether he wanted to or not, Max was about to take a road trip. And in this case, the journey wasn't half so worrying as the destination.

After a bit of stop-and-go driving, the truck accelerated up a ramp and hit a long stretch of smooth travel—a highway,

Max guessed. He had climbed back into his barrel and pulled the top mostly closed, with just enough space for the diesel-perfumed air to enter.

Once Max heard a rustle from somewhere deeper in the truck cab. Rats? He shuddered and fit the lid onto his barrel as tightly as he could. The last thing he needed was rodent company.

Finally, the vehicle rattled down an off-ramp and proceeded to wind its way along what must have been country roads. Either that or Deep Voice's hangover was getting worse.

Max cursed his bad luck in getting so spectacularly sidetracked. He hoped that wherever she was, Cinnabar was having better luck at locating LOTUS's base.

They stopped briefly, and Max heard other voices outside. Someone pounded the side of the truck twice, then the vehicle accelerated up a gentle hill, made a Y turnabout, and came to a stop. The engine cut off.

Max had never been big on prayers—in his experience, foster kids' prayers were rarely answered—but he sent a plea to his mother's spirit: *Please don't let them find me.*

The truck's back door clattered upward. New voices greeted the drivers, and in short order, the drums were unloaded. Max had a bad moment when the man carrying his barrel set it down on an edge and the lid began to slip off.

But the worker must have been looking elsewhere. Max

caught the lid with his fingertips and slid it back into place. *Thanks, Mum.*

The voices receded. Two metal doors boomed shut, a lock clicked, and all was still. Max waited as long as he could bear it, then popped the lid off his drum. He climbed out and stretched, his joints creaking in release.

He found himself in some kind of storage space, about twice the size of his last foster family's garage. Dim afternoon sunlight filtered through a high window, and with its help he made out tidy rows of drums, steel tables piled with boxes, and a gleaming storage tank with DIESEL stenciled onto its rounded surface. The place smelled of scorched earth and petrol.

He took stock of his resources. A sketch pad and camera pen, a phone, a lock-picking kit, some loose change, his lucky rock, and some pocket lint.

That was all.

Challenges? Locked in a storage space in an unknown location, surrounded by heavily armed bad people, and being completely weaponless.

Max sighed. "Full marks, mate," he said aloud. "You've really stepped in it this time."

A muffled "Max?" came from one of the drums. An icy finger of dread touched his spine, and for a second he froze in place. Irrational thoughts flashed through his mind: The rat talks? And it knows my name?

"A little help?" said the muffled voice.

Max located the barrel and pried off its lid. The scent of orange blossoms wafted up, followed by a head of wiry black hair. He took a step back.

The figure unfolded itself, turning to face him. "The shock absorbers could use some work, but still in all, not a bad ride."

"Cinnabar?"

"Don't stand there gawping like a tourist; give a girl a hand."

Max helped her climb out of the barrel, and she brushed herself off. Disheveled and dirty, but definitely Cinnabar.

Questions jostled and collided in Max's mind like crazed shoppers at a half-price sale. "What are—how did—where are we?" he finally managed.

She favored him with a radiant, incredulous smile. "Why, LOTUS headquarters, of course. I'm going to rescue my sister and, if he's here, your long-lost father. Are you in or out?"

IT'S A MAD, MAD MISSION

"DUH," said Max, trying to conceal his surprise. "Of *course* I'm bleeding well in!"

"I didn't know whether you'd sort it out that this Nullthium shipment was headed here," Cinnabar said. "And if you did, I wasn't sure you'd know to stow away in the drums."

Max replaced the lid of Cinnabar's barrel and tried for an offhand attitude. "Yeah, well, give a guy some credit, why don't you? Think I'd let you have all the fun?"

A skeptical look flitted across Cinnabar's face, but a smile won out. "I'm glad you made it. Let me clue you in."

As they waited for the spy's best friend—the cover of darkness—Cinnabar told Max her tale. Back at the museum, she had watched the other door of the workroom until Jensen took a bathroom break, then picked the lock and searched the place. After finding a bill of lading for the Nullthium-Ninety, she guessed that the barrels were bound for LOTUS HQ, so she stowed away. She hadn't been able to text Max because the janitors interrupted her.

"So, how did you know to hide in the drum?" she asked.

"Oh, uh," he said. "Pretty much the same thing."

Unlike Max, Cinnabar had come prepared. She'd brought along her book bag, complete with snacks, smoke bombs, and bottled water. Unfortunately, she'd packed everything but a plan. They sat, backs against a cold concrete wall, and shared an energy bar, talking things over.

"So what happens after?" Max asked at last.

"After?"

"You know, after we rescue them and escape?" He took another bite. "My dad will take me out of the orphanage so we can live together. How about you?"

She frowned. "You'd just go?"

"Well, duh. Wouldn't you?"

Cinnabar brushed crumbs off her lap. "It's not that simple. I'm still a few years away from being old enough to live on my own. And, well, everyone at the orphanage is like family to me."

Max snorted a laugh. "Even Nikki?"

"Sure. The idiot cousin."

They shared a smile. But then Max glanced away. "But look, they're *not* family, okay? Not *blood*, and that's what counts."

"Is it?" said Cinnabar, eyes flashing. "You—" Her phone

vibrated. "Hello?" she said cautiously. "Wyatt? Yeah, we're at the HQ now, so we don't— What?" She looked up at Max. "He says you turned your phone off."

"Well, yeah. Bad guys tend to notice little things like a phone ringing."

Cinnabar smirked. "You never heard of vibrate mode?" She swiveled her phone at a ninety-degree angle to her ear. "Here, he wants to talk with both of us."

Max leaned closer. A tinny voice said, "Max?"

"Yeah."

The phone voice cackled. "Cowabunga, mate! You made it, eh?"

"Um, yeah," said Max. "Listen, we're just about to—"

"I know, I know," said Wyatt. "Hey, you were wondering how I knew you were at the museum earlier?"

Max frowned. "Sure, but—"

"I slipped a GPS tracker in that button I gave you—just in case."

"You bugged him?" said Cinnabar. Max felt the warmth of her cheek next to his, uncomfortably close.

"What are friends for?" said Wyatt. "Oh, and I know why no one could pin down LOTUS HQ."

"Why?" asked Cinnabar.

"Officially, it's the home of Baron Chudleigh Lovat-Belcher."

Max whistled. "With a name like that, no wonder he turned criminal."

Wyatt's tone became elaborately casual. "So tell me, would a layout of the Lovat-Belcher estate grounds and buildings be of any use?"

Max could feel a smile spreading across his face. "Well . . ."

"It wouldn't be a total annoyance," said Cinnabar.

"Right then, Cinn," said Wyatt. "Tell lover boy to turn on his phone and I'll send it right over."

"Lover boy?" said Max.

"Am I brilliant or am I brilliant?" crowed Wyatt.

"You're brilliant," said Max and Cinnabar together.

"Too right," said Wyatt. "And we'll see if we can't hook up some transportation for you, too. Cheers!" He hung up.

"Good thing he stayed behind," said Cinnabar.

"There's more than one way to be a spy," Max agreed.

He switched his phone back on, and a minute later they were looking at a detailed schematic of the LOTUS mansion, grounds, and outbuildings.

"Nice map," said Max. "Now all we need is a plan."

Two hours later, it was full dark. Clouds hid the moon like a street-corner magician with an ace up his sleeve. Max and Cinnabar crouched behind a prickly blackthorn hedge, staring up at a country mansion.

It had fewer windows than Buckingham Palace and a little less glitz than the Taj Mahal, but it would do for keeping the rain off of one's head. Tasteful spotlights illuminated its ivy-covered walls, turrets jutted from various corners of the immense structure, and the general impression was that of overwhelming power and unlimited resources.

"Wow," said Cinnabar.

"I believe the phrase you're looking for is, 'Money, money, great stonking heaps of money,'" said Max.

They watched a solitary guard follow her flashlight beam down a path between the mansion and the outbuildings, headed for the rear of the property. When the woman had gone, Max tapped Cinnabar's shoulder and pointed to a small box mounted on the nearest corner of the structure.

"Cameras," he whispered.

She winced. "Infrared. That means they'll detect our body heat."

"Lovely. So how do we get past them—take a dip in ice water?"

In answer, Cinnabar unzipped her book bag and drew out two black, rubbery garments. "Try these."

"Wet suits?" Max gave her a look. "Who brings a wet suit—no, *two* wet suits—to a museum stakeout?"

Cinnabar nodded primly. "A good spy is prepared for anything."

"But *two*?"

"I had a feeling you might want to come along."

They wriggled into the ultralight neoprene bodysuits, looking like a couple of lost surfers praying for a swell at a country estate. Max worked the rubber hood over his head, leaving only an oval of face showing.

"Let's move," he said. "I'm hot."

Cinnabar smirked. "Cute, maybe. Hot? Don't get bigheaded."

"Oh, ha-ha." Max led the way along the hedge's perimeter, hugging the shadows and working his way closer to the rear of the house, Cinnabar right behind him. They paused beneath a gnarled oak tree.

About thirty feet of open lawn separated them from the rear patio. The grounds were as quiet as a mortuary at midnight, and except for the lights illuminating the house, as dark as the inside of a pocket.

Crouching low and keeping their faces hidden, Max and Cinnabar crept across the perfectly manicured grass. Max felt like a rabbit under the eyes of a watchful hawk. The skin between his shoulder blades prickled with anticipation.

Halfway there, he stumbled over a croquet wire and had to plant his hands on the grass to keep from sprawling headlong. Spies playing croquet? he mused. What's next—a volleyball court?

As they stepped onto the flagstone patio, bright light suddenly flooded the area. Motion detectors! Max dove behind a barrel-shaped potted shrub, and Cinnabar flattened herself into the shade cast by a chaise longue.

They froze, barely breathing. A minute passed, then another. Finally, locks clicked and the back door creaked open, not ten feet from Max's hiding place. His heart was drumming so hard, he felt sure the guards could hear it.

Heavy footsteps scuffed onto the stone. "Bloody badgers," a man's gruff voice complained. "See, nuffin' at all. Told you."

A peevish woman's voice answered, "Well, we had to check, didn't we."

"Wretched creatures. Third time this week. I'm goin' back in."

"Wait." Lighter footsteps brushed the stone, growing closer.

"Aw, what now, Dijon?"

Max could see her around the shrub, a tall, model-thin white woman in black and silver, her pretty face hard as a karate chop. It was Ruthless Ruth—or Ruthless Dijon, he supposed.

"Just being thorough," she said. The woman stopped two feet from the chaise, peering into the night. Max tensed. Could she see Cinnabar?

"I'm cold," the man whined.

"All right, you big baby," said Dijon. "I'm coming." She spun on a heel and strode back the way she'd come. The door closed on the couple's argument. Locks clicked.

Max risked a glimpse around the corner of the pot. When he saw that the back door lacked a window, he hissed at Cinnabar and scrambled as quietly as possible for its shelter.

She poked her head up, annoyed disbelief plastered across her face. When Max gestured urgently, she joined him, scowling.

"They'll see us, you cabbage head," she whispered, her breath hot in his ear.

He shook his head. "We had to get over here before the lights went out, or we'd trigger the sensor again."

Staying snug against the door, Cinnabar slung her book bag off her back and dug through it for her lock-picking kit. The floodlights snapped off; the yard was dark. Then Cinnabar and Max set to picking the surprisingly basic locks.

A few minutes later, the tumblers aligned. Max grinned. His teachers would be proud. Slowly, slowly, he eased open the door and peeked through the crack. A faint bluish night-light revealed the edge of a stove. The kitchen.

They crept inside, all senses on high alert. The kitchen was smaller than your average aircraft hangar, though not by much—a vast space full of gleaming appliances and dangling pots, some of them large enough to boil a small walrus. Max guessed there were a lot of bad guys to feed at LOTUS HQ.

He and Cinnabar peeled off the wet suits and stuffed them back into her bag. Then they crept along a corridor leading farther into the house, their footfalls muffled by a plush ivory carpet deep enough to drown in. Half-open doors revealed a pantry, a formal dining room large enough to seat the United Nations, a den, and what smelled like a cigar storage room.

The hall opened into a cavernous entryway dominated by a grand staircase three stories high. An ornate lotus the size of a Bentley was woven into the carpet. In case they forget the name of their organization, thought Max.

On the far side of the staircase, light showed around the edges of a closed door. Behind it, familiar voices argued.

"Friendly couple," muttered Max. Cinnabar raised an eyebrow.

They searched the ground floor, wandering past lounging rooms, game rooms, libraries, and a great room spacious enough to seat two branches of government with room left over for a family of hippos. In the half-light, a section of the floor threw off a rippling sheen, almost as if it were water.

Max shook his head in wonderment. *Rich people's houses.* When he thought of all the dumps he'd lived in . . .

At last, Cinnabar stopped before a stout door secured with a sliding bolt and dead bolt. She indicated a black wire that snaked from the corner of the upper doorjamb, up to the joint where wall met ceiling, and along the hall out of sight.

"Surveillance," she whispered. "This must be their jail."

A thrill buzzed through Max. Could his father really be on the other side of this door?

He opened the sliding bolt, and Cinnabar fished out her picks. While she worked on the dead bolt, Max dragged a chair over from the library and stood on it to cut the wire with her penknife.

At last the lock gave way. Cinnabar wiped her hands on her skirt. They exchanged a long look and a tight smile. Max turned the knob and they stepped together into the darkened room.

CHAPTER 25

ALL THE BEST HQS HAVE ONE

THE FIRST THINGS Max noticed were a strong salty odor and a faint sloshing sound, rather like water in a bathtub. The dim glow from the hallway petered out rapidly, illuminating nothing but a few feet of carpet. Hands extended before him, he cautiously shuffled forward—one step, two steps, three. . . .

"Jazz?" whispered Cinnabar.

"Dad?" said Max.

The next thing he noticed was the plush carpet turning to rough concrete. "Me, I'd fire the interior decorator." His hushed voice echoed oddly.

Cinnabar closed the door and switched on a laser flashlight. Its red beam revealed a pool that took up half the room, a low guardrail, a variety of pool-cleaning tools, and a tin bucket.

No Jazz. No Simon Segredo.

"What is this place?" said Cinnabar.

Max scratched his head. "A high-security pool room. Go figure." He turned and headed for the door.

At that moment, muffled voices came from the hallway. Cinnabar shielded her flashlight.

". . . just a short," said the male guard's voice. "It's not the first time we've lost the bloomin' feed."

"I don't care," said Dijon. "Mrs. Frost says check everything, so we check everything. Do it, Humphrey."

"Nag, nag, nag," said Humphrey, his voice growing louder. "You're not the boss of me."

"No, but *she* is. Open the door."

Max's eyes widened. In no time at all, the guards would spot the severed wire and picked lock. Then the game would most definitely be up.

"You shouldn't have clipped that wire," whispered Cinnabar.

"*Now* you tell me."

Max tugged on her arm, edging backward until he bumped into the guardrail. She followed.

"Hey! What utter prat went and left the door unbolted?" Dijon's sharp voice came from right outside.

"Wasn't me," said Humphrey.

"Well, it sure wasn't *me*," said Dijon.

"Oh, so it's always *my* fault? What about that time with the Taser—whose fault was that, then?"

Max and Cinnabar stood at the pool's edge, fresh out

of options. In seconds, the guards would burst in and catch them. *Unless* . . .

"Come on," Max whispered.

As quietly as possible, they ducked under the rail, boosting themselves over the side and into the chilly water, still fully clothed. The door swung open as Max gulped a huge breath and submerged himself. He hugged the side like a limpet in love.

The room lights flickered on, and just like that, the inky water turned a pale, translucent green. Max could make out Cinnabar beside him, tight curls drifting about her head like seaweed, and beyond her, a dark, submerged passageway.

The water warped the guards' voices into Martian talk. All these bickering agents had to do was step forward, and Max and Cinnabar would be revealed like a couple of hooked trout, ready to be hauled in.

Max had no intention of being caught.

He tapped Cinnabar's shoulder and indicated the tunnel. She nodded. Together, they sidled crablike toward it, trying not to cause ripples. Max's heartbeat hammered in his ears. It felt like a large rubber band was slowly tightening across his chest.

The Martian voices rose to shouts. Max pushed off the side and surged forward, stroking and kicking his way into the mouth of the dark tunnel. He swam through blackness, on and on, fingers occasionally scraping against rough cement.

Max's suffocation nightmare was back, but this time it was real. His chest was being squeezed as though it were in a vise. His body screamed for oxygen, and if he didn't take a breath *right now*, he thought he'd freak. He held out as long as he could.

And finally he couldn't take it anymore. Lungs bursting, he kicked toward the surface, expecting at any moment to smack his head on concrete.

Instead, air. He gasped, sucking sweet oxygen into his lungs. In another couple of seconds he heard an answering gasp to his left, as Cinnabar's head broke the surface of the pool.

Watery moonlight shone through picture windows onto the ghostly forms of sofas, armchairs, and coffee tables. Max tossed his wet hair back. He'd seen this space before. It was the great room with the rippling floor.

"Who . . . puts a swimming pool . . . in their living room?" Max panted.

Cinnabar shook her head, scattering droplets. "LOTUS, apparently." They paddled toward the edge.

"Don't crowd me," said Cinnabar.

"Who's crowding you?"

"You kicked my leg."

"Did not," said Max.

"Then what . . . ?"

Something brushed along Max's back. Something lengthy, muscular, and distinctly nonhuman.

He flinched and made a sound like a ferret choking on a chicken bone.

"What is it?" said Cinnabar.

"Shark," said a man's voice.

"But then, you'd expect that from a shark tank," a woman added.

Overhead lights switched on, momentarily blinding Max and Cinnabar.

"Of course," said Max. "All the best spy headquarters have one." Shading his eyes, he made out Dijon's lean figure standing beside Humphrey, a buff, V-shaped man clad in black-and-silver spandex. They looked like catalog models for Victoria's Evil Secret.

But, of course, what really captured Max's attention were the two six-foot gray-and-black reef sharks circling around him and Cinnabar like hungry diners at a buffet table.

"Max!" Cinnabar's voice was tight and high.

"Aw," said Dijon, "have the baby spies gotten themselves into a pickle?"

"Don't splash," Humphrey said helpfully. "Splashin' attracts 'em."

Max remembered from some long-ago science class that sharks feed at night. And judging by their eagerness, these sharks hadn't eaten yet.

Cinnabar slipped off her book bag, readying for action. One of the sharks veered toward her while she was occupied.

"Behind you!" cried Max.

Just in time, she spun and whacked the creature with her bag, right on its snout. The predator retreated in confusion.

"Watch out!" said Cinnabar.

Max twisted to find the second shark gliding straight for him, its mouth a wide, wicked slash, its eyes blank and staring, like a demonic doll's. What had Wyatt read to him about shark attacks from that stupid spy book?

Max racked his brain.

The shark swam nearer, until it seemed all Max could see was a mouthful of razor-edged teeth. At the last possible second, *bam!* He clouted the beast in its eyes with both fists, as hard as he could.

The shark jerked back and swam off to join its comrade. Before the predators struck again, Max and Cinnabar paddled to the lip of the pool and hoisted themselves onto the tile apron surrounding it.

Chk-chhk. The unmistakable sound of a slide racking a bullet into a chamber froze them in their tracks.

"Hold it right there," said Dijon, covering them with her pistol. "If you drip that nasty water all over this nice clean carpet, the boss will kill us."

Bundled in enormous fluffy white bath towels, Max and Cinnabar were marched at gunpoint to a triple-locked room on the second floor. There, Humphrey pushed the orphans inside and left them to their own devices.

"Sleep tight, pumpkin seeds," he crooned, closing the door. The triple locks clicked. The guards had taken Cinnabar's book bag, their phones, their lock-picking kits, their pen cameras—even Max's lucky stone. All he had left were some coins and pocket lint.

Their prison proved to be a spartan one: twin beds in a cramped, windowless chamber, with a little nook on one side that barely fit a toilet and sink. Cinnabar sat down on the bed and bit her lip. Her soggy curls dripped, and her narrow shoulders were hunched inside the towel. She stared at the floor.

Max awkwardly patted her back. "There, there."

"I'm not despairing, I'm *thinking*," she snapped.

He held up his hands in surrender, then went and sat down on the other bed. Max was thinking too. He was thinking: It'll take some kind of miracle for us to get out of this alive. But he decided not to share that thought.

They sat in silence for a long minute, until a soft hollow tapping sounded from the inner wall beside Cinnabar's bed.

"Rats," said Max.

Cinnabar cocked her head, listening. "Not likely. Rats are more *scurry scurry* than *tap tap tap*."

"Water pipes, then?"

"Shh!" Cinnabar held up a hand.

The rapping continued, taking on a sort of rhythm. Some taps were long, some short, and they seemed to repeat.

Cinnabar scooted over on the bed and placed an ear against the wall. Then she tapped out a rhythm of her own, frowning in concentration.

"I never took you for a rapper," Max said, trying to lighten the mood.

"Will you *shut up*!"

When a flurry of answering taps sounded from the wall, Cinnabar's face lit up like a Christmas candle. "She's alive!"

"Who is?"

"Jazz!" Cinnabar bounced to her feet, beaming, and gave Max a quick hug.

He felt a warm rush. He didn't know what to do with his hands. "Let me get this straight: You know your sister's alive because someone tapped on the wall?"

Cinnabar slapped his arm. "Not *someone*; Jazz. We used to use Morse code to talk whenever our foster parents separated us. She's in the next room!"

"Brilliant!" said Max. "Oh, Cinn, that's great. What'd she say?"

"So far, only that she's all right."

He put a hand on her shoulder. "Don't you worry. We'll get her out—and us too."

More taps came from the wall. Cinnabar hopped onto the bed and began rapping her response with a knuckle, but she stopped short at the sound of a key in the lock. She and Max stared at the door.

Cinnabar came and stood beside him as the other two

locks clicked and the door opened. A menacing black pistol entered, followed by Humphrey's V-shaped form. They backed up.

"Right, then," growled the guard. "Seems you two have a visitor."

A tall figure brushed past him and into the room, dressed in an impeccable navy blue suit with faint chalk stripes. His cordovan shoes gleamed, but not as much as his smile. "Max!"

Max's jaw dropped. "Agent Taylor?"

"You know this guy?" asked Cinnabar.

"He—uh," said Max, momentarily dumbstruck.

"Max and I are old friends." The dapper agent turned to Humphrey. "You can release him. He's on our side."

"What?" said Cinnabar.

Max wanted to say something—something definitely needed to be said—but his throat felt as dry as petrified tree bark.

Taylor raised his eyebrows. "You didn't know? Yes, our Max has been quite the double agent. With his help, LOTUS picked up Dr. Eisenheimer today and brought him here. Soon, they'll have his Process as well."

"Max?" said Cinnabar. Her milk-chocolate skin had gone chalky, and her golden eyes were huge, fixed on his.

He couldn't hold her gaze. "He promised to help me find my father," he said in a strangled voice that sounded nothing like him.

"Traitor."

His hands flapped uselessly. "All I wanted was to be with my dad, and for once have a real family." He searched Cinnabar's face. Surely she'd understand?

Her eyes glistened and her mouth was tight. "You *had* a family. And you just threw it away."

"Cinn—"

She turned her back, gripping her upper arms as if she were cold.

Agent Taylor laid a sympathetic hand on his shoulder. "Come on, Max."

Numbly, he let himself be led from the room. This was it. He was free again; he was getting what he'd always wanted. Right?

So why did it all taste like ashes in his mouth?

CHAPTER 26

JACK OF ALL TRAITORS

AGENT TAYLOR guided Max to a comfortable sitting room on the same floor. It looked like a photo spread from *Fancy Mansions* magazine. A cheery fire crackled in the fireplace, shelves of burnished leather books lined the walls, and on a table between two armchairs rested a pot of tea, hot chocolate, and a basket of fresh blueberry scones. All that was missing was a faithful spaniel.

The delicious, homey aroma of the scones filled the room, but even though Max hadn't eaten since splitting an energy bar hours ago, he wasn't hungry.

Traitor. The word echoed in his head.

"I know this must be rather trying for you," said the tall spy. "Quite the day you've had. Sit down; have some tea. Or would you prefer hot cocoa?"

Like a robot, Max bent his knees and folded himself into

the chair. He accepted the teacup and saucer and looked down at them like he'd forgotten what they were for.

Traitor.

From a drawer in the cherrywood writing desk, Taylor produced a yellow legal pad and silver pen. He set them on the table beside the scones.

At that, a brown-and-white spaniel with chocolate-drop eyes emerged from behind the divan. Oh, please, thought Max. It sniffed hopefully at the baked goods, but when Taylor snapped his fingers and pointed at the doorway, it padded off.

"Not right now, of course, but when you're ready, we shall require one more thing from you: a sketch of the internal security at Merry Sunshine Orphanage. A source gave us most of it, but we don't know if we can trust its accuracy."

Numbly, Max looked from the pad to Agent Taylor's thin lips. He heard the words, but his brain was busy processing something else.

"You used me," he said.

Taylor had the good grace to look slightly abashed. "It's, ah . . . not as simple as all that. Each of us gained something from the bargain."

A vertical crease appeared between Max's eyebrows. "You used me to betray Hantai Annie. You don't care about me at all."

Oddly, the tall man looked stricken. "Max, that's not—"

"You didn't even find my father." Max stood, and the

teacup fell forgotten from his lap, spilling Earl Grey onto the Persian rug. "He's been captured by LOTUS, dead, for all I know, and I had to learn that for myself."

"He's not dead."

Max clenched his fists. Hot words bubbled up like bile. "Right, like I should believe you? Mr. Trustworthy? You've done nothing but string me along. You'd spit on me and tell me it was raining if it suited you. You have no idea where my father is, you liar."

"I do," said Taylor.

"Liar!"

"Max." The tall man took a step toward him, his face twisted with some strong emotion. *"I'm* your father."

Max barked out a laugh. "Yeah, *right.* And I'm Tinker Bell's long-lost twin."

"No, it's true. I—" Agent Taylor slipped a hand inside his suit jacket and drew out a gleaming calfskin wallet. He unfolded it.

"And now you're trying to *bribe* me into believing you?" Max shook his head. "Man, you *are* desperate."

Without speaking, the spy held the wallet out like a cop's badge. On the right side, under clear plastic, was a small photo—a photo of a smiling Asian woman with lustrous black hair.

"Do you remember her?" he asked.

Max felt like a horse had kicked him in the chest. He took

a wobbly step back. *It couldn't be.* The same photo that rested in his book bag.

The photo of his mother.

"She loved you very much," said Taylor hoarsely. He cleared his throat.

Max bit his lip. No, he *wouldn't* cry. "Look, this family reunion stuff is all really touching," he said. "But if you truly are . . . who you say you are . . ."

"I am."

"Maybe you'd answer one small question."

"Anything," said Agent Taylor, his sad brown eyes soft.

"Where the heck have you been? I've been in and out of foster homes for six years, and you couldn't even drop me an e-mail? A phone call?"

The man winced and rubbed his long jaw. "I've been on the run."

"For *six years?*" said Max. "That's not a run, that's a marathon."

"LOTUS was trying to kill me, so I had to flee the country—leave you and your mother behind, and disappear. Even the slightest communication was too dangerous. They might have traced it."

Max raised a skeptical eyebrow. "And so now you're *working* for LOTUS? Huh. For a professional spy, that's a rubbish cover story."

The tall man—Taylor, Segredo, whoever he was—gave a

rueful chuckle and stepped over to the fireplace. "Fiction is so much tidier than truth. In point of fact, I returned a month ago, searching for you. I had hoped that LOTUS would have forgotten about me after all this time, but apparently I was wrong."

Max folded his arms across his chest. "And then you figured, 'Well, if you can't beat 'em, join 'em,' and you started working for the bad guys."

"Oh, Max." His father gazed at him with an unreadable expression. "There are no 'good guys' or 'bad guys' anymore, just shades of gray. Everyone wants something. All that separates us is how far we're prepared to go to achieve it."

"No," said Max. "You're wrong."

"Am I? Look what you were willing to do in order to get what you wanted."

"That's not the same thing." Max tamped down a tickle of guilt that writhed in his belly. "You think I'll overlook your little switch to the dark side just because you're my father?"

Pain was etched on the elder Segredo's face. "They threatened to hurt you."

Max made a dismissive noise, a little *pff* of air.

"And as proof of their intentions, they burned down your last foster family's house. I saw it all on video."

He was telling the truth—Max could feel it in his marrow, could read it on the man's face, plain as print. Max stumbled backward, and just like that, the pieces of the puzzle began clicking together. That mysterious black car he'd seen the night of the fire—and on the way to the train station. The way Agent Taylor had fought the LOTUS agents on the train, to keep them from kidnapping him.

It was true. Agent Taylor really *was* Simon Segredo.

Max collapsed heavily into the armchair, his thoughts and feelings roiling about like the load in an industrial washing machine. In all his fantasies, somehow he'd never pictured the joyful father-son reunion quite like this. His head throbbed.

"I did it all for you, Max," said Simon Segredo. "Just give them this last piece of information and we can be free of LOTUS. We can be together."

He was wrong. They would *never* be free of LOTUS—Max knew that now. The shadowy organization was holding half of his friends captive, and it wouldn't rest until the School for S.P.I.E.S. had been leveled to the ground and Hantai Annie was buried in her grave.

Max thought of all he'd done to help LOTUS, and the tickle in his stomach turned into a queasy roll. He shoved the legal pad off the table. "Leave me alone," he muttered.

"You've had a shock," said his father, stepping closer. "But think about it for a while, and you'll—"

"No!" Max snapped. "Get out." His lips pressed together. All the feelings bottled inside him were trying to blast out, like a shaken-up can of Coke.

Simon Segredo's face went blank and still, as if a mask

had dropped over his features. "Very well. We'll talk later." He strode out the door, closing it behind him. A lock clicked.

Max grabbed a throw pillow and covered his face. And for the first time he could remember—maybe the first time since his mother's death—he cried, full out. Big heaving sobs, ropes of snot, the whole deal.

And when at last the tears were done, he wiped his face with the sleeve of his damp blazer and sat up straight. The world had thrown him for a major loop, no question.

But now, Max knew what he had to do.

STYX AND STONES MAY BREAK MY BONES

SIMPLE HOUSEHOLD objects can be so inherently useful. Scissors, hairpins, forks, and pencils. Even the lowly paper clip. Who knew how handy it would turn out to be for picking locks?

Max discovered this when he fashioned some paper clips he'd found in the desk drawer into crude picks and unlocked the sitting room door. Ever so cautiously, he slipped into the dim hallway, feet noiseless on the thick carpet. It must have been nearly midnight. Not a soul wandered the hallways of the great house.

He paused outside Cinnabar's door, but kept moving until he located an empty bedroom that overlooked the backyard. Max eased open a window, lifted a book from the nightstand, and flung it as far as he could into the night.

Instantly, the floodlights snapped on.

He raced to the stairwell and crept down to the landing on tiptoe, listening intently. Before long, the guards emerged from their room near the foot of the stairs, bickering away.

"Fine, but if it's another bloomin' rodent, you can go it alone next time," Humphrey grumbled.

"A badger's not a rodent, you prat, it's some kind of weasel," snapped Dijon.

Their voices faded. Max cat-footed it down the stairs and across to the guardroom door. With his hand on the knob, a sudden thought struck him: What if there's a third guard?

He peeked through the door crack. All clear. Max crept inside. His eyes roamed over the video monitors and coffee cups, the electronic gear and corkboards, the purple Barney doll (A *Barney* fan? At LOTUS?), and at last, the ring of keys that hung from a nail.

Snatching the keys, he turned to go, when he noticed Cinnabar's book bag on a shelf beside the door. On impulse, he rummaged inside the zippered pouch, retrieving his lucky stone and an eraser smoke bomb.

Every little bit helped.

After checking the hallway, Max trotted up the stairs, his senses alert for any sign of the returning guards. In fact, he was focusing so intently on what lay behind him that when he reached the top of the stairs, he ran smack into the last person on Earth he expected to see.

"*Wyatt?!*"

The blond boy recovered his balance and grinned from ear to ear. "Blast, mate! A simple handshake would do."

Max grabbed Wyatt's arms. He laughed in delight and disbelief, then clapped a hand over his mouth. "What are you doing here?" he whispered.

"Rescue mission. When you didn't answer my texts, I thought maybe you could use a hand."

Max frowned. "But how did you . . . ?"

"I had some help," Wyatt said. "Someone got separated from his rescue team, and we met someone else on the way."

"Huh?"

From around the corner lumbered the bearlike figure of Styx, and beside him, looking even more like a fireplug than usual, Roger Stones. Both carried Beretta pistols.

Max had never been so glad to see anyone in his life.

"All right then, cupcake?" whispered Mr. Stones.

Max bobbed his head, grinning like a fool. "Cinnabar's just down the hall, and Jazz is next door."

Stones hooked a thumb past his shoulder. "There're two other locked doors down that way. I expect that's where we'll find the rest of our crew, eh, Styxie?"

The big man glowered. "Don't call me Styxie."

Max held up the keys. "Let's open some doors." He strode past the men, heading for Cinnabar's room.

"Oh, I think not," said Styx in a loud voice.

"Shh!" hissed Mr. Stones. "You want to wake the whole bloody house?"

"Yes, actually, I do," said Styx.

Max spun, alarms clanging in his brain. Something was definitely out of whack here.

Mr. Stones cocked his head. "What's gotten into you, Styxie?"

"Don't"—the big man's gun coughed twice—"call me *Styxie*."

Roger Stones staggered back from the impact, staring in disbelief. For an endless moment, he swayed. Then he crumpled in a heap on the plush ivory carpet, blood pooling beside his unmoving body.

Max gasped and clutched his hands to his chest as if he'd been the one shot. Astonishment froze him where he stood.

"No!" cried Wyatt, dropping to his knees.

"I told him and I told him, but he wouldn't listen," said Styx calmly. "I *hate* nicknames."

Max and Wyatt stared in horror. Stones's eyes gazed unseeing at the ceiling, his body as still as a lifeless mannequin. At last, Max's paralysis relaxed its grip, and he took two quick steps toward the fallen teacher. "Maybe he's—"

"Ah-ah-ah," said Styx, training the Beretta on him. "One more step and it's your last."

"What—*why*?" said Max, feeling absolutely gutted. "How could you?"

"Can't guess, brain drain?" sneered Styx.

Wyatt's blue eyes were huge with shock. "Cor . . . you're a double agent."

"You're a bright spark," said Styx. "Got it in one."

A memory rose in Max's befuddled mind. "Then, last night . . . at The Eye with Dijon . . ."

Styx's eyebrows rose. "You were there? Yeah, we was makin' the deal." He gestured roughly with the pistol. "Get a move on."

Wyatt and Max raised their hands, because it felt like the proper thing to do, and shuffled down the hall toward Cinnabar's room. On the way, Max considered and abandoned a half dozen escape plans. The Beretta was a bit of a wet blanket.

"Y-you're going to shoot us?" Wyatt's voice trembled.

Styx scowled. "'Course not. Not if you mind me. What do you take me for? I even helped you, Max, by sending those coded messages that your dad was alive."

"You did?" Max craned his head around to look at Styx. "Why?"

"Well"—the big man grimaced—"didn't want you to lose heart."

"But you . . . but then . . ." Max groped for the words. "Why did you betray Annie, the school, everything?"

"Why did *you*?" Styx growled softly.

Max's heart dropped into his stomach like a stone cupcake.

"Max, turn traitor?" said Wyatt. "That's hilarious. I'd

bust a gut if I wasn't about to pee myself with fright. It's a joke, right, Max?"

Max could feel Wyatt's gaze on him. He kept his own eyes fixed on Cinnabar's door, just down the hall.

"I did it for family," he muttered, half to himself.

Styx grunted. "And how'd that work out?" When Max didn't answer, he continued. "*I* did it for respect. Well, and the moolah, of course—*lots* of moolah."

"Respect?" said Max. He still couldn't bring himself to look at Wyatt, who had fallen silent.

The bearlike man gave an irritated snarl. "Hantai Annie never let me in on the big projects. I was always the general dogsbody—'wash the dishes, Styx'; 'drive the car'; 'empty the rubbish bin.' LOTUS at least respects me."

They reached the door.

"Enough jabber," said Styx. "Unlock the door and hand me the keys. Now, empty your pockets."

He gave them a rough one-handed pat-down and removed Wyatt's phone, as well as the paper clips that Max had tucked into his jacket. "You can keep the change and the pocket lint. I'm not a robber."

"And the eraser?" said Max.

Styx chuckled. "Fat lot of good it'll do you. But all right, for old times' sake." He unlocked the door and shoved them inside. "Ta-ta, kiddies."

And then he locked them in.

◌ ◌ ◌

"*You,*" said Cinnabar. She sat on the bed, face blotchy and eyes red, like she'd been crying. But she wasn't crying now.

"I know you must hate me," said Max.

She shot him an incredulous look. "I don't hate you."

"You don't?" Hope gave a lift to his tone.

"I *loathe* you. I *despise* you— No, even that's not strong enough. I'd have to make up a word, like . . . um . . . Help me, Wyatt."

"Detesticate?" Wyatt said, in a small voice.

Cinnabar clapped her hands. "Yes! I *detesticate* you. I . . . *abhorminate* you."

"I'm sorry," said Max.

Cinnabar rose and planted her fists on her hips. "Oh, it's *way* beyond sorry."

Max glanced from her to Wyatt, who wore a look like a whipped puppy. "I was so, *so* wrong. I made a huge mistake."

"Colossal," said Cinnabar. "Gi-*nor*mous."

"And I want to make it up to you."

Cinnabar snorted. Wyatt, still in shock, said, "He shot Mr. Stones."

"*Wha-a-at?*" said Cinnabar, aghast. "I know you're a traitor, but shooting a teacher . . . ?"

"Not *me,*" said Max. "Styx. He's a double agent." The impact of it hit him afresh, and he reached out for Wyatt's shoulder. "We were standing right there, and Styx just shot him point-blank. We have to do some—"

Wyatt shrugged off Max's hand. "I don't want to talk to

you right now." He curled up on a bed with his face to the wall. Cinnabar sat on the other bed, arms crossed over her chest, staring at the floor.

"I'll get us out of here somehow," said Max. "I'll make things right."

"Hah!" said Cinnabar.

"I'll pick the locks."

"Be my guest."

Max examined the door. Only one of the three locks was accessible from the inside. "Okay, scratch that. Then I'll . . . take off the hinges?"

"Painted over, and we've got nothing to pry with," said Cinnabar. "I tried, traitor."

Max prowled the ten-by-ten room, methodically inspecting everything—the beds, the walls, the toilet and sink. No helpful tools presented themselves, no secret escape hatch said, *Here I am*. He went over it all again, and this time he stopped by a small grate above the baseboard. "What's this?"

"The heating vent, brain drain."

Max squatted in front of it. He measured the width with his hands and compared that to his shoulder span.

"Oh, brilliant," said Cinnabar. "I already thought of that, traitor. We've got nothing to undo the screws with."

Max fished in his pocket and held up a coin. "You call this nothing?"

DOWN IN THE DUCTS

TEN MINUTES and two broken fingernails later, the three orphans were making their way slowly and painstakingly through the heating ducts. It was too cramped to crawl on hands and knees, so they slithered on their bellies like reptiles.

Max's heart was in his throat. Not only did his friends hate him, but he hated tight spaces, feeling sure that the metal would collapse at any moment and spill them into the bowels of the mansion. The duct creaked alarmingly, but somehow their luck held. On and on they crawled, down and down.

Once, a series of deep booming sounds from far below froze them in place.

"What was that?" whispered Cinnabar.

"Target practice?" said Max.

In less than a minute they had their answer, as a rush of

warm air made its way up the ductwork from the boiler room beneath. As they crept onward, the metal surface of the duct around them grew hotter and hotter.

"Ow!" said Wyatt.

"Shh!" hissed Max and Cinnabar.

Max was dripping with sweat. He tried to pull his sleeves over his fists for protection, but they kept slipping back. His neck ached with the effort of keeping his face off the hot metal.

"I feel like a microwaved burrito," he muttered. Wyatt snorted.

"Shh!" hissed Cinnabar.

Still they crawled onward, and eventually the heater switched off.

Wyatt had a bad moment, when he got stuck at a bend in the ductwork. But somehow he managed to wriggle free.

They crept past many offshoots leading to darkened rooms, until at last Max reached a certain side passage that caught his attention. The room beyond was bathed in the glow of a familiar bluish night-light.

Could that be the kitchen?

With much awkward back-crawling and maneuvering, Max managed to squirm around so that he was traveling feetfirst. Then he inchwormed down the tunnel on his back until he could go no farther. He rested with his feet on the grille.

"What are you waiting for?" whispered Cinnabar, her face just inches behind his head.

"Cover."

"What?"

Max drew his knees as far up as the duct would allow. "You'll see."

And a minute later, when the deep booming sounds returned, Max added to them by kicking—once, twice, three times!—at the grate.

It clattered onto the kitchen floor.

He wriggled after it, praying that the guards hadn't heard the noise. He tried to help Cinnabar, but she swatted his hands away and crawled out on her own. Finally, a red-faced Wyatt squeezed through to join them.

"If we make it out of here alive . . ." he said.

"When," Max corrected.

". . . I'm getting right to work on some escape gizmos. Duct crawling is strictly for ducks."

Max took it as a good sign that Wyatt's sense of humor was returning. He removed the eraser smoke bomb from his pocket.

"What's that for?" asked Cinnabar.

"Diversion," said Max. "We need to steal the keys again. Picking three door locks would take too long."

Cinnabar scoffed. "We don't need one of *your* diversions. We need a *real* diversion. Wyatt, raid the fridge."

"Thought you'd never ask," said Wyatt.

Cinnabar placed a saucepan on the stove and turned the burner up high, while Wyatt located several slices of lunch meat and, after taking a bite, dropped them into the pan. Next, Cinnabar doused a dish towel with rum from the pantry and splashed the alcohol liberally around the stove and wall. Meanwhile, Wyatt hunted up a box of old-fashioned wooden matches.

"What's the pan for," said Max, "if you're only going to torch the place anyway?"

"You'll see."

Max spread his hands. "Hey, who's supposed to be the pyro around here? Why bother with . . . ?"

"If it looks like a duck and quacks like a duck . . ." Cinnabar cocked her head like an artist examining a painting. She draped the dish towel on the hood of the stove so that it hung above the pan.

"How's that again?"

Wyatt struck a match and touched it to the soaked towel. It burned fast, with a hot blue-and-yellow flame. "It has to look right—like a midnight snack gone wrong."

"Exactly," said Cinnabar.

The flames spread from the towel to the wall. The lunch meats sizzled.

Max backed up. "I think it's time to—"

"Go," Cinnabar agreed.

They hurried down the hallway and ducked into the murky cigar room, as the piercing *beep-beep-beep* of a smoke alarm echoed up the hall. The guards' footsteps thundered past their hiding place. Voices carried.

"And I suppose this is my fault too?" Humphrey whined.

"That's it!" Dijon snapped. "I'm putting in for a new partner."

When the agents had passed along the hall and out of sight, Max, Cinnabar, and Wyatt dashed down the corridor to the guardroom and snatched the key ring. They took the stairs two at a time, pounding upward.

"Jazz first," panted Cinnabar.

Outside Jazz's door, Max fumbled with the ring.

"Here, let me." Cinnabar grabbed the keys from his hand and, with a minimum of trial and error, found the proper ones. She pushed the door open into a dim room. "Jazz?" she whispered.

"Cinn?" came the answer. A tall, brown-eyed girl with curly hair and skin a shade darker than Cinnabar's milk chocolate stepped into view. "It's *you!*"

The sisters collided in a fierce hug. They rocked each other, laughing and crying at the same time—some kind of girl thing, thought Max. It tickled him to see Cinnabar reunited with her sister, but this was no time to plan a party.

"Keys!" he hissed urgently.

A Cinnabar-shaped arm peeled away from the Jones-sister amoeba and held out the ring. Max took it and trotted down the hall, Wyatt beside him.

"Mr. Stones"—Wyatt paused to gulp at the name—"said the other locked rooms were down this way." He turned into an intersecting corridor. Halfway along, they found two doors with multiple locks, right across from each other.

The first room yielded Rashid and Tremaine, the students kidnapped during surveillance exercises. Max felt a surge of fierce joy at seeing them unharmed.

Tremaine gave a whoop. He bounced off the bed, seized Max in a bear hug, and lifted him off the floor. "Yesss, Maxwell!"

Rashid was still wearing his red tracksuit. He flashed a rare grin and pumped Wyatt's hand. "Glad you could make it, gentlemen."

They went to unlock the second door, but it swung open at a touch. The room was empty.

"We heard voices out here an hour or so ago," said Tremaine.

"They must have moved Dr. Eisenheimer," said Max. "Let's split up and search for him."

Rashid caught his arm. "No time. If we're going, we've got to go now."

For a handful of heartbeats, Max stared at the empty room, jaw clenched. Reluctantly, he nodded at last. He wouldn't be able to make everything right, after all. The four teens hurried back down the hall to join the others, but just before they reached the intersecting corridor, a door opened to their left.

Out stepped a yawning, older white woman. Her pixie-ish gray hair was sleep-tousled, and a satiny sapphire robe swaddled her thick body. She looked like an upscale grandmother roused from her nap.

"Oh, my!" she quavered, clutching the top of her robe together at the sight of them. "Who are you boys? What's the matter?"

"We . . . uh," said Tremaine.

"That is," said Max.

Wyatt stepped forward, all curly blond hair and wide blue eyes. "We're houseguests, mum," he said politely. "We couldn't sleep, so we thought we'd hit the kitchen for a bite. I hope we didn't disturb you."

Max glanced at Wyatt in disbelief. That was one smooth lie. He only hoped the woman didn't notice the smoke alarm's faint beeping in the background.

"Oh, you poor dears." It seemed that Sleepy Gran bought the story. She patted Wyatt's cheek and turned to reenter her room. "I'll just ring the chef and have her whip you up a midnight snack."

"Don't!" blurted Max. When the woman peered around quizzically, he continued. "Uh, don't . . . bother her. We can make our own snacks."

Sleepy Gran flapped a hand. "Why, it's no trouble, child."

"Stop her!" Suddenly, Jazz appeared with Cinnabar at the hall corner.

Max and the others turned to stare. "What?"

"That woman," said Jazz, striding closer. "That's Mrs. Frost, the head of LOTUS. Don't—"

Click.

The door closed and a dead bolt snapped shut. Sleepy Gran had gone.

"—let her go," Jazz finished, throwing up her hands. "Super. Now she's calling the guards."

"Oops," said Wyatt.

"Run!" cried Max.

They sprinted around the corner and up the next corridor. "We'll never make the main doors," said Rashid. "Is there another exit?"

Max pictured the mansion layout Wyatt had e-mailed him. "Uh, there's a balcony. Past the stairs and down the other wing."

"Then let's get cracking!" said Cinnabar.

She and Max led the group as they rounded another corner and closed in on the stairs. But they stopped dead when they saw what was coming up the steps.

"Oi!" barked Styx. "Hold up." He stood on the landing, legs spread, cradling a serious-looking assault rifle. Dijon flanked him, similarly armed. Two steps above them, Agent

Taylor—a.k.a., Simon Segredo—wielded a bulky yellow-and-black Taser.

The orphans skidded to a stop. Wisps of smoke billowed up the stairwell, and smoke alarms wailed below. Everyone stood frozen, waiting to see what would happen next.

CHAPTER 29

MAKING A BIG BANGARANG

"MAX," said Simon Segredo. "You disappoint me."

Max snorted. "Think how *I* feel. I wait half my life to meet my old man, and he turns out to be a ratbag."

His father winced. "This is your last chance. Come with me right now, and I can make amends with LOTUS. All you've done, really, is start a fire."

Max threw up his hands. "Why does everyone think *I'm* the firebug?"

"Come with me. I can protect you."

Max glanced at Cinnabar standing next to him. "And what about her?" He jerked a thumb at the other teens. "And them?"

His father shook his head. "Just you. Not your scruffy orphan friends."

Max turned to look at the group. Red-faced Wyatt, serious Rashid, athletic Tremaine, and lovely Jazz, standing panting in the hallway, expressions of defeat written on their faces. And prickly Cinnabar, right beside him.

"These guys?" he said. "They're not my friends."

Cinnabar flinched like he'd slapped her.

"They're my *family*," said Max. "Do you know what that means?"

He dug in his pocket, and Dijon pointed her gun at him. "Relax," he said. "This is my good-luck stone. I want you to have it." Max tossed the rock to his father, a little high and wide.

Simon Segredo stretched to catch it, and for a moment, Styx and Dijon were focused on him.

Max pulled apart the eraser bomb he'd palmed, gave it a twist, and lobbed it at them. Light flashed, and bluish-gray smoke billowed up, obscuring the little group below.

"Go!" cried Max.

Tremaine hefted a potted rubber tree that stood near the top of the stairs and hurled it into the cloud. A thud, and someone grunted. Max hoped it was his dad.

He raced toward the balcony, with the other orphans hot on his heels. An automatic rifle stuttered, startlingly loud, stitching a line of holes along the wall.

"Don't shoot!" Mr. Segredo coughed on the smoke. "Take them alive."

With a hiss, ceiling sprinklers burst into action, raining down on pursuers and quarry alike. The orphans fled pell-mell down a corridor lined with expensive-looking paintings of the type found in museums. The artwork was getting royally soaked.

"Mrs. Frost won't like that," Max panted.

"What a pity," said Jazz.

The balcony lay dead ahead, behind a pair of posh French doors. Tremaine flung them open and scrambled over the railing, onto the thick ivy vines that covered the house. Jazz and Rashid quickly followed.

With one leg on the railing, Wyatt hesitated. "I really don't like heights."

"How do you feel about torture?" said Max.

Wyatt blanched. "I'm going, I'm going."

Max and Cinnabar made to join him, but they were just a shade too slow.

"Don't . . . bloody well . . . move!" Styx stood about ten feet off, sopping wet, panting heavily, and mad as a grizzly bear with a toothache. His rifle was aimed straight at them, its black muzzle yawning as wide as a train tunnel. "I don't . . . care . . . what your dad . . . says. You budge . . . an inch, I shoot."

Simon Segredo stopped beside the double agent, Taser held loosely in his hand. The lines of his long face looked like they'd been carved in granite.

Max gulped. Was this it? After all he'd survived, all his narrow escapes and awful foster parents, would his short, checkered life end here, in this absurd mansion, surrounded

by enemy spies and his turncoat father?

He squared his shoulders. All these years he'd been helpless, shunted from foster home to foster home, never in control. But he *could* control *something*. Max Segredo raised his chin and stared his father in the eye—with a look full of complicated feelings, regret, and rebellion.

And then he deliberately turned his back and stepped to the balcony railing.

"No!" cried Simon Segredo.

Max's shoulders tightened, expecting a gunshot.

Gzzztch! A strange buzzing crackled instead.

He whirled to see Styx slump to the floor, flopping like a hooked marlin. The big man tried to form words but could only sputter. Mr. Segredo calmly picked up the rifle and clouted Styx on the temple, knocking him senseless.

"Don't say I never gave you anything," he said, with a bittersweet look.

Max gaped, rooted to the spot.

"Go on, then."

"But won't you—" Max began.

"I'll survive. Spies, like cats, have nine lives."

Cinnabar tugged on Max's sleeve. Together they clambered over the railing and down the stout vines to their friends below. Max's last image of his father was a long pale face above the balcony railing and a hand lifted in farewell.

◌ ◌ ◌

The grounds of the mansion jangled with activity, like a hurricane in a wind chime factory. Klaxons blared, spotlights swept the bushes and walls, and black-suited guards trotted here and there. The six teens crouched in the shadow of a yew hedge.

"I won't lie," said Rashid. "Getting out of here might be a bit tricky."

Max turned to Wyatt. "How did you guys break in?"

"Over the wall. Mr. Stones had a gizmo that fooled the security system."

"Brilliant," said Cinnabar. "Where's the gizmo?"

Wyatt's face crumpled. "With Mr. Stones. The car keys too."

They all fell silent for a moment, remembering their teacher. Max felt a heaviness in his heart that he knew would stay with him for a long while. But they had to soldier onward, as Mr. Stones would've wished.

"Okay." Max rubbed his jaw. "So . . . all we need are wheels and an escape plan. Shouldn't be too hard."

"Truth, Maxwell." Tremaine poked his head around the hedge, down low. "I count four cars up here. We could steal one, but we'll need a bangarang."

"A big gun?" asked Cinnabar.

"A big diversion."

"How about an explosion?" said Jazz.

"That'll do," said Max. "Anybody have a bomb?"

Everyone shook their heads.

And then a faint smile stole across Wyatt's face. He rested a hand on Max's shoulder. "Did I ever mention I Googled Nullthium-Ninety?"

"Uh, Wyatt?" said Max. "Not the time for science-nerd factoids."

The blond boy's grin stretched wider. "And you know what I found? Among other things, Nullthium-Ninety is highly combustible. Like petrol."

Everyone's head swiveled toward Wyatt.

"Cinn," said Jazz. "Where was that shipment you and Max stowed away on?"

Cinnabar pointed at a building through the trees. "Right there."

"Beauty." Wyatt pulled a box of wooden matches from his pocket. "Who fancies a bonfire?"

"I do," said Max. "And may I just point out once more, this was not the pyromaniac's idea?"

Ten minutes later, the orphans were crammed into a stolen black Mercedes, speeding down the driveway and leaving a most satisfying explosion in their wake.

Max counted heads. "Hey, where's Rashid?"

"You'll see," said Tremaine, at the wheel.

They squealed around a wide curve, and suddenly the guardhouse stood dead ahead, lit up like Christmas and staffed by a burly LOTUS agent. A massive wrought-iron gate stood closed behind it.

"Uh, that doesn't look good," said Cinnabar.

"Do we bust through?" asked Max.

"You'll see," Tremaine repeated. He slowed the car as they approached the shack, and the guard stepped out, a dead-eyed man with gray hair, a neat beard, and a high-tech automatic rifle.

"Where do you think you're going?" he said.

"Out, mon," said Tremaine, laying on his Jamaican accent with a trowel. "We raw hungry, feel like ice cream."

The guard shook his head and raised his rifle.

"Ah-ah-ah." Rashid emerged from the shadows of the hedge, holding a pistol in a two-handed grip. "Drop it."

When the man laid down his weapon, Tremaine said, "You look stressed, dada. What you need is a little kip."

And with that, Rashid whacked the man with his gun butt in the side of the head, and the guard dropped like a stunned ox. Rashid opened the gate and hopped into the car.

The six teens whooped as they sped off into the night.

Cinnabar punched Max's shoulder. "Not bad for a first mission," she said. "Not bad at all."

CHAPTER 30

FAMILY IS WHERE YOU FIND IT

DAWN'S FIRST LIGHT dusted the tallest buildings with a pinkish hue when at last the black Mercedes sedan pulled into the driveway of Merry Sunshine Orphanage. The team piled out, yawning and stretching.

"The first thing I fancy is four hours in a hot bath," said Jazz.

"Glad to hear it," said Tremaine. "'Cause I was looking for a subtle way to tell you." Jazz elbowed him in the ribs. But from the way they walked to the front door with little fingers loosely hooked together, Max guessed they were more than just friends.

The other kids followed, but Max took a moment to gaze up at the orphanage. Less than a week ago, he'd surveyed this building with doubt and apprehension. But now the sight of its soot-stained bricks, roof spikes, and surveillance cameras left him with a different feeling, a feeling he couldn't quite put a finger on.

It was a shame, really. Because Max knew that despite his role in the daring escape from LOTUS headquarters, he probably wouldn't be staying on. He had a *lot* to answer for—betraying the school, getting Dr. Eisenheimer kidnapped and Mr. Stones killed—and now that he was back, these things weighed on him like a sackful of stones.

Inside, the warm air was rife with the aroma of bangers and scones, omelets and Belgian waffles. When Max entered the dining room feeling like four miles of bad road, he saw white linen, a candelabra on the table, and a cheerful blaze crackling in the fireplace.

The entire school had turned out for the feast. Miss Moorthy and Victor Vazquez bustled from kitchen to table, bearing endless platters of hot food. Standing by the door, Max spotted Jensen and Shan, Dermot and Nikki Knucks, and all the rest of his fellow orphans.

A growl like low-flying aircraft alerted him to the presence of Pinkerton the dog. The huge beast stalked over stiff-legged, sniffed Max's hand, and gave it a tentative lick.

Some kids patted Max on the back as he made for an open seat by Wyatt and Cinnabar. Some glared or fixed him with wary expressions. The story of his betrayal and change of heart had apparently made its way around the school, in the mysteriously instant way that these things spread.

As Max passed Nikki's chair, the redhead caught his forearm in a hard grip. "Don't think I don't see what you're doing," she said.

"What?"

"Pretending you were a triple agent all along." She glowered. "I'm on to you, Segredo. You want to hog all the glory."

A laugh caught in his throat. Max felt such a strange mixture of sadness, relief, regret, and peace that not even Nikki Knucks could get a rise out of him. "You fancy the glory?" he said. "You can have it."

Already, Wyatt was brimming with the latest intel. Between forking huge bites of waffle into his face, he told Max that LOTUS headquarters was still in an uproar over the rescue, and over the high-ranking enemy agent Miss Moorthy had captured at the museum operation.

"She used their comm devices and intercepted a transmission," he said, chewing mightily. "They're hunting for your dad. He *escaped*, mate. Isn't that bonzer?"

"But they've still got Dr. Eisenheimer," said Max.

"True," said Cinnabar. "But without the Nullthium-Ninety, they'll have to start from scratch."

Max chewed a few bites of the omelet but found he didn't have much of an appetite. A thought struck him, and he scanned the room. "Hey, where's Hantai Annie?"

And just like that, the director appeared at the head of the table. *"Mina-san,"* she said. "Everyone, pay attention." The chatter subsided, and she continued. "Today, we thankful for return of all our students." A shadow crossed her face. "Cost was high, very high. But we *gambatta*. Congratulations to away-team for successful mission!" She straightened up, lifted a glass of orange juice, and toasted. *"Banzai!"*

"Banzai?" a few students echoed.

"Banzai!" Hantai Annie repeated, more insistently.

"Banzai!" This time, half the room replied.

The director shook her head in disbelief, raised her glass high, and bellowed, *"BANZAI!"*

"BANZAI!" the students yelled back.

Hantai Annie nodded brusquely, satisfied. She took a long sip of juice, and the rest of the room followed suit.

"What did we just say?" muttered Jensen.

"Something about little-bitty plants?" Wyatt guessed.

"Morning Warm-Ups is canceled today," the director continued. At that news, a couple of the rowdier students crowed, *"Banzai!"* but fell silent under her glare. "Max Segredo, Cinnabar Jones—my office, now. Rest of you, enjoy breakfast!" And with that, she executed a precision turn and marched out the door.

Max and Cinnabar swapped a worried look. Max pushed back from the table. "No use postponing the inevitable."

"I suppose not," Cinnabar said.

"Luck, mate," said Wyatt.

Max patted his shoulder. "Thanks."

Hantai Annie brought Cinnabar into her office first, while Max sat on the stairs waiting for what felt like at least half an Ice Age. He was too tired to pace, too keyed up to relax. Would she have already called his caseworker, Mr. Darny, to come pick him up? Should he start worrying about juvenile hall, or did the director have something worse in mind?

An orphanage couldn't shoot orphans, could it?

At long last, the office door opened, and Cinnabar stepped out into the entryway. Her face was impassive.

"Well?" said Max.

"I'll wait for you."

That didn't sound good. He took a deep breath, drew back his shoulders, and strode into the office with as much calm as he could muster. How ironic, he thought. I find a family at last, only to lose it. But that was a foster kid's lot. He knew that; they all knew that. No point in wasting tears.

He closed the office door and parked himself on the same overstuffed couch where he'd sat that first night at Merry Sunshine. He ran his fingers over the velvety fabric. By the window, Hantai Annie stood in her usual stance, looking out at the new day, hands clasped behind her back.

Finally she turned, her expression sober. "Some call you hero, some call you traitor. *Docchi da*? Which is it?"

Max shrugged. "Both?" He honestly had no idea.

Hantai Annie held up her hands and gazed at them, ticking off positive points on the right-hand fingers, negative points on the left. "You disobey orders, but you find LOTUS headquarters. You rescue students, but you get Stones-*san* killed."

Max bit his lip and gazed at the carpet, recalling the jovial, sarcastic teacher.

"You get doctor kidnapped, but you destroy Nullthium-Ninety." Then she added one more finger to the negative side. "And you break school's *ichi-ban*, most important rule: Loyalty Above All." The director shook her head, disbelieving. "Max-*kun*, what I do with you?"

"It's okay." Max sighed, put his hands on his knees, and pushed up to standing. "I'll go pack."

"Wait."

"'Wait'?" He felt a stirring of something like hope, but quickly smothered it. Hope was a dangerous animal.

Though stern, Hantai Annie's face held a trace of something like sympathy. "Why you betray school?"

"For family."

She gave him a reproving look. "Max, *we* are your family."

He gulped, trying to swallow the softball-sized lump in his throat. "I . . . I know that now."

"Family is messy," she said. "We fight, we make mistakes, we don't always like each other. But somehow, we forgive."

Max nodded. For some reason, he was finding it hard to speak.

"You forgive your father?"

This startled him into speech. "That ratbag? He was working for LOTUS. They're evil—you know . . . murder, controlling the world, and all that?"

Almost fiercely, Hantai Annie said, "But he is your *father*."

Max frowned. He gazed at Hantai Annie with deep bafflement. "I don't get you at all."

The ghost of a smile played across her lips. She sat in her office chair and reached over to straighten the already perfectly aligned in-box on her desktop.

"You know where my nickname comes from?" she asked.

"Your nickname?" Max was thrown by the sudden change of direction.

"You know what means *hantai*?"

Max shook his head.

"*Opposite*," said the director. "Long ago, they call me Hantai Annie because when you expect me to do one thing, I do opposite. Like, I half-Chinese, but I speak Japanese."

"Huh." Max had no idea what to say to that.

She stood and stretched out a hand. "Max Segredo, you passed your tryout. Welcome to School for S.P.I.E.S.— Systematic Protection, Intelligence, and Espionage Services."

Automatically, he met her grip, but his brain wouldn't process her words.

"I . . . uh . . . what?"

"You staying," said Hantai Annie, as if talking to a three-year-old. "Don't make me regret it."

Relief flooded him. "No. No, I won't. But . . . the Process? Dr. Eisenheimer?"

Her eyes twinkled. "Not real doctor."

"Okay, so he had a fake degree," said Max. "I don't see—"

"Not fake degree, fake *doctor*," said Hantai Annie. "We use your distraction to smuggle real one out of country."

Max's head spun like a cartwheeling schoolgirl. "Then the guy they kidnapped wasn't . . . ? And you knew that I had planted . . . ?"

"A good spy anticipates everything." The director tapped her temple. *"Sumaato dakara."*

"But how—"

"Isoge!" she said, waving a hand in dismissal and taking her seat. "You go. I very busy woman. Many messes to clean up."

In a daze, Max wandered to the door. When he glanced back at Hantai Annie's face, half obscured by the computer screen, he could have sworn she was smiling.

Cinnabar rose from her seat on the stairs and came to meet him. "So?"

"Well . . ." He ran a hand through his hair, bemused. "Looks like I'm staying."

A whoop of joy escaped Cinnabar's lips, and she gave Max a fierce hug and a kiss on the cheek. Midway through it, both realized they were actually touching, skin to skin. They separated with a start.

"Uh, I'm glad," she said, flushing and avoiding his gaze.

The spot where she had kissed him tingled, cool and invigorating, the way a mint felt on the tongue. "Me too," said Max.

"So."

"So."

Cinnabar brushed back a stray curl. "What next, rookie?"

Max looked down at himself. His private-school clothes were filthy and smoke-stained. He was sleepy and wired, wrung out like a dishrag, but with it all, strangely peaceful. In the silence, the clatter and chatter of their classmates drifted in from the dining room, and his belly grumbled.

"What next?" he said. "Maybe I'll learn to crack the Unbreakable cipher, maybe I'll help Wyatt invent some escape gizmos, or maybe I'll even look for my father and try to help him. But right now?"

"Yes?"

"I believe I'll have a waffle. Care to join me?"

Cinnabar suppressed a smile. "If you insist." Side by side, they walked back into the happy ruckus of the dining room, where the hearth fire was burning bright.

Caesar Cipher or Caesar's Code

Codes have been in use as long as people have had to communicate something they didn't want the whole ruddy world to know. One of the oldest and most widely used is the Caesar cipher, named after Roman emperor Julius Caesar, who used it in his private letters.

This simple encryption technique relies on substitution. Each letter in the plaintext (original message) is replaced by a letter some fixed number of positions down (or up) the alphabet. For instance, with a shift of two, A would be replaced by C, B would become D, and so forth.

This code is easily broken, especially in our computer age. However, in Caesar's day, when many people could barely read, it proved effective enough in protecting his military messages from prying eyes. This is an excellent cipher for the beginner to start building his or her experience of cryptology.

To encode a message in Caesar cipher, first align two alphabets; the cipher alphabet being the plain alphabet shifted left or right by a designated number of spaces. For instance, here is a Caesar cipher using a right rotation of two places:

> Cipher: YZABCDEFGHI J K LMNOPQRS T U VWX
> Plain: ABCDEFGHI J KLMNO PQR S TUVWX Y Z

When you're encrypting a message, look up each letter in the "plain" line and replace it with the corresponding letter in the cipher line, like so:

> Ciphertext: UCR ZGPBQ DJW QMSRF
> Plaintext: WET BIRDS FLY SOUTH

To enable deciphering, tell your contact person the key—the number of spaces shifted left or right—and he or she will perform the process in reverse.

Excerpted from:
Survival Skills for the Modern Spy, 3rd Edition
by Giacomo Fleming, Belle Maclean, and S. Gromonowitz

Foreign Languages

Any spy worth his or her salt must learn to communicate effectively in a variety of languages. Foreign languages constitute a sort of code of their own—although the wise spy will never assume that bystanders cannot understand the language he or she speaks.

Intensive study and a good ear is required to master languages; however, even a smattering of words in a foreign tongue can come in handy when you find yourself behind enemy lines. To get you started, here are a few common phrases in French:

Qu'est-ce que c'est?: What is it?
N'est-ce pas?: Isn't that so?
Je m'appelle Brigitte: My name is Brigitte
Donnez-moi le fusil: Give me the gun

And in Japanese:

Gambatta!: Go for it!
Damare!: Be quiet!
Ikimashou: Let's go
Toppu himitsu: Top secret

**For more spy information and activities,
please visit www.school4spies.com.**

ACKNOWLEDGMENTS

BEFORE I wrote this book, I always wondered why people wrote long acknowledgments in their novels. Now I know.

I'd like to thank my beta readers, Justina Chen, Sofia Headley, Robin LaFevers, Susan Lipson, and Lee Wardlaw, for telling me what they liked, as well as what they didn't. Major mahalos also go out to Kristin Clark Venuti, Kathy Jackson, Ashley Ullrich, and Michelle Arndt, who helped me understand the world of foster care and deepen Max's character.

Many thanks to my international consultants—Christopher Cheng (Australia), Annie Sung Bernstein and Janette Cross (Japan), Nigel Waymouth and Kevin Childerley (UK), and Elizabeth Coburn (Ireland)—for helping me understand how characters from those countries might talk. Any errors that found their way into the book are purely my own.

Thanks, too, to Stephanie Lurie for offering the kind of editorial support Goldilocks would've loved (not too little, not too much; just right), and to ace agent Steven Malk, for coming through when it counted the most. And most of all, thanks to Janette, who puts up with my writerly wackiness and keeps the home fires burning.